JUÁREZ DANCE

JUÁREZ DANCE

a novel of borderland noir by
Sam Hawken

Juárez Dance copyright © 2013 by Sam Hawken

Published by Pax River Books

ISBN-10: 1484106377

ISBN-13: 978-1484106372

Cover design by JT Lindroos

ACKNOWLEDGEMENTS

The author would like to thank Mariann Hawken and Svetlana Pironko for their contribution to this work.

1.

Cooper drank Canadian Club because it seemed the closest thing to real liquor the minibar had to offer. A fifteen-year-old whiskey was better than something blended, or cheap vodka or something flavored out of a chemical lab. He poured the little bottles over ice and sat in an uncomfortable chair with a pistol balanced on the armrest.

He was in Dallas and from the window of the hotel room it was possible to see the control tower for the expansive Dallas rail yards. The triple-underpass was nearby and the cursed triangle of Dealey Plaza. One of these days Cooper planned to visit the museum at the old book depository because that was one hell of a hit, even if they caught the wrong man.

The sound of a television turned too loud came through the wall by the bed. The room was not a big one and didn't even have a writing desk. This was a place to go when accommodations didn't really matter, when luxury wasn't even a secondary concern. There was a bed, four walls, a chair, a round table tucked into the corner and the minibar. Thank God for the minibar.

It was almost nine o'clock. Cooper finished his drink. He clinked the ice around in the bottom of the glass for a little bit and then tipped it back again to catch a little melt-off and a drop or two of whiskey. Then he put the glass aside.

His pistol was a SIG Sauer P226 with a threaded barrel. He had a matching sound suppressor for it, just an unassuming black cylinder the size of a tube of toothpaste. This he screwed onto the end of the gun until it was fitted tightly. He checked the magazine: Glaser Safety Slugs with blue polymer tips. The bullets were filled with No. 12 birdshot and expanded rapidly on impact. They couldn't penetrate a wall or a door but they would rip and tear soft tissue like a metal claw. They also left no round that could be typed for ballistic purposes. If he collected the ejected brass there would be nothing to link him to any shot he fired.

The gun went back on the armrest. He wasn't new to this and he wouldn't clutch his weapon until his hand sweated and the grips were slick with moisture. He considered making himself another drink, assuming he could find more Canadian Club. Somewhere in the back of his mind he remembered seeing magazine ads about cases of the stuff left in exotic locales for adventurers to find. If he remembered correctly, that was a very good ad campaign.

Cooper wore a simple suit made of a polyester blend. It was not a good suit and it had been fitted off the rack. He wore it because it was the kind of thing seen on men in hotel rooms like this one. When he lingered in the bar downstairs he'd seen at least ten suits exactly like it in everything but color. Bland, horrible blues and red ties. So many red ties.

He was waiting for a man named Bingham. They had met for the first time yesterday and had lunch together shortly thereafter. Bingham had worn a wedding ring when they started talking, but the ring was vanished into some pocket before they were done. A white mark remained on tan skin. This was something else Cooper took care not to notice, or at least he didn't say so.

Bingham was a tall man, widening in the middle and thinning up top. He smiled a lot, Cooper could tell, because the lines were cut into his face. He said he played a lot of golf and, frankly, he looked the type. He looked less like the type to meet strange men in hotel rooms for a suck and fuck, but Cooper knew that sometimes that wasn't the sort of thing you could pick up on right away.

Next to almost anyone Cooper was forgettable. He wasn't tall and he wasn't short. He wasn't thin or fat or balding and he had no tattoos. His wristwatch was the only thing he wore that might be called ornamental; no rings or bracelets or neck chains. When he wasn't dressed down he looked good in suits made to order by a Mexican tailor. He wore expensive shoes. Clothes were his weakness and he did not like to be without good ones. Just wearing this ugly blue suit and red tie made him unhappy.

It was past nine now and Bingham hadn't arrived. Cooper imagined him in the lobby below, pacing out his anxiety or maybe taking his time in the bar as Cooper had earlier in the evening. Maybe he would have a double shot of Canadian Club to soothe his nerves. Whatever the case, it annoyed Cooper. He wanted to get this over with.

He wasn't bothered by the killing — that was as simple as turning off a light switch — but by the man himself. He didn't *like* Bingham, and it wasn't because the man was a closet case. There was something about country club white guys that got under Cooper's skin. Maybe he had just spent too much time in Mexico. Maybe that was it.

The rap on the door was a relief. Cooper collected his pistol and went to the door. He looked through the peephole to be sure it was Bingham and to be sure he was alone. The hallway on either side of him was empty.

Cooper undid the safety latch and the lock. He held the door open for Bingham. The man was flushed, bright with tiny spots of perspiration and smelled like alcohol. So it was the bar, then.

"Come on in," Cooper said and he smiled to let Bingham know he was sincere.

Bingham passed Cooper in the door. When his back was completely exposed Cooper put the muzzle of the SIG Sauer right behind the man's ear and pulled the trigger. The gun made a thumping noise and Bingham pitched face-forward onto the carpet.

Cooper let the door close itself.

He put the gun on the bed and stood over the corpse. He rolled Bingham over onto his back. There was no exit wound, but a stream of blood trickled from one nostril where the dead man had banged it on the way down. Bingham just stared.

Cooper took the man's watch and wallet and put those on the bed, too. He checked Bingham's belt to see if it was the kind that hid money, but it wasn't. Then he rolled Bingham back over onto his face.

Once upon a time Cooper might have used the cord from a lamp to bind the dead man's wrists and ankles, but now the wall lamps were molded in place. Cooper used his knife to cut the curtain cords and these he used to do the tying. Anyone who cared to check would be able to tell ligature marks before death from those made after, but no one would care. They would see what they were meant to see, and by the time anyone knew better it would be too late.

The watch was a Seiko and would have gone with the suit Cooper wore. The wallet had $200 in cash and a full complement of credit cards. He put wallet and watch into his pocket even though he didn't want them. It would look strange if he left them behind.

The only things he had touched in the whole room apart from the body was the minibar, the little bottles of Canadian Club and the glass he drank from. These he wiped down carefully. He went to the inside door handle and wiped that, as well, just to be certain. He dropped the clean plastic room key on the bed and let himself out.

Down the hall he descended four flights of stairs and left by a side entrance with a security camera watching it. The lens of the camera was a layered in black spray paint. Within a few minutes Cooper was driving and he did not look back.

2.

Cooper took his time driving. He took I-30 west until it connected to 20 and then rode nearly five hundred miles to I-10, which would take him the rest of the way. On the road to El Paso he went through Abilene and Big Spring and Midland, where the second President Bush met his wife for the first time, and Odessa and Pecos. Not a one of them was as big and spread out as Dallas and Fort Worth. The character of the landscape changed even though it stayed flat, flat, flat. Colors went from green to brown to yellow as the land petered out to something akin to desert, but not quite. The towns seemed to dry up with it.

His car was a rental, a burgundy-colored Chevy Impala with 12,000 miles on it. For a cheap car it was a good one and Cooper found he didn't have to stop and fill it up as much as he thought he would. This gave him more uninterrupted time on the road, which was mostly straight and mostly empty and marked with speed limits meant to eat up the miles as fast as possible.

He drove ten hours straight through the night and into the following morning. He was on the Bridge of the Americas early and got across the border without too much trouble at all. If he had been of a more poetic mindset he might have said that he breathed easier once he was over the bridge into Ciudad Juárez, but the truth was he had never breathed hard the whole time from shooting Bingham to where he was now. He could have been driving anywhere.

Traffic was dense, the streets close and busy. Signage stacked up on signage over storefronts and *farmacias* and tourist shops selling plastic junk to a thinning population of American *turistas*. Cooper passed three trucks with mounted machine guns on them and the words POLICÍA FEDERAL emblazoned across doors and windshield. He had not been in Juárez since the big federal crackdown and he could never remember seeing so many cops on the streets. He saw army vehicles, too, though strangely they were not as intimidating as the deadly black of the federal police.

He drove to the Triunfo de La Republica where things eased off and a driver could afford to take a breath. He pulled into the Hotel Lucerna. It was ten stories and white and out back there was a broad, cool pool that would feel wonderful when the temperatures hit 100 degrees later in the day. Cooper tipped the valet parking attendant with American cash and the bellboy, too. He didn't have much luggage.

His suite was ready and they took him up to the eighth floor. Cooper walked the broad, sun-splashed front room and looked at the city gleaming under the climbing sun while the bellboy put his bags away. Just for the hell of it, Cooper tipped him again.

There was a full wet bar in the suite and not just a few little bottles tucked away in a miniature refrigerator. As a nod to Bingham, Cooper brought out the Canadian Club and poured himself a generous portion over ice. He put himself in a comfortable chair and enjoyed the quiet and the air conditioning.

There wasn't the first sound of the outdoors audible and no loud television in the next room.

He took the drink slowly and when he was finished he put the empty tumbler away on a glass side table. His eyelids were drooping now and he let himself fall asleep in the chair with his feet up in the sun.

When he awoke it was probably closer to noon. He was sweaty and his mouth didn't taste good. The hotel provided toothbrushes and toothpaste and he brushed twice before using complimentary mouthwash. That was better.

He took a shower to get the dusty driving off his skin. He used a lotion that made him smell a bit like apples, which pleased him a little. He was glad to be shed of the cheap suit and put on khakis and a white cotton button-up from his bags. The shirt was a little rumpled, but that gave it character. He put on loafers without socks. Bingham's watch and wallet went into the trash along with the horrible red tie.

Cooper decided he would take lunch by the pool. He would have a big, fruity-tasting margarita and something spicy. And then he would wait for Barriga's man to call.

3.

He went swimming after lunch and sunbathed for a while. Cooper could hear traffic sounds coming from the road, but that wasn't too much of a distraction. After a while he even managed to doze and only woke when the waiter was clearing away his empty margarita glass. Cooper ordered another.

Out in the city proper there was dying in the streets like no one had ever seen. They were averaging two or three thousand murders a year here, just one drug cartel warring against the other. But at the hotel it was as though there was nothing going on except leisure.

There was one woman in the pool: a mother watching two children. She was American in a way that was immediately obvious even though she had dark hair and olive-colored skin. Something about Americans always stood out in the way they moved, in the way they spoke Spanish with an accent or without. Cooper knew he had the American way about himself, too, despite the fact that he lived in Monterrey and knew Juárez well.

The woman wore sunglasses, but Cooper could tell when she looked his way. He smiled at her and nodded and idly wondered what it would be like to take her up to his room and fuck her. It wasn't that she was beautiful, because she wasn't, but just the idea of turning a nice mother around and putting it into her from behind amused him and turned him on at the same time.

Eventually the woman and her children left the pool and Cooper was alone. He lingered a while longer hoping someone else would come along. His habit was people watching and he could do it all day. But no one came, so he dipped into the pool and took a few laps around before getting out, drying off and heading back upstairs.

He had time to kill and tried sleeping some more. Cooper wasn't much for naps, but it seemed the day for them and he slept on top of the sheets with the air conditioning and the turning ceiling fan stirring the hairs on his arms. When he woke it was still hours from dinnertime, but he was hungry. He ordered a sandwich from room service, and ate it in the front room in front of the television.

The news wasn't something he paid much attention to but he watched it now in Spanish for an hour or two, just letting the stories drift by along with the time. He was beginning to think about where he'd take his evening meal by the time the phone rang.

"*¿Bueno?*" he asked when he picked it up.

"Señor Townsend?"

The voice was not familiar to Cooper, but he didn't worry; Barriga rarely used the same courier twice. It was better that way, because it didn't reveal patterns in their dealings with each other.

"*Sí.*"

"My name is Amador. You are available?"

"I'll meet you in the bar."

Cooper washed his hands and face in the suite's bathroom before heading downstairs. The bar was called El Acueducto and was fine as far as hotel bars went. There was a little stage for live music, plenty of seating and a long bar made of black stone and wood. The only man in the place was the one calling himself Amador, seated at a table with his back to a corner. Cooper sat across from him.

"Señor Townsend," Amador said.

"*Mucho gusto,*" Cooper returned.

"Señor Barriga sends his regards."

"How is he?"

"He is well."

A server came to the table. Amador had nothing in front of him except a square paper napkin and an ashtray, though he wasn't smoking. He waved the server off. Cooper ordered a screwdriver.

He looked at the man across the table. Amador had nothing unusual about him that might make him stand out. He wore a broad mustache that sat on his upper lip like a dark slab. His eyes were dark brown and flat, as though he was incurious about everything. And perhaps he was. Amador was a courier and little else. A lack of curiosity benefited him.

"Okay," Cooper said, "let me have it."

Amador produced an envelope from inside his jacket and passed it across the table. Cooper slipped a finger under the fold and checked inside. There was a printed receipt with a series of numbers on it and a strip of paper with a handwritten note. Cooper checked the first and read the latter.

"Why does he want to meet with me?" Cooper asked.

"I couldn't say, señor," Amador replied.

"When does he want to meet?"

"As soon as possible. The matter isn't urgent, but time is a factor."

"Where?"

"Señor Barriga intends to take a suite here at the hotel. You need not bother going anywhere; he will come to you."

"That's new," Cooper said.

"I wouldn't know anything about that."

Cooper considered. His screwdriver came. He didn't touch it. He played the envelope and its contents between his fingers, then tucked the envelope away in the breast pocket of his shirt. "All right," he said. "I'll meet with him. It's just unusual, that's all."

"Señor Barriga apologizes in advance."

"He does?"

"Yes."

That was new, too. Cooper nodded and was silent a moment. "Okay," he said.

"You'll be informed when Señor Barriga has checked into the hotel," Amador said.

"By you?"

"Most likely not. But we may see each other again."

Cooper looked at Amador anew. The man was older than the usual courier and more self-possessed. Or maybe it was just because he brought unusual news. Cooper couldn't be sure. He couldn't see if the man was carrying a weapon, but he might be. Many people went armed in Juárez these days.

"I guess we're done here," Cooper said.

"Yes. Thank you for your time, señor."

"*De nada.*"

With that, Amador rose from the table and headed for the exit. Cooper turned to watch him go and once the man was out of sight he returned his attention to the table and his drink. He brought out the envelope again. He sipped at the screwdriver. It tasted fresh and good and made him feel better.

4.

Cooper killed another day at the hotel, lazing and eating and generally letting his mind wind down. One night he heard gunfire from somewhere not far away from the hotel, but he was high above it all and it didn't affect him.

On the morning of the next day he received a message under his door from the hotel: his reservation for dinner at the hotel restaurant had been set for nine o'clock that night. Ignacio Barriga had arrived.

He didn't dress up for Barriga, but he made sure he was shaved and put on a pressed shirt for their meeting. There was no real reason for it — Barriga had never paid any attention to Cooper's appearance before — but Cooper felt more comfortable having put forth some effort.

That day passed slower than the one before. Cooper didn't drink as much as he might have otherwise. He watched a lot of television. A parade of stories about killings marched across the screen. People with missing heads and limbs and a whole panoply of mutilations. Sometimes it seemed like this was the only news the stations had to report.

Finally it was time. He turned off the lights in his suite and went downstairs to the restaurant. The place was fine as far as such restaurants went, but it was still in a hotel just as the bar was still a hotel bar; there was a limit to how luxurious it could be.

He asked the maître d' for Señor Barriga. He was directed to a table slightly away from the others, one large enough to seat six or eight, but with only the man himself there. A place was set for Cooper and he sat down.

Ignacio Barriga was in his fifties, growing a little heavy around the jowls but still with the look of someone who might play golf or otherwise stay active. He was tanned from time spent in the sun. His hair was cut short and his mustache was neat. He had extremely dark eyes that sometimes glittered. Cooper got the impression that Barriga could be a cruel man.

They didn't shake hands. "Cooper," Barriga said, "it's good to see you again."

"The same, Señor Barriga," Cooper replied. "You're looking fit."

"I do my best," Barriga said.

"I was surprised when you said you wanted to meet."

"Not yet, Cooper. Let's have something to eat first."

There were pre-meal drinks and then a savory tortilla soup. For his main dish Cooper had rotini with salsa di limone. Barriga opted for a steak. They passed the meal without much to say to each other, though Cooper would have liked to fill the space with something, even small talk. Barriga was not one to do so, and so there was silence.

The dessert was fried ice cream in a portion big enough for two. Cooper picked at his, while Barriga attacked the sweet with gusto. Again there was quiet, and Cooper wondered if they would have their after-meal coffee before Barriga got down to it.

Then Barriga spoke: "I have something for you, Cooper."

"I thought so."

"My people are very happy with the job you did in Dallas. It was clean. My people appreciate that. I know you like to take some time after you work, but time... time is against me here and I need someone quickly. You were the first person to come to mind."

"I'm flattered," Cooper said. Though he did not care for the ice cream itself, the honeycomb it was flecked with was tasty.

Barriga finished off his ice cream before Cooper had even gotten halfway through his. He signaled for the server and ordered coffee for them both. It was after ten o'clock.

"When is the job?" Cooper asked.

"One week," Barriga replied.

"It's a hit? Where?"

"No hit," said Barriga, "and it will happen here in Juárez. There's a gated community in the country, they call it Los Campos, it will happen there. For the most part."

Cooper was curious now. He left off eating the ice cream; he didn't want it anyway. "If it's not a hit, I don't understand."

The coffee came. Barriga took his with three creams and three sugars. Cooper preferred his almost black.

Barriga continued. "In a week I'm to meet with a man named Sandalio Ruíz. You know the name?"

"No."

"I didn't expect you would. Señor Ruíz is a wealthy man, a landowner. He also has interests in the *maquiladora* business. It's the latter that interests my people, but I won't bore you with the details. What you need to know is that I will take meetings with Señor Ruíz for some time — perhaps a week — and when we are finished I may need you to do what you're good at."

"He's a target?"

"He may be or he may not. It will depend upon the meetings."

"Why not just contact me when you know for sure?"

"Our meetings will take place in Ruíz's home. I will want you with me. You'll enter as my bodyguard, see what there is to see inside the place and proceed from there. You should also take time to survey the environs. This you will do on your own."

"I'm not a bodyguard," Cooper said. "I've never done that kind of work."

"It doesn't matter. I will be safe during these meetings. Anything else would make my people very angry and Señor Ruíz is well aware of this. Bringing a bodyguard is just a formality, and half-expected given the conditions in Juárez right now."

Cooper nodded. "You could use a real bodyguard."

"I am not concerned."

"What about payment?" Cooper asked.

"You'll be paid a per diem for your time. If you're called upon to act at the end of the meetings, then you'll be paid the usual rate. My people will pay half if you aren't."

"So I'll be paid no matter what," Cooper said.

"That's correct."

Cooper considered this. He finished his coffee. It was bitter and not very good. He expected more from an expensive restaurant like this one, but then it *was* just a hotel. He'd had worse.

"I will need a decision before we part this evening."

"I'd like more time than that."

"How long?"

"A day. I want to consider the situation."

"What is there to consider? If I may ask."

"This isn't the usual work I do. It has different risks."

"I see. I can give you a day, but I must have an answer by tomorrow night. If you aren't going to take on the job, I will need to find someone else to fill your position."

"I understand. I won't make you wait."

"See that you don't."

5.

Cooper was growing dissatisfied with the hotel. He had too much to think about, his brain wasn't idle, and a hotel was not a good place for serious matters. For Cooper, the hotel and Juárez at large was a place to let his mind go blank.

He thought about going out, but the Juárez he liked did not come out until dark. The character of the city had changed over the last few years with the commencement of the cartel wars and it wasn't safe to simply wander the way he might have otherwise. Soon he might not be able to visit Ciudad Juárez at all and the thought made him sad.

If he were asked he would be hard-pressed to explain why he kept coming here. It was once his tradition to come back to Juárez after every job to spend a week in some hotel or the other. He would prowl the Avenida Juárez near the Paso del Norte footbridge among the drunken Texans and college boys and tourists with a taste for the adventurous. He would pay for drink and sometimes drugs and sex with one or two women.

There were cleaner, safer places to go. His apartment in Monterrey was in one of the safest districts in the entire country, though it was not untouched. He could walk there at all hours and never hear a gunshot, never fear a mugging or a murder. But Monterrey was in other ways different from Ciudad Juárez. It lacked Juárez's filth, and it was that filth that attracted Cooper if only for a little while.

After his first job he'd come here. He was twenty-seven years old with a payment in cash in his overnight bag. He got high on cocaine and partied for two days straight in a brothel called the Panama. He had a string of girls over that time, four or five at least. It was like living in a fever dream of flesh and it had never left him.

It was not time for him to make his visiting rounds. That was for when his mind needed to go blank. Now he had to consider and that meant he would have to put off pleasures of any kind.

He didn't drink that day and he didn't go down to the pool. He stayed in his room with the television turned on and sound shut off. The news had begun to blend into itself anyway and he didn't care for the endless string of *telenovelas* that crowded the other channels.

For the most part it seemed like a simple enough task to perform and nothing to fear. He would be paid whether he delivered a hit or not. He would be idle for a week that he would have spent drinking and whoring and that was all right, too, even if it meant breaking with his habit. Money was more important. Money meant time to relax and he could always play later.

Cooper didn't like the way he would be exposed. His work was based on the walk in. He would locate the client, watch and learn and when the time came he would deliver the package and move on. No one knew his face. But for this he would spend a week exposing himself. No one would have to know his name, but they would learn what he looked like and if he had to hit, memories would be long. He might not be able to come back to Juárez anymore.

Ignacio Barriga and his people were his most frequent patrons. They had long memories, too. If he did this, they would appreciate it. His rate might go up. They might consider him for even more work. Maybe he could afford to lose Ciudad Juárez. Maybe it was time to move on from here. He had almost gone already.

He took most of the day thinking about the job. When he made up his mind he made himself a drink at the bar and enjoyed the taste of it sip by sip until it was gone. He had another and then a third until there was a pleasant cloudiness at the edge of his thoughts. When he was working there would be no drink.

Señor Barriga left a number to call. It was not to his suite at the hotel, but a number in Mexico City. The phone rang three times on the other end before a man picked up.

"This is Townsend," Cooper told the man.

"Have you made a decision, Señor Townsend?" the man asked.

"I'll take it."

"Very good. I will let Señor Barriga know."

"I want some time to go home, get some things."

"You have a four-day window, Señor Townsend. The schedule is set."

"I can make it."

"Very well. You'll be contacted when it's time."

"Where?"

"Your suite will be held for you. The expense will be part of the package."

"Four days?" Cooper asked.

"Four days, Señor Townsend."

"All right, then."

He hung up the phone and considered another drink, but he did not want to get drunk. The glass went into the bar's little sink. Though it was early, Cooper got ready for bed. Tomorrow morning he would be out of the hotel early.

6.

Cooper drove the cheap rental car from Ciudad Juárez to Monterrey in Nuevo León. By now the rental-car company would realize the credit card he used was stolen and the car wasn't coming back. In Monterrey he parked across town from his apartment and left the doors unlocked and the keys in the ignition. By nighttime it would be gone and by tomorrow it would be in pieces.

He called for a cab, and paid cash with a generous tip. The driver did not ask what an American man was doing in a bad neighborhood with his luggage in the middle of the day. Cooper's building was near downtown and had a doorman and brass-fitted elevators that might have been at home in a luxury building in Manhattan. The streets bustled, but they were wide and clear and not at all like the hive of Ciudad Juárez. He was home again.

It hadn't been long since he left so the air had not had a chance to grow still. His place was neat, appointed well and kept clean by a maid service that came twice a week. He enjoyed a drink from his own bar and turned on the television for company. He took a shower and put on fresh clothes.

The apartment had a good view of the city and the rising mountain that marked the city center. They called Monterrey the City of the Mountains because the foothills of the Sierra Madre

Oriental punctuated the skyline. Cooper had lived here for ten years.

With four days to himself Cooper had plenty of time before he had to pack, but he browsed the contents of his closet anyway. He would not be able to dress casually; a bodyguard would be as formal as his charge, so Cooper would need suits. Of course he would be able to carry his gun and knife, but depending on security he might be relieved of his weapons. He had to consider ways to bring something in that wouldn't be found in a pat down.

He picked out three suits that would likely fit the bill. Tomorrow he would send them out to be cleaned and pressed. He matched silk ties to them and the right shirts. Looking in the mirror he wondered if perhaps he ought to get a haircut before going back to Juárez; his hair was getting longish. In the end he decided to leave it alone.

When he was done doing that he still had hours to kill before bed. He lingered in front of the TV for a while and then used the phone. He called a number he had memorized. A woman answered.

"This is Cooper."

"Hello, Señor Townsend. How are you?"

"I'm fine, thank you. Is Valencia available?"

"I will check. Please hold."

Cooper listened to the flat silence for almost a minute. When the hold was released, it was Valencia on the phone. She had a rich, Castilian accent to her Spanish. To Cooper she sounded like class. In person she was short and going round like a Mexican grandmother, though her hair was still jet black and her face smooth. Once he had gone to dinner with her and she had matched him drink for drink and course for course. She was a woman he respected because she had earned it from him.

"Cooper! How are you?"

"Hello, Valencia. I'm fine."

"You haven't called in a while. I was worried that you didn't love me anymore."

"You know that will never happen."

"This I am very happy to hear."

"I was wondering if you had anyone available tonight," Cooper said.

"Tonight? Let me see."

Cooper imagined Valencia with a great, leather-bound ledger full of names and secrets. He saw her in his mind's eye licking her fingers and turning the pages. He heard the click of a computer keyboard and then she was back.

"Have you met Olivia?"

"No."

"Then you must!"

"All right, then. We'll have dinner at the Presidente Monterrey. The Wall Street Steakhouse."

"What time?"

"Ten o'clock? No, make it eleven."

"I will arrange it."

"*Gracias.*"

"Think nothing of it. You are my favorite, Cooper, and don't forget that."

Cooper didn't believe this. He shook his head and said, "We'll have to go out together again soon."

"You'll take me to the Presidente Monterrey?"

"Somewhere better."

"Then we will have a date. Good-bye, Cooper. Be well."

He had hours before he had to be anywhere so he took shower and a nap and then picked up a book he'd been trying to read before his trip to Dallas. It was a thriller by some author he didn't know and it was all right, but nothing special. It filled the time, and that was enough; many times in Cooper's life it was just a matter of waiting until the next thing. Some might have found this boring, but Cooper was used to it.

Dining at the restaurant at the Presidente was formal. Cooper decided to wear one of the suits he would take with him back to Juárez. He put on a little cologne and a touch of gel into his hair. When he was happy he left the apartment and went down to the garage where his car was. He drove a BMW 750 and was glad to be behind the wheel of it again. He turned the sound system on and listened to Bach as he navigated late-evening traffic.

7.

The hotel Presidente Monterrey was located in the heart of the city's financial district, the Zona Valle. This fit with the building itself, because to Cooper it looked like a bank: lots of white stone facing and mirrored glass windows tinted blue. It was luxuriously appointed inside and its rooms were the best Monterrey had to offer, but it was not friendly from the outside.

He parked at the valet station and tipped the boy there to be sure his car would be well taken care of. Passing through a set of automatic doors, he slid into the quiet atmosphere of the hour. People were still coming and going, because Monterrey stayed up late, but it was a different kind of busy from the height of the day.

The hotel had two restaurants. Cooper had chosen the one with the most American atmosphere: a steakhouse styled like an exclusive clubhouse. There were billiard tables and a fully stocked bar, lots of richly colored wood and comfortable chairs and the smell of well-cooked meat.

He found Olivia in the bar. Without asking he knew it had to be her. She was tall, encased in a black sheath of a dress that flattered breasts and bottom. He saw she was wearing silk stockings, a thin line of seam traveling up her calves to the line of her dress. A heady scent floated around her and when Cooper got close it surrounded him, too. She had long hair and her lips were painted red. No one would call a woman like this a whore.

"Sorry I'm late," Cooper said, though it was only a few minutes past eleven. Out in the restaurant proper there were still a few quiet dinners going on, some people finishing their coffee or smoking cigars. He leaned in and kissed Olivia on the cheek, smelled the fresh scent of her skin beneath the perfume.

Olivia smiled a little. She had white, white teeth. "It's all right," she said. "Would you like a drink? I'm having something myself."

Cooper signaled to the bartender. "Double Glenmorangie on the rocks," he told the man. "Send it to my table."

He offered Olivia the crook of his arm and she slid into it. Cooper could look at her some more and then some more without growing tired of her. If she was not the most beautiful woman he had ever seen, then he could not remember who was. He could not imagine this woman anywhere else but in a place like this one, where luxury was always at hand.

They got their table in a secluded corner well away from the others still occupied. The server brought Cooper his drink and he let himself enjoy the smell of the single malt before tasting it. Across the table Olivia drank something with a twist. Cooper wasn't sure what it might be.

"I'm surprised. I wouldn't expect you to be available on such short notice."

"I had plans," Olivia admitted, "but they fell through at the last minute."

"I'm lucky then," Cooper said.

"Maybe we both are."

When it came time to eat, Cooper ordered a porterhouse and Olivia had a salad with grilled chicken. He was able to talk to her and she to him, and it was as if they were both acquainted with each other, and used to the rhythms of idle conversation. Cooper found that he loved the sound of Olivia's voice and the delicacy of her laughter, which did not come so often that it seemed like she was flattering him. They shared a slice of cheesecake for dessert and had coffee and then Cooper took care of the check.

"I already have a room," Olivia said. "If you'd like to come up."

"I would."

They took the elevator. Cooper put his hand on her waist and she let him draw her to him for a kiss that tasted clean and cool. They touched tongues and then the kiss was over.

"Do you want me?" she whispered in his ear.

"I want you."

At the room she could not be quick enough with the key. Inside Cooper wanted to take his time undressing her, but he found he lacked the willpower. He pawed the top of dress down and freed her breasts and put his mouth on her nipples as they grew stiff in the dark. Her hands were on his belt, on the buttons and the zipper and then she was on her knees sucking him urgently to the point where Cooper thought it might all be over too soon.

They shed clothing from the sitting area at the front of the room to the bed. She brought a condom out of somewhere and slipped it on while working him with her hand. Cooper grabbed her knee and raised it and pushed into her and made her gasp with the suddenness of it.

He kissed and she kissed him back, but their lovemaking was not tender. Cooper clutched at her as if she would slip away from him and pressed her into the mattress with his thrusting. Her ankles were crossed at the small of his back, pulling him into her and he could not stop himself.

When he finished Cooper fell over Olivia in a lather of exertion-sweat. His heart sped against his ribs and he could not catch enough breath. Olivia covered his mouth with kisses and held him close to her. As he softened and slipped from her she collected the condom and vanished it away somewhere.

Cooper wanted to have her again, but had exhausted himself. She stayed with him as long as he offered his arm to her and after a long while she rose from the bed and dressed in the half-light from the windows. Cooper watched her, thought of calling her back, but the sweat was dried now and he was too spent. He was getting older.

"Thank you for the evening," Olivia told him when she left.

"Thank you," Cooper said. And when she was gone he went to sleep.

8.

When he returned to Ciudad Juárez he drove his own car. The trip was pleasanter behind the tinted windows and with the sound system piping gentle classical into the cabin. Coming into the city he was reminded again of what a blight it was, like an enormous urban scab on a landscape that was none too beautiful to begin with. Without Juárez there it would have been a rolling expanse of desert and scrub unfit for life, but somehow a city had been settled there and somehow it had grown.

Juárez was more populated than El Paso across the border and more densely packed. In some places it was almost an echo of America, but in most it was hardscrabble buildings on buildings and people sweating out their living. In the *colonias*, where there was little electricity and sewage, the buses from the *maquiladoras*, the factories free trade built, ran to them day and night.

It was not the city center or the *mercados* or the *colonias* that interested Cooper. He wanted to see the place they called Los Campos, the Fields. There were many places like it, well away from the reeking air and close streets of the city proper, sealed off from the bustle and kept immaculate with the power of money.

Eventually Cooper found it behind a long march of barred fencing topped with razor wire growing out of the hill country. He passed the gated entrance with its armed guards. He circled around a while getting a feel for the place. Here and there he saw the white walls of estate houses set down among green trees and broad expanses of water-hungry lawn.

He parked at the far end of a length of fence and walked up to it. On the other side were trees marching up the side of a low hill, the ground underneath them just dirt and rocks with a few patches of starved grass. Twin coils of razor wire made the barricade look like the first line of defense around a prison. But a man who knew what he was doing could pass through that without being hurt.

Not for the first time he wished he had a better idea of where Ruíz's home was, what surrounded it and how he could approach from the outside. He knew he would have to come at the place on foot, cross somewhere like here and cut a path through the trees to the target. If he could find enough of a vantage point he might be able to use a rifle. If he could not, then he would have to mount the wall of the house itself — because there would be a wall without question — and go in with close weapons like pistol and blade.

The house would have security. The reserve would have security. Getting out would be more difficult than getting in, particularly if things did not go smoothly or silently. He did not like the idea of fleeing through brush and trees with a search party just behind.

He would know more once they were inside. With luck they would show him the parts of the estate that he needed to see. The right window or the right set of French doors, the right spot on the back lawn or the right approach up the front drive.

The heat of the day made him sweat. Cooper got back in the car and turned up the air conditioning.

His suite at the Hotel Lucerna was still being held. Cooper was glad to get inside, to shower off the road dust he imagined on himself and change into something casual. He ordered a meal in his room and sat staring out the window at the city while the television droned on in the background. He was thinking about Los Campos and the home of Sandalio Ruíz and part of him was also thinking of Olivia. He wondered if he would see her again. Valencia would arrange it.

When he was finished eating he went to the bedroom to look over his weapons. He had decided to carry the P226 with him, but not the silencer. A bodyguard would have no use for a sound suppressor and to bring one along would be to raise suspicions he didn't need to deal with. He had a knife shaped like a dart, eight inches from tip to pommel, that he could lash to his forearm. It was possible security might even miss it. The blade was almost six inches, and the weapon could be used effectively to kill up close. He would not want to fight with it, but it would suit his purposes now.

Broken down into three sections inside a hard case he kept locked was the rifle, an Armalite AR-30 chambered in .308 caliber. This was the distance weapon he would use if he managed it. One shot would be best and then he could just walk away. He could kill the man with the pistol or the knife, he wasn't afraid of that, but the rifle bought time he could use to slip off into the mesquite trees and just disappear.

9.

That night he went to the Avenida Juárez.

There was talk about turning the district into a city within a city. With so much violence, the tourists weren't coming the way they used to. They didn't feel safe, and who could blame them. The proposed solution would put up walls and gates between the city at large and the brothels and bars and restaurants just across the footbridge.

Cooper thought of the district as a sore, where the city rubbed up against El Paso and raw flesh was exposed. On every corner someone was offering to sell roses or candy or pills or just directions to the best place to get pussy. Booths were set up to sell tourist crap: papier-mâché marionettes and straw sombreros and cheap beaded necklaces and a hundred other little things that were meant to remind you of Mexico, but were just sad.

Once Cooper would have come here like the lonely men and college boys to get sex and see the floorshows. He would drift from strip club to strip club dropping dollars more and more quickly as he grew drunker. Once this was Cooper's grotty playground, but now... now it was just a reminder.

He went looking for the club called Panama and found it without too much trouble. The taxi overcharged him for the ride, but it was just a few extra bucks and he didn't mind paying. The club had a cover charge that he paid and then he was in the under-lit, noisy guts of the place.

A girl was dancing on the little stage. She had small tits and the beginnings of a belly. She looked like she had Indian blood. A handful of young white men clustered around the rail putting up dollars and hooting every time the woman did something remotely sexy. They would be drunk off the cheap booze and maybe high on pills. There were places to buy pot, too, but there were too many cops to smoke it on the street.

Cooper went to the bar and ordered. A place like this did not have fine liquor and he didn't expect any. His eyes were adjusting, but every once in a while the whirling dance lights would flick across his face and he would be dazzled again.

Women prowled the club, some naked to the waist, offering lap dances and the occasional hand job. One approached Cooper, but he signaled for her to move on and she did so. There were enough people in the place that she didn't need to make the hard sell.

Cooper was thirty-nine years old. He had first come here twelve years before, but it seemed like twice that. Whenever he came he saw the familiar things that never changed — the dingy bar and the little round tables with red cloths on them, the girls with interchangeable faces — and it reminded him of that first time in a way that seemed hollower every passing year. One day he might stop coming here altogether. Maybe the name of the place would change or someone would spare the money to remodel. It would be too different, too distant, and he would lose the thread entirely.

He nursed his drink and another girl came out to dance. The music booming through the speakers changed, but only a little. It was either heavy metal or rap or techno, always American. Cooper did not know a single place that played Mexican music.

"Hey," the bartender said. "Hey, mister, you want a blue pill? Make you rock hard for the ladies."

"No, thanks," Cooper replied. "I don't need that."

"You want a good time, ask for Luisa. She'll make you happy."

"I'll do that," Cooper said.

He put away his glass unfinished and left.

Out on the street he was free of the stink of cigarette smoke and cheap liquor. In the evening the smog that lay over Ciudad Juárez eased off and it was possible to breathe. It was not so bad here as it was in Mexico City, but it was getting there as the years passed.

He wandered the string of blocks, ignoring the talkers on the sidewalk that tried to lure him into to see girls, girls, and more girls. In his mind he still saw Olivia and her breasts and felt the way she moved under him as he fucked her. There were not a half dozen sad whores in this entire district who could equal that.

Cooper wasn't sure when he made the decision, but it happened by the time he reached the end of the lights and business and the avenue petered off into quiet shadows. He knew that he would not come back to Juárez again after this. Perhaps he would work here, but he would not return to the Panama to have a reminder that he no longer needed. He had outgrown this place.

It was easy to find a taxi: they were everywhere. He asked the driver to take him back to the Hotel Lucerna. The radio was on full blast, playing *norteño* without regard for the comfort of the passenger. Cooper hated *norteño* but he didn't ask for it to be turned down or the channel to change. In a way this was just like Juárez: loud and thoughtless.

Dropped off at the hotel, Cooper paid the driver with a stingy tip. He did it out of spite for the radio and after he had done it he wished he could call the man back and pay him the rest. The urge passed quickly.

He was not ready to confine himself to his suite so he went to the pool and lingered there. A waiter came out to him and he ordered something with more class than he could ever get at the Panama. He took a seat and watched the water cascade from the mouth of a *faux* aqueduct into the lighted blue pool.

Cooper thought he would feel some kind of loss knowing that he would never come back, but he didn't. A part of him felt freed. He was not the young man who partied with abandon among the cheap strippers and whores of the Avenida Juárez. He was something different, better, and he no longer needed a reminder to know this.

10.

He had the rest of the week to spend at his leisure and by the time things were ready Cooper was about to go out of his mind from the wait. A note came from Barriga when it was time. Cooper gathered his weapons the way he planned and armed himself.

His suit was clean and pressed and he wore an understated tie. A bodyguard's role was to see and not be seen. He didn't want to stand out beside Barriga. The less notice Ruíz's men took of him, the better off things would be.

Barriga had a car waiting, a Mercedes S600 sedan in glossy black. Cooper tipped the valet and took the wheel. Barriga sat in the back seat. He wore white.

They drove in silence for a while. Cooper didn't put the sound system on and the car was utterly quiet. Even the noise of the street didn't penetrate the cabin. Traffic was slow because of a police checkpoint. Cooper ran the air conditioning.

"You know the way now?" Barriga asked.

"I do."

"What did you find?"

"That he's very secure there. I haven't seen the house, but the whole place is locked down."

"You can get in?"

"If I have to go that way."

"Perhaps you won't have to at all."

Cooper wanted to ask about the meetings, but he knew it was just idle curiosity. Knowing would make no difference one way or the other to what he was being asked to do. He glanced into the rear view mirror and saw Barriga looking idly out the window. There was stillness there.

It wasn't that Cooper was jumpy. He was used to waiting, used to taking his time executing a job. He did not rush things when rushing would disturb the natural order. It was better to let events happen as they would and react to them accordingly than to try and make something happen a certain way at a certain time. In this he and Barriga were clearly alike. Barriga would be thinking ahead, but he would never *be* ahead. The future hadn't happened yet.

When they reached the roadblock Cooper put down the window. Air conditioning whipped out and daytime heat replaced it. The temperature would hit 100 degrees or more today and already it was above 80. There were cops and soldiers manning the barricade. Cooper showed his ID to the soldier. The man didn't ask for Barriga's papers.

"*Buenos días,*" Cooper said and put up the window again.

Traffic picked up and Cooper found himself making better time. He was aware of Barriga at his back always. Anyone else he might not have allowed to sit behind him. It was too easy to put a bullet in someone's head from the back seat, or drape a garrote around the neck. Even though he knew Barriga would do neither, the possibility was always in the back of his mind.

"They'll never catch anyone that way," Barriga said at last. "The *narcos* don't travel with papers that say who they are, what they do. It's a waste of time and money, what they're doing. I don't know how people stand for it."

"It makes them think they're doing something."

"That must be it. If they see the police keeping busy, then everything will be better. They don't seem to notice that while they have soldiers stopping cars and demanding identification they're having ten murders a day."

"I think they notice," Cooper said. "They just don't know what else to do."

Barriga made an assenting noise and fell quiet again.

From time to time Cooper speculated on the people Barriga served and the work he passed on to Cooper. He wondered how different it was from what was happening in Juárez: the beheadings and the mutilations and the bald-faced shootings. But he knew: what Cooper did was cleaner, squared away, kept small. In Juárez a gang of cartel members would spray bullets into a crowd of people just to kill one person. For Cooper it would take one shot and no one would even hear it.

He thought about Bingham in Dallas. Bingham hadn't heard the gun.

Cooper felt better than Juárez again. The same way he felt superior to the *turistas* dragging their drunken asses along the Avenida Juárez and the sorry college kids hollering at the dancers in the Panama. There had never been a time when Cooper had been so crude, or at least he chose not to remember it. It was a dance in his mind, partnered to his memories of the place and never able to pass more than an arm's length away from them.

Maybe he would never come back to Juárez again for any reason. Not to work, not to play. He wanted different things now. He wanted Olivia and fine hotels and the comfort of his apartment in the relative safety of Monterrey. He didn't want to hear gunshots in the night or have to pass through roadblocks marked with trucks and sandbags and guns. He wanted the gentility of this Mercedes with its V12 engine and cat-silent running. Glancing back at Barriga, he knew he wanted that thing the man in the white suit had.

They drove out of the city center, away from the dirty, crowded streets and into the country. He navigated automatically, letting his mind go on wandering. When he reached the house he would have to be alert, but now he drifted.

When they reached the gates of Los Campos, he slowed and stopped. He put down the window again. The air here was even hotter and drier than it was in the city. A man with an Armalite slung underneath his arm approached the car. "This is private property," he said.

"Señor Barriga to see Señor Ruíz."

"You are on the list?"

"Check it and see."

The man retreated to an air-conditioned guardhouse where more men were on duty. They conferred and Cooper saw the man with a clipboard in his hand. When he returned, his manner was easier. The gate swung wide on electric hinges.

"Have a good day, señor," the man said.

Cooper put up his window without saying anything in return.

11.

The house was broad and white with pillars in the front and many windows. It had a separate wall, as he expected, and the house was set well back from it behind a long drive lined with trees, real trees and not the twisted hunchbacks of mesquite that dominated the landscape. There was a wide expanse of perfectly maintained lawn where the drive curved up to the front of the house. A second, smaller wall divided off the rear; Cooper saw it as he drove up.

Three men in suits waited at the head of the drive. They wore sunglasses and had identical short haircuts. Two had mustaches and one wore a full beard. Cooper could tell they were armed without having to see the guns; they moved like men with weapons.

One held up a hand for Cooper to stop twenty feet shy of the front doors. Another came around the side and stooped to look through the tinted rear window at the silhouette of Barriga. He signaled for Cooper to put the window down. Cooper obeyed.

"Ruíz," Barriga told the man at the window. The man nodded and Cooper put the window back up.

Cooper killed the engine. He left the keys in the ignition when he got out, and then he went around to open Barriga's door. Barriga stepped out onto the white-gravel drive and straightened his jacket. When he stepped forward toward the men, Cooper made sure he was within grabbing distance. A bodyguard would never let his client step outside that invisible circle.

"We must search you," said the man with a beard.

"Of course," Barriga replied. He put his arms out from his sides.

One of the other men patted Barriga down. When he was finished he nodded to the man with a beard. Barriga was able to step through the line of them, but they stopped Cooper from moving ahead.

Cooper put his arms up and let them pat him down. They found his gun and took it like he expected they would, but they didn't run their hands down his forearms and missed the dart-shaped knife he had strapped there. This was good to know and Cooper smiled a little at them when they were finished.

"Follow me, please, señor," the man with a beard said to Barriga.

They went up the front steps of the house. On the porch were a couple of rocking chairs that Cooper was certain had never been used. The men with mustaches opened the double doors onto a two-story-high foyer marked at the far end by twin staircases leading up to the second floor. Everything was open and breezy though the line of French doors in the back — four sets in all — was kept closed tightly against the heat of the day. The house smelled like a museum; it was sealed off and kept perfectly cool.

A woman came down from the second floor. She was in her fifties and dressed for summer. Handsome in the way rich women were who were beautiful in her youth, tending a little toward fat. Streaks of silver were in her hair, left uncolored. Not many women in her position would have done that.

When she came close her eyes flicked over Cooper as if he was a companion dog and she smiled at Barriga.

"Señor Barriga," she said to Barriga. "It's good to see you again."

"Señora Ruíz," Barriga returned. "It is good to see you, too."

They exchanged kisses on their cheeks and Señora Ruíz took both of Barriga's hands in hers. "It's been too long since you visited us and now you come just for business? When will you come as our guest? We're having a party next week."

"I would be happy to attend," Barriga said.

"Good. I will tell Sandalio."

"What will you tell me?" a man asked. He entered from a side hallway. Cooper hadn't seen him approaching because of a pillar in his way. The men with suits were still around him, which made him uncomfortable, and he did not like being taken by surprise. He almost put a hand in his pocket to have something to do, and then he stopped himself; bodyguards never put their hands in their pockets.

"Señor Barriga will come to our party," Señora Ruíz said.

"Ah, good, I'm glad to hear it."

Cooper took his first real look at Sandalio Ruíz. Like his wife, he was in his fifties and like her his hair was going silvery white. His was thick through the middle and had strong forearms covered in hair. When he shook Barriga's hand, Cooper saw gold rings. The man wore an open-collared shirt that was untucked and his grayed chest hair was prominent. His mustache was the neatest thing about him, his hair pomaded and short.

"How are you doing, Joaquín?" Ruíz asked Barriga.

"Very well," Barriga replied.

"That's good. Always good. As for me, I'm gaining weight." He slapped a hand on his belly. "I swim twenty laps a day in the pool and still I grow fat. What am I supposed to do about that?"

"I don't know," Barriga said diplomatically.

"Well, enough about that anyway. I have a place set aside for us to talk in the library. We won't be disturbed. This is your man?"

Ruíz turned his gaze on Cooper and Cooper had the sense that he was actually being seen for the first time. Señora Ruíz had forgotten him the moment she saw him, but Ruíz was different. He had sharp eyes like Barriga and those eyes assessed what they saw. He did not offer to shake hands with Cooper.

"Yes. His name is Cooper."

"We'll take care of him," Ruíz said.

"Have you had breakfast?" Señora Ruíz asked Barriga.

"Only a little something."

"Then you must eat. I'll take care of it."

Señora Ruíz bustled away. Ruíz himself remained calm. He had a placidity about him that reminded Cooper of the saying about still waters running deep. He grabbed Barriga's arm for a moment and smiled. "It is good to see you again," he said. "Come with me. Rudolfo, see to Señor Cooper."

Barriga and Ruíz went away. Cooper was left with the men in suits. They surrounded him on three sides as if they expected him to make a break for it. He wondered if they were disappointed when he didn't move.

The man with the beard spoke to him, "Señor Cooper, my name is Rudolfo. If you need anything, ask for me. If you have concerns, ask for me. I will be available to you during your time here."

"I'll need somewhere to wait."

"That has already been arranged. Follow me."

They led Cooper through the foyer toward the back of the house and the French doors. One of the men with mustaches opened the door for him and held it open and then they were out on the lawn.

Cooper saw now that the house was shaped like a capital I turned on its side, with the narrowest point being that part where the foyer tied it all together. The house had two stories all around, the windows blank to his wandering eye. He saw a camera watching the approach to the house. There was probably a second somewhere else. Vines climbed the walls and made for good hiding places.

Rudolfo walked first along stepping-stones that splashed into the green grass as in a pond. These marked the way to an extensive patio area shaded with trees and punctuated by table sets and chairs with umbrellas. The patio embraced a sizable pool that reflected harshly the way the mid-morning sun angled in. Later it would be a painful temptation to dip a toe in, especially as the day grew cruelly hot.

"You may sit wherever you like," Rudolfo told Cooper.

"How about here?" Cooper asked, and pointed toward a chaise longue with black-and-white stripped cushions. He noticed the pool had a black-and-white design in the center, the shape of a stylized tortoise. "Is this all right?"

"Wherever you like," Rudolfo repeated.

"Okay."

51

"If you're hungry, I can arrange for breakfast to be sent out to you," said Rudolfo.

"I'd like that."

"Very well. Can I get you anything else, Señor Cooper?"

"No, thank you. I'm fine."

With that the men in suits left Cooper behind. He thought one of them might stay, but they all retreated into the house and left him on his own. Turning slowly in place, he spotted a black post running up close to one of the trees. A camera was mounted atop it, the lens pointed directly at him. He was not alone.

After ten minutes a maid appeared from inside the house coming from the far wing. She had a tray with covered dishes and set it down on a near table. "Would señor like coffee or juice?" she asked. She had a pot of one and a carafe of the other.

"Both," Cooper answered. He sat at the table.

The dishes went out for him and coffee and juice were poured. He peeked under the cover of one dish and found *huevos rancheros*. It smelled delicious.

"Cream or sugar in your coffee, señor?"

"I can take care of it," Cooper said. "Just leave them."

"Is there anything else?"

"No."

"I will be back for your dishes when you're ready, señor."

"Thank you."

Besides the eggs he had chorizo sausage, refried beans, corn cakes and wheat tortillas. Slices of tender avocado adorned the side of his egg plate. For a touch of sweetness there was *cajeta de membrillo* and *dulce de leche* for spreading on bread. The coffee was from some rich, aromatic bean and the juice was freshly squeezed.

He ate and went on eating until he was full, but there was still food on his plates. After a while the maid came back and offered him more coffee, but all he could do was wave her away. Finally he was left on his own with just the camera for company.

Because he had never been a bodyguard or anything like it, Cooper was not prepared for what came next: boredom. He strolled the edge of the pool for a while, taking an opportunity to survey the wide back lawn and the white line of wall that marked off the Ruíz property from the greening hill country beyond. He marked the spot where the gentle swell of a hillock made for a perfect spot for sniping. Looking back he found that he could survey the entire back of the house from that position. It had a northerly exposure so it would be possible to set up by morning or evening and not be blinded by the sun.

When he had nothing else to see and the pool failed to mesmerize him, he sat on the chaise longue and simply stared off into space. The sky was a perfect blue and unspotted by even the smallest cloud. Once he saw a bird and it was the most exciting thing he could imagine. For a few seconds, at least, and then it was gone from sight.

Despite himself he drowsed on the chaise and even closed his eyes for a few minutes that stretched into twenty. When he woke up he was embarrassed even though there was no one to see. He wondered if Barriga could see him from the window of whatever room he was sequestered in. Did he know Cooper had been sleeping? Cooper forced himself to stand and walk around some more. The day was scorching.

It was coming close to lunchtime and Cooper had begun to think about food again when Rudolfo reappeared. The man crossed the wilting green lawn by himself. He didn't smile or offer any greeting. "Señor Ruíz and Señor Barriga have completed their business for the day," he told Cooper. "If you will come with me?"

Cooper went and was glad to see the back of his time by the pool.

12.

When Cooper and Barriga were back in the car and headed away from Los Campos, Cooper watched Barriga in the rear view mirror. The man was not quick to speak up and for a long time they rode without speaking to each other. It was Barriga who broke the quiet.

"What were you able to learn?"

Cooper took his eyes from the mirror and cast his gaze out over the road. They were headed into sandy flats dotted with scrub. The trees around Los Campos thinned out. They were back in the kind of desert that lived underneath the concrete and asphalt of Ciudad Juárez.

"I found out that they have a lot of electronic surveillance on the ground," Cooper answered. "They have cameras in the front and back, probably watching inside as well as outside, but I'll have to try for another look tomorrow. There are floodlights at the wall and on the house. It doesn't look like they use animals. I didn't see any sign of them anyway."

"How many men do you estimate Ruíz has around him?"

"I'd say six to eight. He didn't keep his men on me which means he couldn't spare them to keep watching. They used cameras instead."

"What does this mean to you?"

They reached a fork in the road. Cooper touched the turn indicator and guided the car into the right branch. They passed over a spray of gravel on the roadway and he heard rocks rattle against the underbelly of the car.

"I'd say that a direct hit would be impossible for one man to pull off. There's too much electronic security on the grounds for anyone to just walk in unless they had a connection on the inside. If I had someone like that, then I could guarantee a close delivery of the package, but as it is it'd have to be long range."

"You have ideas?"

"I saw one or two likely spots."

"Can you reconnoiter them?"

"Maybe. Is that what you want me to do?"

Cooper caught the movement of Barriga's hand in the mirror, waving the question away. "There's no need right now."

"What's the likelihood that I'll have to make the hit?"

"It's difficult to say. We are in the early stages of our discussion and much depends on how that discussion proceeds. I will try to give you some warning, but it's possible there may be a short turnaround time. You will be able to adjust to this?"

"Has it ever been a problem before?"

"That's not an answer."

"It won't be a problem so long as I can gather more intel. I don't know the man yet. I don't know his habits. I can't learn these things overnight."

"No one expects you to," Barriga said. "And don't worry yourself too much about it, Cooper. Like I said, I will try to give you fair warning."

"That's all I can ask for," Cooper replied.

A *colonia* grew out of the edges of the city ahead of them. Ramshackle buildings made of scrap piled onto one another in close patterns that barely allowed for foot traffic between them.

A rickety wall of sheet metal and plywood passed along a dirt roadbed. Cooper saw a barefoot child playing with a skinny dog, a stick and a length of rope.

Some of the *colonias* around the city were almost like real neighborhoods: there was water and power and someone came to collect the trash. Others were like this one, just an accumulation of humanity crashing against the more developed parts of Juárez. Huge mounds of garbage marked the edges of the *colonia*. A welter of cables stretched across many roofs and collected at a single post where electricity fed off to whatever homes were lucky enough to be connected.

Cooper had to slow because a trio of buses out of the city were making broad U-turns in the road and blocking traffic. These buses carried workers back and forth to the *maquiladoras* along the border. Americans would recognize the names on the goods that came out of those factories, like GM and Magnavox and General Electric, but they probably overlooked the *Made in Mexico* label as meaningless.

Maquila workers made 70 pesos a day. They worked twelve-hour shifts. Most of the employees were women and many of them came from the *colonias*, and before that from the country. Not good country like the wooded hill country around Los Campos, but hard country where very little grew and it was hard to scrounge together a meal for one, let alone a family.

Juárez was not the cheapest city to live in, either, and *maquila* wages were often not enough to afford an apartment close to work, a place with running water. The *maquiladora* buses came night and day.

The buses kicked up dust and for a moment they vanished in a sandy colored cloud. A fine film settled across the windshield. The car would need to be washed after a few days of this.

"What did you think of Señor Ruíz?" Barriga asked suddenly.

"I didn't get much of a chance to form an impression," Cooper answered.

"Tell me what you gathered from your first meeting."

Cooper didn't know why Barriga would want to know. He hesitated with his hands on the wheel as the buses trundled across the roadway and finally cleared aside. A cluster of women in *maquila* uniforms waited in the shade of a three-sided bus shelter made of metal and plastic.

"He's wealthy. He seems secure. He worries about his safety. Nothing unusual for a man in his position. Rich people always worry about their safety."

"Sometimes they have reason, though, don't they, Cooper?"

"Sometimes they do," Cooper said.

He drove on.

13.

On the morning of the second day Cooper went down to the little shop off the lobby of the hotel. He browsed the books and magazines and finally settled on a thick doorstop of a novel by an author he'd heard vague things about. When it was time to drive Barriga again he put the book on the passenger seat.

"How are you feeling today?" asked Barriga.

"Fine. Ready," Cooper said, thinking of the book. It made him feel foolish, bringing it along, but he recalled the boredom of yesterday and didn't wish to repeat it.

"That's good. I plan to have a productive talk today."

It occurred to Cooper that he could ask what Barriga and Ruíz talked about, but he knew Barriga would never answer. Moreover, just asking would violate some unspoken agreement between them never to delve too deeply into the doings of the other. They could talk about the security surrounding Barriga and even the hit itself in a vague way, but they would never speak of personal things or the details of delivery of the package.

They were immediately caught up in morning traffic and the going was slow. Trucks and cars crowded in around them, weather-beaten and sun-blasted. Cooper could not remember the last time he saw a new car out on the street just driving. In the circles of the Barrigas and Ruízes of Ciudad Juárez it was a different story, but among the regular folk that plied the lanes, not at all.

"I don't like this city," Barriga said after a while.

Cooper had nothing to say to that. He kept his eyes on the back of the truck in front of them. It was piled high with pipes, the load held down by barely adequate straps that showed much fraying. Barriga could go on if he wanted to.

"It's not like Mexico City. At least there you get the sense of progress. Here... I don't think there's anything progressive about Juárez."

A flick of the eyes toward the mirror and Cooper saw Barriga looking out the window with a deep frown on his face.

"It's dirty here. The people are dirty. And it's not just the *colonias*. There's a stink about the place. I wouldn't want to walk the streets here. What could I find, anyway? Tourist holes, and places cheap enough for the *maquila* workers to patronize. It's the poverty of the city, do you know, Cooper? There's being poor and then there's being without class. The people here are without a shred of class."

"It's a hard place to live," Cooper offered.

"There are worse places. At least in Juárez there are jobs to be had. Go south, Cooper, and you'll find whole sections of the country where the *peones* are living off government generosity. They can't scratch out enough of a living on their farms to pay the rent and they come with their hands out. They should come here and try to work for a living."

"Some do."

"Some do," Barriga agreed. His tone was sour. "But what about the rest of them? I could do without them."

Barriga had nothing else to say and eventually they crawled through the worst of the traffic and escaped into the countryside. Driving to Los Campos this time seemed quicker than it had before, or maybe Cooper was just getting used to the route. At the gate he had only to roll the window down so the guards could see his face before they waved him through.

Landscapers were working on Ruíz's great lawn, cutting grass with riding lawnmowers and edging with gas-powered tools. The noise was annoying when Cooper and Ruíz exited the car. The men didn't stop for guests.

Once again Rudolfo and the other men greeted them at the front door. This time there was no welcome from Señora Ruíz and Ruíz himself was slow to come to the foyer. Cooper used the opportunity to look around. He saw a camera near the front door and yet another at the top of one set of curving steps to the second floor. He wondered how many men Ruíz had detailed to watch these cameras, whether all of them were even connected or if some were just dummies to intimidate guests.

Barriga went away with Ruíz and Cooper was led out to the pool. "I'll send you breakfast," Rudolfo said without much enthusiasm.

When breakfast came it was just as expansive and hearty as it had been the day before. This time there was more fruit to choose from, but Cooper couldn't possibly eat it all. He thought the kitchen must think there was two of him.

A maid came out to collect the dishes. She was the same one from the day before. She saw Cooper's book and nodded. "It's nice to read out by the pool, isn't it, Señor?"

"Yes," Cooper said.

"Señor and Señora Ruíz have many parties out here. The view is so pretty. You get a good breeze through the trees."

Cooper didn't know what to say. "Yes," he repeated.

"I won't bother you, señor. I was only talking."

"It's all right," Cooper said. "I could use the company."

"They talk for a long time," the maid agreed. She gathered up the dishes onto the broad tray. "Señor Ruíz always has such meetings. Every time it is someone new. Sometimes the men who come with them have to sit outside by the pool. Like you. It must be very boring for you."

Cooper held up the book. "That's why I have this."

The maid smiled. "Yes. Have a good day, señor."

She left him alone with his reading and the slight stirring of a morning breeze. Sometime soon it would become still and hot and the pool would beckon again. What if he brought his swimming trunks? What would Barriga and Ruíz think of that? He found the fantasy amusing and smiled to himself and then he read the hours away.

14.

He was surprisingly engrossed in the book, unaware of his surroundings and the time. Only when he heard the scuff of a sandal on brick did he look up suddenly, cognizant of how much he'd let slip. His heart raced.

The girl flinched when Cooper looked up, as much surprised by him as he was of her. "I'm sorry," she said. "I didn't mean to startle you."

It was difficult to know her age exactly, but she was young, maybe eighteen or nineteen. Not yet twenty. She wore a white dress that stirred with the remnants of the warm, dry breeze and she was in sandals. Her hair was long and her features delicate. She could have been a sister to Olivia; they looked much alike.

Cooper half-rose from his chair in respect. "No, don't apologize," he said. "I wasn't paying attention."

"I didn't know anyone was out here," the girl said.

"I'm... waiting," Cooper replied.

"Waiting for my father?"

"Something like that."

Barriga hadn't said Ruíz had a daughter, but there was no reason for him to. Daughters or sons, they didn't figure into the hit he might be asked to perform. And sometimes it was better not to know. Knowing could only be a distraction.

The girl smiled a little. She was light, as if she didn't spend much time in the sun. When the breeze blew again the dress clung to her. "I see. You're not waiting for him at all. Not really."

"What makes you think that?"

"You are the hired help," she said at last.

This made Cooper smile. "Yes, I am. The hired help."

"Whenever someone comes with a bodyguard, the bodyguard gets tucked away. In the kitchen sometimes if the weather isn't good. You're lucky to be out by the pool."

"That's what they tell me."

"What's your name?" she asked.

"Cooper."

"I'm Lorena."

Lorena offered her hand. Cooper got up from his chair again and took it. It was slight. "Pleased to meet you," Cooper said.

"You're American?"

"I live in Mexico now."

"You speak very good Spanish for an American."

"I try."

Lorena looked back toward the house. Her hair drifted into her face and she brushed it back. "Have you been waiting here long?"

"All morning."

"I thought about going swimming before it was too hot. I don't like to swim when it's burning out. Do you?"

"I don't think I've ever given it much thought," Cooper admitted.

Lorena regarded him for a moment, looking as though she had something else on the tip of her tongue and was unsure if she should say it. Then she showed her white teeth. "You're an

American working for a Mexican. How exactly does that happen?"

"I'm not sure. It's just the way it worked out."

"Doesn't it usually work out the other way?"

"You ask a lot of questions," Cooper said.

"You don't have to answer if you don't want to, Cooper."

She said his name easily and this was pleasurable. Lorena was young, younger still than the girls Valencia sent to him, and perhaps too young, but he was already taken with the thought of what it would be like to have her. The feeling, the speculation, was automatic as it was with every woman he met of a certain age. Would he or wouldn't he? It was immature, even insulting, he knew, but it didn't stop him from thinking it.

"Señor Barriga has money," Cooper replied after a moment to consider. "Money buys a lot of things. Cars, houses... sometimes an American bodyguard."

"Are you very good?"

"At what?"

"Being a bodyguard."

"No. Not really."

The answer made Lorena look at him funny. Cooper wasn't able to read the expression, but he liked the way it made her face look: as if she had been asked to solve a very difficult math puzzle in her head.

"Will you be coming to the party?"

Cooper remembered Señora Ruíz asking about a party the following week. If Barriga went, he might bring Cooper along just to make a show of him as his bodyguard. The thought didn't appeal, but he was playing a part and it couldn't be disrupted. "I don't think I'm invited," he said finally.

"I hope you'll come. They'll have it by the pool. There will be barbecue because my father loves to cook with the pit over there. You see it? The brick stand with the metal cover? He can roast a whole pig in there. He'll spend all day at it."

"If I can come then I'll come, but I don't think I'll have much of an opportunity to mingle. I *am* the hired help."

"You can talk to me," Lorena said, and with that she turned and went. Cooper watched her go from his seat, the paperback book forgotten and everything else — the pool, the barbecue pit, the burgeoning heat and the dwindling breeze — pushed aside for the moment. She was lovely. He saw very little of her parents in her.

When she was gone it was quiet for a while, but Cooper's concentration was mussed and he wasn't able to return to the book. He read a page or two but couldn't remember what he had just read and finally he simply put the book down. Like he had the day before he strolled the edge of the pool out of shadow into light and back again.

He stopped at the barbecue pit. It was a solid construction of red brick and was set up so the great iron lid could be raised with a counterweight. Cooper did that now and from inside came the smell of charred mesquite and ash. It was big enough for a full-sized pig or even a man. For an instant Cooper had the image of Sandalio Ruíz spitted and dripping with grease as his heat-browned body roasted over glowing red coals. It was more comical than horrible.

Cooper put down the lid and then he saw Rudolfo advancing across the grass toward him. The man's face was unreadable even when he drew close. Cooper expected a rebuke for speaking to Ruíz's daughter. It wasn't to come.

"Señor Ruíz and Señor Barriga are going to work through lunch," Rudolfo said. "I've been instructed to provide you with a meal."

"That's kind of you."

"I'll send the maid out to you. Ask for whatever you like."

Truthfully, Cooper wasn't hungry for another meal. The huge breakfast was still settled into his belly and the thought of eating didn't appeal. But there was time to kill and they would be insulted if he refused.

"You are comfortable?" Rudolfo asked.

"As comfortable as I can be."

"Enjoy your meal, señor."

"I'll do that."

Rudolfo left and Cooper was alone again.

15.

Cooper read most of his novel by the time Barriga and Ruíz were done. The same good-byes were said and Cooper got behind the wheel of his car with Barriga in the back seat. It was then that Barriga told Cooper of the party.

"They'll expect to see you there," Barriga said. "It would be unusual if you didn't come."

"What am I supposed to do? Mingle?"

"Of course not, but it might be useful to you all the same."

Cooper couldn't imagine how, but he kept this to himself. Instead of saying anything else he drove on and let Barriga decide if he wanted to talk anymore. Eventually he did.

"The discussions are going well. Today was very productive."

Cooper nodded, though he wasn't sure if Barriga saw.

"I don't anticipate we will have to have to continue this for very long."

"What about the client?"

"I'm positive about that outcome. He's more useful to my people alive, anyway."

It wasn't that Cooper was wedded to the thought of killing Ruíz. He wasn't a psychopath, though he'd known a few. They were the sorts who began to see every situation as one that could be resolved through the careful application of violence, or sometimes not so careful. These were the ones riding the edge of it, untrustworthy at the trigger because they were unstable. No, Cooper wasn't one of them, but he didn't like the idea of sitting idle.

"How is your book?" Barriga asked.

"It'll do."

"Sound more cheerful, Cooper. You've being paid to eat Sandalio Ruíz's food and lounge by his pool. Anyone else would consider this a vacation."

Cooper considered. "It's just not my way, that's all."

"You're a professional, Cooper. It's why I like you."

"When is this party?" Cooper asked by way of changing the subject. He did not like to talk about himself or to be the subject of a conversation he didn't control. It wasn't modesty, but a way to keep from being spotlighted. He worked better at the corners, tucked away, not in the center.

"Sunday night. It will be a formal affair, so you'll need a new suit."

"I can do that."

"Tomorrow you'll have off. Ruíz has business elsewhere. Do you need the name of a good tailor?"

"I know one."

"You can add the expense to your bill when we're done," Barriga said. "My people won't mind. Think of it as a gift."

"I don't need any gifts," Cooper said more sharply that he intended. Then he said, more calmly, "I can take care of it myself."

"It was only an offer." If Barriga was insulted, he didn't show it. They never spoke much when they had dealings before. Usually it was a meeting in person or on the phone discussing a potential client, and then the deposit would arrive via courier.

They rarely talked about a job afterward; it was just another courier and another payment.

He wanted to talk about Lorena Ruíz and their strange meeting by the pool. Certainly Rudolfo and the other security detachment would have known to stop her from going out, or maybe she had just dismissed them. Nonetheless it was odd and odder still because she did not have the aversion to strangers that seemed endemic among the rich. Cooper didn't have the sense that she was being anything less than forthright, as if he was a real guest and not just "hired help."

Finally Cooper said, "I met Ruíz's daughter today."

"Oh?"

"It was nothing. She said hello, I said hello."

"She's a very beautiful girl, is she not?" Barriga asked. "But she's only seventeen, Cooper. A bit young for you."

Barriga's answer irritated him. He immediately regretted having said anything at all, but now it was out there and had to be dealt with. "I wasn't thinking that," he said.

"Of course not. And I never think it, either."

Cooper let the subject drop. There was a mocking tone to Barriga's voice that Cooper didn't like, even though what Barriga said was the truth. He *had* thought of her that way and he *had* chastised himself for it. What he didn't like was the way Barriga saw through him immediately, as if he were just a man and all men thought the same thing when confronted with a lovely girl like Lorena.

16.

The next day Cooper slept late and ordered breakfast in his room. It wasn't the sprawling feast he would have gotten at Ruíz's home, but it was enough. The hotel delivered more American flavors and less Mexican. He had eggs over easy and bacon and American-style pancakes with a side of strawberries and cream. He drank his orange juice and finished his coffee in front of the television news.

He had time before he to leave on the day's errand and so eventually he switched off the talking heads and fetched out his unfinished novel. With his feet up on the couch he polished off the rest of it and then set it aside. When he left the room he would probably just leave it behind and the maids would throw it away. Too bad, because it was actually pretty good.

It was after eleven when he left the hotel and navigated the Mercedes to a narrow downtown street a block away from a little park where office workers took their lunches under the shade of a few scattered trees. He parked by the curb and keyed the alarm and walked past dusty storefronts until he reached the one he wanted.

The shop of Claudio Garza was tiny and lined with pocketed shelves from which jutted bolts of fabric in various colors. A clothing dummy stood just inside the door, visible through the front window, and was the only indication that there was a tailor here; the business did not even have a sign.

Garza himself was a short, thin man with skin like tanned leather. His face was a heavily wrinkled and he wore thick glasses. When he saw Cooper the wrinkles pulled into a smile and the man came forward around the small counter to give Cooper's arms a squeeze. "Cooper! Cooper, how are you?" he asked. "It's been a long time."

"Four years?" Cooper asked. That seemed about right.

"At least," Garza said. His shop smelled faintly of pipe tobacco and hot metal. From where Cooper stood he could see part of the crowded back room where measurements and fittings took place. There was an ancient-looking sewing machine made of black steel. "I get your Christmas cards. That's how I know you're still alive."

Garza plucked at Cooper's suit. He took Cooper by the wrist of one arm and held it out from his side, examining the way the fabric hung from Cooper's body. He did the same on the other side. Then he looked Cooper up and down. His eyes blinked behind his lenses.

"Still fits," Cooper said.

"It could fit better. You've gained some weight?"

"Maybe a couple of pounds."

"You want me to let it out a little? Give you room to breathe?"

"I'm breathing fine now."

"So you say. It's no trouble."

"Don't worry about it."

They talked for a little while about things. Garza had two sons, neither of whom had gone into the trade of their father.

One lived in the United States and another in Ciudad Victoria. Garza informed Cooper of their accomplishments while he collected Cooper's new measurements. He did not need to write them down, but kept them stored in his head.

Cooper had almost forgotten how he first got Garza's name. It was a year after his first trip to Juárez and he had been indulging at the Panama when he made the acquaintance of a businessman in a nice suit. Cooper asked him where he could get a suit like that, more to make conversation than anything else, and the man had written Garza's address and telephone number on a slip of paper. All of Cooper's suits came from Garza's shop. Twice he had recommended the old man to others.

They went over fabrics together, matching them to the character of Cooper's tan and the season. Cooper wanted something in basic black, but Garza argued for something with a little more life. Eventually they settled on an olive-toned stripe that would match well with a subtle green tie. It was a two-button, non-vented cut. Again Garza took measurements to be absolutely sure.

The work was nearly done when Cooper glanced out the front window of the shop. He wasn't sure what drew his eye — maybe the flicker of a car driving past, or some too-quick shadow from a passing bird — but he saw the man immediately and knew he was watching.

The man was across the narrow street, eyes behind sunglasses, dressed like one of the businessmen and office workers that frequented these blocks. For a moment he and Cooper looked right at each other and then the man turned away to examine the shop window nearest to him.

"When will you need this?" Garza asked.

Cooper walked to the window. He looked left and right down the street for another watcher, but there was just the man, now wandering slowly along the storefronts and deliberately keeping his eyes averted. But he could see in the reflections.

"Cooper?"

"Uh, Saturday," Cooper said.

"So soon?"

"Yes, sorry," Cooper replied. The man was nearly at the end of the block and while Cooper watched he rounded the corner without glancing back. He entertained the thought that the man hadn't been watching him at all, but the way he looked in the front window of Garza's shop was too obvious, too purposeful to be an accident. "I have a party to go to."

"Ah, a party. I understand the hurry."

"You can do it?" He kept his eye on the corner. The man didn't reappear. Again the suspicion that he was out-thinking himself, but he knew he wasn't.

"Of course I can. There will be a rush fee. I'm sorry, Cooper, but business is business."

"I can afford it."

"I didn't doubt it, my friend. It will be done. And you must need new suits to replace those old ones. Four years is too long to wear the same clothes."

Cooper turned back into the shop. His eyes were dazzled from the slant of the sun outside and the shop looked dark all over again. "I have to go," he told Garza. "I have to go now. I'll talk to you again on Saturday."

With that he was out the door. Garza's voice followed him: "Allow time for a fitting!"

Out on the street it was hotter than inside Garza's shop but not so close. There was not the comforting odor of pipe tobacco. Cooper crossed the street, leaving his car behind, and went to the end of the street. He paused a moment at the corner he'd seen the man vanish around and then took the turn himself.

He saw the man lingering at the end of the block. The man saw Cooper see him and he immediately moved away from the little taco trolley where he'd been standing. He lost himself around another corner. Cooper pursued.

By the time he reached the end of the block, the man was moving away fast. Cooper thought about following himself still farther, but he didn't want to run down a sidewalk beginning to fill with workers on their lunch break. He went back to his car.

A look up and down the street showed no cars that hadn't been there when he pulled up, or at least none he recognized as new. When he got into the car and started the engine he looked in the mirrors for movement and then again when he pulled out. There was nothing.

17.

On his return to the hotel Cooper circled five times before he was convinced there was no one trailing him. It occurred to him then that someone might already know where he was staying and therefore wouldn't have to follow him, and the idea made the back of his neck itch.

He went to his suite and stalked the space. There had been no one in the lobby that moved like someone following him and he passed his floor on the elevator before taking the stairs back down. The itch would not go away.

His rifle case was still where he left it, and the lock still clasped. He opened it up anyway and inspected the weapon for tampering, knowing as he did it that he was letting his paranoia get away with him.

When he was done with that he put the rifle away and looked underneath the edges of the bedside tables and behind the headboard of the bed. He checked the tables in the front room, as well as the marble lip of the bar. There was nothing. Finally he took the room phone and disassembled it to see the ear and mouthpieces. Again nothing.

Speculation followed. He had no way to tell if the man on the street had been one of Ruíz's men or not. If it was Ruíz then he would likely know where Cooper and Barriga were staying and so could afford to send just one or two followers to see what they did when they were away from there. Or perhaps it was some interest Cooper didn't suspect, which made it worse.

He'd been sweating and he wanted to get out of his clothes and into the shower, but as long as the itching was there he couldn't turn his mind to more mundane tasks. He considered calling Barriga and letting the man know what had happened, but until he had more it was just his wheels spinning and catching nothing. Barriga would say he was too suspicious and he would not be far wrong.

Not for the first time, Cooper regretted letting the man go. He would have looked crazy running the man down in the street, but then he would know one way or another what was going on. Maybe he was mistaken about everything and the man was nobody. Cooper couldn't get himself to believe that.

He burned hours running over the details in his mind, stringing back week-by-week. Ruíz was the first and most obvious culprit, though Cooper was unsure when the follower had picked him up. Cooper chastised himself for missing it; he should have been more aware. Moreover, Cooper didn't know why a follower would be interested in a bodyguard, unless the cover story had already cracked. At least they had not gotten to the rifle. The rifle would expose everything.

Mentally Cooper rolled back the clock to Dallas. The Bingham hit had been as clean as such things went. He had surveilled the man for three weeks before delivering the package and everything was just as he planned for it to be. Cooper picked up on Bingham's habit of cruising the same business hotels, working the bars and finding men like himself: away from their wives, looking for that thing they could not do for themselves. It been almost too easy and no one had been watching, or at least no one Cooper had seen.

Had someone been watching? Cooper worked at the idea now and it made the itch worse. Why would they watch and not do anything? Or was it worse than that: had Cooper left some trail that could be picked up and acted upon? Were they just now catching up to him? How? When?

A drink slowed down the turning of his mental wheels and a second did still more. Cooper was pouring a third before he considered where that third drink might lead him. Tomorrow he would be back with Barriga and back at Ruíz's estate. He did not want the throbbing headache, the sharp stabbing of light in the eyes, the infinitesimal slowness, that lethargy, that no amount of home-brew cure could master. This was why he did not drink on jobs.

He looked out the window at the city. It was getting toward evening and the sun cast a hot orange and red across the buildings and streets below. The colors made the city look almost attractive in a way it was not usually, but Cooper was not thinking about beauty; he could only think of the follower.

If he saw the man again he would know him. This much Cooper could be absolutely certain of. But now the man knew he was burned. He would be rotated with another follower. Maybe he would take the wheel of a chase car and another man would do the street work. The thought was infuriating and almost set Cooper's mind churning again.

Cooper distracted himself by ordering dinner in his room. By the time it came he had forced a level of calm on himself and he was able to take the meal and offer a tip as if nothing was the matter. He considered calling up the hotel masseuse and arranging for a hot rock massage, but the tension he felt couldn't be disposed of by rubbing muscles.

He ate mechanically, staring at the blank television set he did not turn on. He barely tasted the food. When it was gone he took the shower he'd been waiting for and laid on the bed in his robe just staring at the ceiling.

18.

Sleep didn't chase Cooper's concerns away. He dreamed of being in an open-air *mercado*, convinced that there were watchers just behind him. As many turns as he took, they were always on his trail until he ran off the edge of the market into an unformed gray that stuck to his arms and legs and eventually held him fast. They would be able to come for him in their own time now and kill him. This he was absolutely convinced of, that they would kill him and there was nothing he could about it.

He woke in the night, but he wasn't sweating. Instead he was very cold, with the vent of the air conditioning blowing directly onto him from above. He found an extra blanket in the closet and draped it over himself and lay awake for a long time just listening to the breath of chill air as it cascaded down upon him. Eventually he slept again and didn't dream anything at all.

When he and Barriga met in the hotel lobby, Cooper told the man nothing. They passed morning pleasantries but nothing of substance. The valet brought Cooper's car around. He wanted a chance to check it for devices, but there was no time and he wouldn't know what he was looking for, anyway.

Driving Cooper spent more time watching the mirrors. Once he thought they were being tailed, but the car turned off and they were on their way alone. When they passed outside the limits of the city proper and the road opened up they were truly alone and any follower would have stood out.

Of course they would not need to follow Cooper and Barriga; they would know where they were going. The itch returned.

Everything else was the same: Cooper gave up his gun, Barriga left him and once more he was marched out to poolside where he did not even have his book to keep him company. He found himself growing frustrated because he was only seeing the same rooms, the same stretch of back lawn and the pool itself. He distracted himself now by observing the little hillock off the edge of the property where he could set up with his rifle and sweep the entire back of the house.

He wondered which room was Ruíz's and if the man even had a window facing the rear. While he was looking he thought he saw a woman's shape and a white dress, but it turned out to be a curtain and not anyone at all. He thought of Lorena then, but the image of her annoyed him because he was thinking only of the work, of delivering the package.

This morning he had no taste for the great breakfast they served him. As he had the night before he ate like a machine and left more on the plates than off. The only thing he took more of was the rich coffee.

Cooper looked at the glass eye of the camera watching him. He resisted the urge to give it the finger.

He had decided that the only way to be sure of the tail was to expose himself to it. Somehow they had found him once and so they could find him again if they tried. He had to return to Garza for the suit. Maybe they would pick up his trail there. Maybe they were watching Garza's shop even now.

What he would do once they had him again, he didn't know. He needed to know them, and the first step was by observing how they observed him. If they were aggressive then he'd know there were plenty of them to make up for the ones he burned. If they kept their distance, he'd know they were setting him up for a closer pass by another team entirely, maybe for a hit.

Cooper had never been the target of a hit. He had always been too careful, too clean on exit for that kind of blowback. As when he killed Bingham he left nothing that could be traced back to him. His employer was the only hard link between him and the client.

Given time and space to wonder, Cooper considered whether it might be Barriga that they were after. If he were Barriga's primary cover, then they would want to know his movements, his habits. They might be curious why he left Barriga without cover at the hotel when he went to visit Garza. They might plan to deliver a package the next time Cooper split from Barriga.

It began to make more sense to Cooper, but he wasn't comforted. Of course they were watching Barriga. They had no reason to look for Cooper because he was no one. The last person from Barriga's organization to see him was Amador and before him a string of men whose faces blended into one another and whose names were forgotten. Barriga was the constant and it was only now that they were so close together that Cooper had a tail.

At least it hadn't been him that slipped up. That thought had been screwing itself into his ear for the past twelve hours. Somehow he'd broken his winning streak and they were all over him. He couldn't bear the thought of such a miscalculation. But Barriga... now he could blame someone else.

19.

Each day after that Cooper watched the mirrors and drove with care. Whenever he thought he saw a tail, he made a fresh turn or two to see if they would follow. None did. He would have liked to vary the times they left the hotel, but those were fixed to the schedule between Ruíz and Barriga.

On the Saturday before the party the two men took another break and Cooper was on his own. He left the hotel with the same watchful eye and this time when he visited Garza he parked two blocks away at a meter on a busy street.

The air smelled of heat and car exhaust. As with Mexican drivers everywhere, the car horn was a means of communication and at the knotted snarls of traffic near lights or stop signs there was plenty of talk. Cooper stepped onto the sidewalk and carefully checked both ways before moving on.

He was certain no one was following by the time he reached Garza's shop. He saw no one on the narrow street and all the cars parked there were empty. Cooper was almost ready to tell himself that he had been mistaken all along, but he could not go so far.

The suit fit him perfectly by the time he left the shop. He bid Garza farewell knowing it would be another year or more before they saw each other again. The old man seemed to take this in stride. He was like Cooper and he was not demanding.

Cooper walked back to his car. It was undisturbed. He looked around once again, as if he would suddenly catch the eye of the men following him, but there was no one. A woman passed close by and smiled at him. He smiled back.

There was no tail. He was a fool.

20.

Things were different when it came time for the party. Both Cooper and Barriga were in new suits and when they reached the Ruíz estate the long drive was clotted with other cars waiting their turn before the front entrance. There were Mercedes and BMWs and Rolls Royces but no sign of nouveau riche trash like a Lexus. The people that came out of these cars were all of a type Cooper saw: graying and well dressed and comfortable in their wealth. They were all like Barriga.

Valets worked the front of the house. Cooper didn't know where they were parking the cars. He surrendered his keys and then his gun to the quartet of security men at the door. Rudolfo was nowhere to be seen. Cooper imagined him at the bank of monitors in the nerve center of the house, watching everything, smiling at nothing.

A man in a tuxedo led Cooper away from Barriga once they were inside. They passed down a half-lit corridor toward the smell and sound of a kitchen. Through the door they were in bright light, surrounded by movement.

"Make yourself comfortable," the man in the tuxedo said. He waved his hand to the corner of the big kitchen space and left.

The kitchen had an eating area with a large harvest table and benches on both sides. There were a half-dozen bodyguards sitting there with food and drink in front of them. All of them, like Cooper, were in tailored suits, but all were Mexican.

He looked at them and they at him until finally one said, "Come and sit with us." He made some space for Cooper on one of the benches and cleared back the plate of food he picked at.

Cooper sat among them. He felt tension, or perhaps it was just his imagination. These men were real bodyguards and they all had the same air about them. Cooper lacked that and he was certain they could tell.

He distracted himself by watching the kitchen staff. There were a dozen working in tandem, sliding in and out of clouds of steam. Two prepped hors d'œuvre while a third loaded silver platters that were in turn collected by wait staff in black. The process was quick, mechanistic.

It was difficult to imagine anyone using the kitchen for anything other than party cooking. The room was long and wide with twin banks of grills and prep areas. Bright lights glared down and washed out everything in white, casting down heat of their own. There were two sets of glass-faced ovens the height of a man. Cooking was happening everywhere.

After a while the bodyguards began to talk amongst themselves. Of the guests at the party Cooper saw none. The men were happy enough about that, especially since the kitchen staff were generous with the hors d'œuvre and likewise when the main dishes began to assemble.

Cooper talked with the bodyguards and for their part they seemed perfectly fine having him there. Some talked about their current protection and others about the people they had protected in the past. Several of them were from Mexico City, where kidnapping had been rife for years, but now the money had gone north to the border as the bodies in the streets began to multiply.

"Never mind that no rich man's ever even heard a gunshot," said a bodyguard named Luis. "If they think they need it, they need it."

More joined the table. If he lied to them they would know it, so Cooper told them the truth — that Barriga was his first close-protection assignment — and they were tolerant of that. Two of them were also on their first jobs and the old hands like Luis were quick to offer advice and sympathy.

Food was still moving out of the kitchen. More food than Cooper would have thought a party could consume. He imagined a throng out by the pool, and a massive barbecued pig still to come, served straight out of Ruíz's custom pit. There was so much noise from the great blowers sucking out heat, steam and smoke that he couldn't even hear the distant sound of talk.

Cooper got up from the table as yet another bodyguard came to join them. By now there were more bodyguards than there was space and several were standing up and eating the free food from little china plates. Cooper was reminded of the children's table. "I need the restroom," he said.

"Don't fall in," Luis admonished him. This got a laugh.

"I'll try."

A camera was situated at the end of the kitchen, looking out over the busy cook-staff. Cooper wondered just what the security men meant to see. There were none around.

"The bathroom?" Cooper asked one of the *commis*. The woman pointed him through a metal door with a porthole in it. He followed her finger.

It was unlit in the hallway beyond, with the only light coming from the porthole. He went a few yards until he saw the open door of a restroom, the glint of reflection from porcelain.

He urinated and washed his hands and switched off the light. Standing in the dark he let his eyes adjust until he could see more of the hallway as it led away from the kitchen. He didn't know what part of the house he was in, but it was somewhere new and he was hesitant to leave it.

Cooper went away from the kitchen. He was careful and quiet. Two doors passed on his right and then he was in a wider space that he realized was a staircase. He could hear the party now and light came from up ahead.

The footsteps came too quickly for him to hide from them. They descended lightly down the stairs and stopped on the landing above. Cooper looked up and saw her there, limned against a high window turned orange from the artificial light outside.

Lorena wore a white dress again, but it was different, finer, than what she'd had on by the pool. Her outline was ghostly in the half dark and her eyes totally black. Cooper opened his mouth to say something to her, but nothing came out. She stared at him and he at her.

Without saying anything, she turned back up the stairs and vanished. Cooper put a foot on the step. He heard new footfalls approaching and one of Rudolfo's security men swept into the hallway from the direction of the party. "Hey," he said, "what are you doing out here? You belong in the kitchen."

"I was just in the bathroom," Cooper said. He looked up at the space where Lorena had been, or had he just imagined it? "I got turned around."

"Well, get turned around the right way," the security man said. "Move it."

The man prodded and Cooper went. He left the specter of Lorena behind.

21.

Cooper spent another idle day indoors at the hotel. The feelings of paranoia were back and he didn't want to be seen on the street. He wasn't afraid of the violence. He was immune to the violence. Rather, he thought about the man who followed him and knew that if he went out he would see that man everywhere.

He was anxious for the business with Ruíz to be completed. Sitting with the bodyguards in the kitchen at Ruíz's estate he felt more exposed than he had before. He did not like people knowing his face, learning his name, learning *him* as they would by just observation.

The assignment as Barriga envisioned it was a wash. He knew no more about Ruíz's home today than he did on his first day. Cooper didn't consider learning the layout of the kitchen a positive.

Despite sleeping he was tired and restless and growing angry with Barriga and himself. He wanted to be out of Ciudad Juárez and on his way to anywhere. He missed the comforts of his own apartment, the pleasure of food he cooked himself. There was a point where hotels could no longer provide what a guest needed and he was at that point now.

The day grew hot enough that the glass of the suite's windows became uncomfortably warm to the touch. A sullen layer of brownish smog settled over the city. Cooper didn't want to breathe it anymore.

He took dinner in the restaurant and saw Barriga there. The man waved him over to his table. A place was set for Cooper and a waiter brought him ice-cold water in a crystal glass.

"How are you tonight, Cooper?" Barriga asked.

Cooper weighed his reply before answering. He sipped the water and made a show of unfolding his napkin and putting it in his lap. "I'm concerned," he said at last and he waited for Barriga to say something else before he continued.

"I can tell. It's been bothering you for days, hasn't it?"

Again Cooper was irritated. He did not like being read, did not like being so close to someone that he could be read. "It has," he said.

"What is it?"

The waiter brought menus. Cooper glanced over his without much enthusiasm. "I'm concerned about security," he said. "I don't like being so close to the client for so long. It's not something I'm used to. And I think maybe there's something coming back on us. Ruíz may have his own interest in this."

"Why do you think that?"

Cooper told Barriga what he had seen and felt on that day outside Garza's shop. Speaking it out loud he realized how slender the thread was between what he suspected and what he had seen, but it was a conclusion he could not shake regardless. It felt better to have it out on the table and by the time the waiter took their appetizer orders he knew he had gotten through to Barriga; the man was watching him more carefully, dark eyes glittering.

"How long were you going to keep this from me, Cooper?"

"Until I had more to go on. Or you asked."

"I'm asking now."

"Let me ask you back: how much longer is this going to continue?"

"I can't discuss our business with you."

"I don't need to know the business," Cooper returned. "Just how long it's going to take. We're hanging out on this one, farther than I'd like, and I want to fold it up before one of us gets burned."

Barriga watched Cooper from across the table. He was like a lazy tiger. "Do you think I would let you get burned, Cooper?"

"I think sometimes you wouldn't have a choice."

A silence grew between them. The waiter brought them a spicy tortilla soup that made Cooper's nose run. From time to time he looked up from his bowl and saw Barriga busy with his as if they had not just been talking.

Eventually Cooper said, "I only telling you what I see."

Barriga touched his lips with his napkin. "Can you handle this, Cooper?"

"Yes," Cooper said.

"Because if you can't handle it, I can have someone step in for you. This needn't go any further."

"I can handle it."

"Good. I wanted you because I knew you would be able to. I have confidence in you, Cooper. More than you know."

"I appreciate that, but—"

"No buts," Barriga said. "We continue as before. If you think Ruíz is watching us, then that's all the more reason for my meetings with him to go well. He has a stake in this, too. I would be surprised if he's not trying to find some advantage over us."

"To what end?"

"Why does anyone do anything? To have more. I told you I can't discuss it, but you know this is a matter of profit. Mine. His. The people I represent. Even yours. We're playing games within games and the end result is money."

"I still don't like it."

A man at the table next to them lit up a cigarette. In Mexico it was still acceptable to smoke in places where it had been banned in America. Cooper smelled the cigarette and immediately he wanted one for himself. He hadn't smoked in over two years, but the craving was strong.

This time Barriga's voice had an edge to it that Cooper caught immediately. The man's eyes were darker still. He pushed his empty bowl aside and folded his hands on the table. "You're still concerned?"

"I can't earn money if I can't operate," Cooper said.

"You won't be disappointed," Barriga replied, and when Cooper didn't say anything he pressed on. "Do you think you will? Do you want some guarantee? Because I can't offer you one."

"I don't need a guarantee."

"Trust me," said Barriga. "I will steer you the way to go."

Cooper drummed his fingers on the edge of the table. They itched for a cigarette. "All right," he said.

"Then let's have a nice dinner together and talk about pleasant things."

22.

Cooper had come to see the breakfasts at Ruíz's home as a test of his endurance. On the first day it had been a welcome surprise in its vastness and lavishness, but each time it was repeated Cooper found he had less and less stomach for it. This morning he had no appetite at all.

The maid brought him the loaded tray as usual, but trailing after her was Lorena in a yellow dress with embroidered flowers of white and red on the neck. She was barefoot and came across the grass smoothly, like she had practiced it.

"*Buenos días*," Cooper said.

"Good morning," Lorena replied. The maid paused as if she was confused. Cooper saw Lorena dismiss her with a little wave of her hand. The woman glanced back once and then headed for the house.

Lorena looked over the spread the maid had left behind. "Breakfast," Cooper said.

"At least we know you won't starve to death."

"Would you... would you like to sit?" Cooper asked.

"Thank you."

She took the seat across from him. Without asking she took a coffee cup and poured herself some. Cooper noticed there were two cups to begin with. She added plenty of cream and just a touch of sugar and then turned it all with a lazy spoon.

"You didn't come talk to me at my parents' party," Lorena said.

"I wasn't allowed to mingle."

"I know. They put you in the kitchen with the other hired help."

"That's right."

Lorena sipped. She made a little face and then added some more sugar.

"You must have known they'd never let me out with the real guests."

"I thought they might make an exception for you. Everyone loves to have an American at the party. More than one if they can manage it. Nothing makes a Mexican feel more important than having an American as their guest."

"I didn't know that."

Lorena nodded. "It's true. But usually it's some boring old man from a *maquila* concern. And his wife. They come across from El Paso and make nice with everyone before going to back to where the real money is. Where it's safe. Over the border."

She had a young face, but her voice was bitter. A notch appeared between her eyebrows and then it faded. Cooper saw her watching him and so he busied himself with the process of eating. He still hadn't developed an appetite for it.

"Maybe you can attend another party. As a real guest," she said after a while.

"Somehow I don't think I'm on too many people's guest lists."

"You never know. Everyone's looking for something new and interesting."

"Even you?"

"Especially me."

"How interesting am I?" Cooper asked.

Lorena shrugged delicately. Her coffee was finished. "I don't know yet. And by the time I find out, you will probably be gone. That's the way it works in my father's house; people come and go."

"That's probably true in my case. I'm told not to get too comfortable."

"With all of this?" Lorena said and she raised her hands to encompass the whole of the back lawn, the pool and the looming house, totally empty except for the two of them and the ever-watchful camera.

"I won't be sad to spend my days doing something else," Cooper admitted.

Movement caught the corner of Cooper's eye. He saw Rudolfo marching across the grass. He did not need to think about why the man was coming.

Lorena saw him, too, and the corners of her mouth drooped. "I'm afraid I can't visit with you anymore," she said.

"It was nice while it lasted."

She got up from the table. Quickly, impulsively, she reached out and touched Cooper's hand and then she stepped away from the table as Rudolfo arrived. "You're needed inside, señorita," he said without preamble.

"Of course I am," Lorena said. "Good-bye, Cooper."

"*Despedida*," Cooper said and he watched them go away.

23.

"If my people decide that Señor Ruíz is to be sanctioned," Barriga asked, "how much turnaround time would you need?"

They were on the road back to the city, kicking up dun-colored dust in a plume behind them. The valets at the hotel were keeping his car washed and neat after each foray to Los Campos, but every day brought new dirt that had to be cleaned.

Cooper considered the question. It had never been far from his mind, but he didn't want to answer too quickly. In his mind's eye he saw himself on the grassy hillock with the scoped AR-30 taking aim at a crowd of dressy men and women around the pool. Ruíz was silhouetted against the under-lit blue water. A touch on the trigger and he was dead.

"Twenty-four hours," Cooper said.

"You could get to him so quickly?"

"I'd find a way."

"Even inside his home?"

"If that's what the situation calls for. Does it?"

"You know I can't answer that yet."

If he had go in things would be more difficult. First he would have to get access to the larger confines of Los Campos and make it to the wall of Ruíz's estate. That much would be easy. Evading cameras and motion-controlled floodlights would be something else entirely and if the house's doors were wired — and there was no reason why they wouldn't be — it would take some time to make entry. He still didn't know what floor Ruíz's bedroom was on, or in what wing of the house. It could be done, but it would be a challenge.

"Ideally he could be drawn out in the open," Cooper said. "Somewhere I can work without his security breathing down my neck."

"You have ideas?"

"I may. But it would take you to make it happen."

Cooper glanced in the rear view mirror and saw a new vehicle there: a black Land Rover driving through the ephemera of dust the Mercedes left behind. Its windows were tinted dark and there was no way to see how many people were inside.

Barriga said something Cooper didn't hear. Instead of asking the man to repeat himself, Cooper kept watch on the Land Rover as they plied the same road. There was a fork up ahead; branching off before they reached the *colonias*. One way led to the city, the other off in some direction Cooper didn't know. He took the latter. The Land Rover followed.

"Cooper?" Barriga asked.

"There's someone following us," Cooper said.

Barriga glanced behind them. The Land Rover kept its distance, but it was always the same distance, neither nearer nor farther. Cooper felt his pits grow damp.

The road deteriorated as it looped around to come close to the ramshackle border of a *colonia*. Cooper saw people walking from a well carrying bright plastic buckets filled with water. The Mercedes hit a bad pothole and the whole cabin was jarred. The Land Rover hadn't come any closer even though it could have overtaken them on the uneven surface. The sweat spread to Cooper's palms. He did not like being out here, exposed, with no idea what was ahead. For all he knew the road would simply peter out and stop in a dusty field somewhere and they would be caught.

This was when a bodyguard, a real bodyguard, would know what to do. This was not just Cooper alone, but Cooper plus a principal, Barriga. There was no dash to safety without Barriga; he was part of the equation.

Suddenly the Land Rover lurched forward and began to notch away the distance between them. Sun glared off the windshield and made the Land Rover an orange eye. The driver would be blinded.

"Hold on," Cooper said.

He turned and hand-braked and the Mercedes slewed around on a road surface that was more dirt than pavement. A massive, choking cloud of tan grit billowed around them and for a moment the Land Rover and everything else was obscured. Cooper put the accelerator down and the car surged forward bumpily and when it broke the whirling cloud the Mercedes and the Land Rover were almost nose-to-nose.

The Land Rover swerved hard to the right to avoid a collision. Cooper kept the steering wheel locked straight on. The Mercedes picked up speed and the tornado of dust kicked up by the Land Rover dropped away from them. Cooper took the turn back onto the city pathway with too little brake and too much speed, all four tires skidding in motion.

When he looked back again, the Land Rover was gone, but he didn't slow down. Only when he was on a clean paved road did he slow and then to avoid hitting one of the buses plying the route from there to the maquiladoras.

"What the hell was that, Cooper?" Barriga asked.

"I don't like being followed."

"That car?"

"I don't know. I didn't like it."

Barriga was thoughtful in the mirror. He looked back. Cooper checked the mirrors again. There was no one behind them. "You're on edge."

"I'm just doing my job."

"You think Señor Ruíz has been keeping an eye on us," Barriga said. It was not a question.

"I think someone has. That's twice I've been cruised."

"It's possible that he's watching us," Barriga admitted.

"Someone is."

"You suspect other players?"

"No. I don't know. Maybe. It's hard to tell. Who else is involved?"

"That's not something I'm at liberty to discuss with you."

"Even if it means I'm unprepared? You're paying me to be your bodyguard; I need to know who I'm protecting you against."

That was something Barriga had no reply for. They finished their trip back to the hotel in silence.

24.

The day passed into evening and then into the next morning. He and Barriga met together in the lobby as usual and nothing was said. They traveled together without speaking through the knotted traffic and into the countryside. Cooper didn't see the Land Rover.

Overnight he'd begun to question himself over the Land Rover. Whether it was really following them or just some random vehicle that happened to take the same wrong turn. In his mind Cooper imagined a truck filled with armed men prepared to force the Mercedes into a dirt rut and fill the car with bullets. In practice they had fallen behind and hadn't caught up with them again. He didn't know what to think anymore.

It was the waiting. On the one hand he was used to waiting, but then only on his own terms. This was different, frustrating. He did not have the working knowledge he needed to do his job and this made him angry. Barriga was the one who angered him.

There was still silence between them when they reached Ruíz's home. Rudolfo marched Cooper out to his poolside chair that served as his prison cell and he was abandoned to be stuffed with cooking from the grand kitchen.

He tried to imagine Rudolfo in the Land Rover, but the image wouldn't coalesce in his mind. One of Ruíz's other men would do the job, one of those underneath Rudolfo. Or perhaps Ruíz had specialists of his own.

Cooper didn't like this, the sitting and the thinking that came with it. His mind wouldn't be still now and the hours went by at a crawl. He found himself wishing for Lorena to come out and be with him for even a few minutes because she was at least something different and interesting and lovely to look at. Instead he got the maid and the food and the quiet lawn.

The clock ticked onward and the heat drowsed him. He would have been happy to sleep. When one of the French doors at the back of the house opened, he raised his head.

Rudolfo crossed the lawn. He had something in his hand. When he was close, Cooper saw it was a delicate envelope. The man handed it over. "For you," he said.

"Thanks."

"Is there anything else you want?"

"No, I'm good."

Rudolfo lingered. His eye was on the envelope, but Cooper didn't open it. Finally he turned away and headed back to the house. Cooper waited until the man was completely gone before he slipped a thumb under the flap and tore the envelope open.

He sat with his body between the camera and the envelope. There was no letter inside, but a little square invitation on thick, textured paper. Cooper turned the envelope over again, but it was not addressed to anyone.

The invitation was also unmarked. It had the date and the location printed on it in script, but he did not recognize the name of Rafa Madrigal, the host. The party was set for the coming Saturday.

After a little while the door at the back of the house opened again and the maid reappeared. She didn't bring another tray or even the pitcher of cold tea that she sometimes provided when the weather was especially hot. She seemed almost apologetic when she came close. "You're wanted inside," she said.

Cooper thanked her and gathered his jacket. The woman led the way back to the house and in the cool foyer he found Barriga and Ruíz together. Ruíz seemed jovial. "Ah, here he is!" he said brightly.

"It's time for us to go," Barriga told Cooper. "Bring the car around."

"You will have to come visit us again, Ignacio," Ruíz said to Barriga as Cooper passed. "We'll have a party, a *big* party this time. And you can invite some of your people to join us."

"I don't know if they would want to attend a party in their honor," Barriga said.

"Then we'll make it for something else!"

"We shall see."

In the front of the house a single guard stood sentry in the blazing heat. He'd taken refuge in the shadow of one of the pillars but his face was still shiny with sweat and his jacket stained at the pits. He gave Cooper a twisted look when he came out. "What are you doing here?"

"The car," Cooper told the man.

"It's still early."

"Not early enough for me."

The guard trundled off. After a few minutes he reappeared behind the wheel of the Mercedes. The air conditioning blasted, but the inside of the car had not yet cooled down. Waves of heat rose off the paint.

Cooper got in and waited for Barriga to emerge. Again it seemed like forever. He felt the invitation in the inside pocket of his jacket, stiff there against the material. He would have liked to ask someone about it, but there was no one.

Eventually Barriga emerged. Ruíz still spoke animatedly to him, touching Barriga's shoulder and arm frequently. The contact seemed to cause Barriga pain, but Ruíz did not appear to notice.

"... a vacation!" Ruíz said as Barriga pulled open the rear door of the car.

"I haven't been to Palmilla in a long time," Barriga said.

"Well you must, you must!"

"Perhaps I will. Good-bye, Sandalio."

"Good-bye, my friend," Ruíz said and he pushed the door shut behind Barriga.

"Let's go," Barriga told Cooper.

They drove carefully down the neatly raked gravel drive. The temperature in the car had finally begun to become bearable. In the back seat Barriga loosened his tie and then touched his forehead with his sleeve. He was about to say something. Cooper could sense it.

"He lives," Barriga said.

They drove back to Juárez.

25.

Barriga checked out of the hotel that night. Someone from the staff delivered an envelope under Cooper's door near dinnertime. Inside was a deposit receipt. No note from the man himself, which was no more or less than Cooper expected.

He was free. Free to do whatever he wanted. He could check out of the suite today and Barriga's people would pay the bill. He could go back to Monterrey and sleep in his own bed. But then there was the invitation.

Cooper didn't know the name of the host and after a couple of hours asking around he had his answer. Rafa Madrigal was the owner of several *maquiladoras* operating in the technology corridor on the Mexican side of the border. He had contracts with GM and Magnavox and others, producing high-tech goods for the American market. He was a wealthy man and he lived in Los Campos not far from Sandalio Ruíz.

There was no good reason for Cooper to have an invitation to Madrigal's party, but somehow he knew Lorena had arranged it. The invitation was blank, so it wasn't hers passed along. He was to be a real guest and not just relegated to the kitchen.

He wasn't sure how he felt about it. With the hit called off, there was no need for him to expose himself anymore. He could go back to Monterrey for some quiet time in his own apartment, sleep in his own bed, and maybe take a vacation in Mazatlán.

Lying on the beach would be a good way to forget why he had even come here.

The invitation drew him back. It made him curious, and his curiosity became an itch he couldn't scratch. He extended his stay at the hotel for another three days and went down to the pool for the first time in a week.

Cooper didn't feel the eye of surveillance on him anymore. He had convinced himself that it was Ruíz's men trying to gain some advantage by knowing where he went and what he was doing. Maybe they would wonder why he wasn't always at Barriga's side, or maybe that was a detail they overlooked completely. Certainly they treated him no differently after the close pass.

It occurred to Cooper that he could rent a house here. He had no compelling reason to stay and many reasons to go, but he found himself reluctant to part with this ugly, sprawling city with too many people and too much noise. He wondered if there was something available outside the city limits, in the country where Los Campos was located, free of the crowding and the violence and the smell of exhaust.

He knew the name of a broker who might be able to find something for him. Cooper resolved to call her later in the afternoon once he'd finished his time in the sun, listening to the splash-patter of water from the fake aqueduct and the fountain at the far end of the pool.

Today he was alone, which made his idle time less interesting than it might. At least in this pool he could get in and swim and so he did that, up and down the length of it again and again until his fingertips pruned. Once he imagined he was in Ruíz's pool, thumbing his nose at the watchful camera, making lazy backstrokes. He went under the water and came up again thinking he saw Lorena by the edge of the pool, but it was just a waiter refreshing his drink.

When he left the pool he was relaxed and buzzed from too many margaritas. He stripped out of his bathing suit and took a long nap on top of the covers, naked and suntanned. By the time he got up there was time for an early dinner where he had more drinks, and then he retired to his suite to watch the news until he was tired again.

The next day he called Elena, the real estate broker. He told her what he was looking for and she said she would do her best to find something. "It's a renter's market right now," she told him. "Everyone's looking to lease property."

"It's not long-term," Cooper was sure to tell her. "Just a couple of months, maybe."

"I'm sure I can find something. Wait for my call."

He didn't want to spend another day by the pool so he had a cab brought round to the front of the hotel and instructed the driver to give him a tour of the city. All the tourist spots he'd seen before, but it was a way to shut off his mind and just cruise through the busy streets without having to be aware of anything. He barely even noticed the soldiers and their armed trucks and the thickets of police that manned checkpoints here and there across the tangled maze of downtown.

The driver showed him statues and plazas and famous buildings. The cab's air conditioning wasn't very strong and it grew stuffy inside. Three times they looped through the city and then the driver offered to take Cooper to a place where the best whores could be found. The idea bored him and he told the driver to take him back to the hotel. He paid with a handsome tip on top and went inside to the bar where he could drink until nightfall.

He was falling into a rut. This was what happened when he spent too long away from home, looking at generic walls in the nicest of hotels. It was easy to grow fat and lazy and sodden with alcohol because there was nothing else to do. He could only watch so much TV, could only order so many room-service meals, could only laze by the pool so many times before it felt like a gilded cage.

Cooper thought about this and drank too much and actually staggered a little when he left the bar to return to his room. He skipped dinner that night and fell asleep in front of the television.

26.

He got a call from Elena the next morning with word on a rental house outside the city center. They made arrangements to meet before lunch at the address, which Cooper scrawled on a notepad beside the bed. He had a headache and was irritated with himself. A long, hot shower helped matters, as did a voluminous breakfast ordered from room service. He was reminded of Ruíz's then.

The Mercedes' GPS led him to the place. It was not so far out as Los Campos but enough that the worst of the city's congestion was left behind. There was still more dirt than green, but there was space and a freer sense of being. The house itself sat behind a wall of red adobe with a wrought iron gate closing off the drive.

Elena was in her twenties and had gained weight since Cooper had last seen her. They exchanged pleasantries and went in through the visitor's gate, headed up the front walk under drooping tree branches heavy with the heat.

The front door was carved and ornate and with a tin sun mask nailed to the wall beside it. The steps were tiled. Cooper stood and listened: there was no sound of traffic or even a human voice. It was pleasantly still.

She found the key and let them in. The foyer was wide and sun-splashed. Stairs went up and large rooms opened up on either side. The house was furnished.

"Everything you see comes with the lease," Elena said.

"Where are the owners?"

"Out of the city. They wanted somewhere... safer."

"Have there been problems with crime out here?"

"Not here in particular, but they wanted to feel more secure."

Security was a hard thing to come by along the border of Mexico and even less so in Juárez, but Cooper said nothing about this. He wanted into a brightly lit sunroom scattered with comfortable chairs. A little fireplace crouched in the corner for when the weather turned cold.

Elena told him the rental rate and Cooper found this more than reasonable. "The house has four bedrooms," she said. "Three bathrooms. There's a pool and a hot tub. The house also has two staff who handle cooking, cleaning and anything else you'll need."

"Where are they?"

"Out while I show the property."

"How long can I rent?"

"As little as a month or as much as a year. The owners aren't planning to come back anytime soon."

"And I can decide month to month?"

"If that's what you want to do."

Cooper nodded.

The living room was even more capacious than the sunroom. He went from there to the formal dining room with its massive slab of a table to the sunny kitchen. It was not as large as the kitchen at Ruíz's place, but more than enough for one person. There was much colorful tile. The kitchen had a walk-in freezer filled with food.

"What do you think?" Elena asked.

"I'd like to see the upstairs."

All four of the bedrooms were on the second floor. Cooper looked at each one and checked the sight lines from their windows. From two he could see the front street and from another he got a complete view of the back yard and swimming pool. The house was surrounded on all sides by the wall. He saw security lights at the corners. There had been sensors on the windows downstairs, but none on the upstairs.

The room he wanted was not the master bedroom, but one located centrally to the stairs and whose window provided a long view of one whole side of the property. It was decorated simply, a guest bedroom, but it would do.

"I'll take it," he told Elena finally.

"When would you like to move in?"

"Tomorrow if I can."

"That can be arranged."

They went back downstairs and sat at a big table in the kitchen to work out the details on paper. Elena had contracts with her that Cooper signed. The cost of the staff was built into the rent. He learned their names were Marita and Aurelio. He would meet them the next day.

She left him alone for a little while she went to make a call to her office. Cooper prowled the kitchen, reluctant to touch anything even though he'd agreed to rent the place in writing. He poked his head into the refrigerator and came away with a bottle of pineapple Jarritos that he drank in the splash of light from one large back window. He could see the pool from here; it was small and not as inviting as the one at the hotel, but the hot tub beckoned. Even on a scorching day, a hot tub felt good.

"It's done," Elena said when she came back. "You're the lord of the manor now."

"I guess I am," Cooper said. He finished off the soda and put the bottle in the sink. "For now, at least."

They parted where they met, out by the front gate. Elena gave him a ring of keys. He was alone, but now he had a place to be.

27.

When he checked out of the hotel the bill was already taken care of by Barriga's people. A bellboy carried Cooper's bags out to the car and left with a few folded bills in his hand. The Hotel Lucerna was the nicest hotel in Ciudad Juárez, but Cooper was glad to see the back of it.

He took his time driving out to the house, enjoying the sensation of being alone in his car. Barriga's presence in the back seat made him uncomfortable, as did the role he was asked to play. It was not him and he wouldn't do it again for any money.

Marita and Aurelio were at the house when he arrived. They were an older couple, small and dry-looking like the landscape. Aurelio took Cooper's bags into the house and put them in the bedroom Cooper wanted. Like the bellboy, he showed no sign that he recognized the rifle case for what it was.

Cooper asked for an early lunch and went to his room. He put away his things in an empty wardrobe and chest of drawers. The rifle went below his suits.

It was a different sensation, knowing there were people in the house with him. Ordinarily he might have idled for a long while in front of the television just letting the minutes draw by, but he didn't feel ready yet to do so with others around. Instead he went out to the pool and swam laps, spent some time soaking in the hot tub and then swam more laps when the water still felt icy cold by comparison. He had lunch outside, pork loin in adobo and fresh fruit as a dessert. He drank lots of ice tea with lemon and just a touch of sugar. When he was finished, he felt almost right again.

When he lay down for a nap his brain circled the question of the party again. He had two days until the appointed time and they would be spent here, quietly, enjoying the new house and the freedom from Barriga. He wondered if he would see Ruíz and if there would be questions asked. But then what would it matter? The job was completed, the charade no longer necessary. Let Ruíz think what he wished, though he might be less trusting of Barriga in the future.

Cooper slept. He awoke refreshed.

Marita was in the kitchen preparing ingredients for the night's dinner. Aurelio was in the back fishing leaves out of the pool. It was almost totally still.

"How long have you worked here?" Cooper asked Marita.

"Eight years," she answered. She was mashing her own corn meal with a mortar and pestle. At some point she'd gone out and purchased a whole selection of fresh vegetables and peppers that filled baskets on one counter. If nothing else, Cooper would eat well.

"How long has the house been empty?"

"Almost a year, señor."

"That's a long time."

Marita had no answer. She added more corn to crush between her stones. The pestle was like a hand roller and Marita gripped it at both ends, crushing down along the half-bowl slant of the mortar. The coarse-ground meal collected at the bottom of the mortar and from time to time she scooped it out into a bowl painted with blue and yellow designs on the side.

"I'm not sure how long I'll stay," Cooper said. "Maybe a month or two. It depends."

"Stay as long as you like, señor. We're happy to have someone here."

"I guess the house would seem awfully empty."

"Yes."

Cooper could think of nothing else to add and after a while he meandered out of the kitchen and into a room with large couches and a massive plasma television. He switched it on, flipped through channels until he found the news and tried to do what he would normally do. Every time his brain went numb there was some small sound from the kitchen, or the noise of Aurelio going in and out the back door and he could not maintain it. Eventually he gave up.

He considered going out again. He could order a new suit from Garza, this time in colors more suited to him. This time he could drive without having to look over his shoulder for a black Land Rover or anyone else. The watch was off. In the end he decided against it.

The house had a library. Cooper looked through the books for something likely. Everything was in Spanish, which was fine. Eventually he settled on a novel set during the Porfiriato. It quickly turned out to be a romance, but Cooper didn't much care what it was about so long as it filled the time.

It occurred to him that it would be not much different at home in Monterrey. He spent long hours idle between visits to the gym at the top floor of his building, or trips out to eat. When he cooked for himself it was simple fare and his only real companion for most of his hours was the television. At least here had a chaise longue to relax on in the splash of sun from the library's corner window. He had a woman preparing meals to his liking and a man to look after the little things of house- and groundskeeping.

The book turned out to be quite good and before he knew it the sun had shifted and it was late. He finished it off and put it aside. He got up and stretched. It was too early for dinner, though there was the smell of slow cooking coming from the kitchen.

He went up to his room and looked out the window. He made a note of the cars on the street when they passed. There were no close neighbors so there were no vehicles parked where he could see them. He stood sentry for a while, until the quiet remained undisturbed for a long time and then he went downstairs again.

28.

Cooper decided that he would go to the party unarmed. There were too many questions he would not want to answer if they found him with weapons, so he didn't carry even the flat little dart of a knife up his sleeve. He kept his SIG Sauer in the locked glove compartment of his car. It would cost precious seconds for him to bring it into play if he had to, but he wanted no valet to discover it by accident.

The route to Los Campos remained familiar despite the late hour. The party didn't start until nine o'clock and the sun was drooping low in the west. He drove into it, blood-red light washing over the car.

His invitation got him past the guards at the gate. He recognized two of them, but if they recognized him they gave no sign. The car was just another shiny luxury model and the invitation turned him one of the nameless, faceless rich that came and went all day long. If one of them did think he looked familiar, doubtless they would dismiss the thought; no hired hand would be back to party with a Los Campos family.

He deliberately arrived late. The sun was down now and the streetlights appeared like flickering fireflies among the trees, roads branching off to private estates here and there among the community.

The Madrigal house was lit brightly with strings of white lights in the trees and trailing along the great pillars at the front of the house. Traffic up the drive was light, which bothered Cooper; he wanted to be one of a crowd of latecomers.

A valet took his keys and his car. The broad double doors at the front of the house were open and Cooper could see more lights and people milling about in rich clothes. Cool air from inside blew out into the sweaty night.

A guard with a wand-shaped metal detector waved down everyone who passed inside. He was thorough, getting both legs and arms completely. He was not like the men at Ruíz's home, with their slack body searches and attitudes of complacency. These men were alert, grim-faced and did not even spare a few words to wish partygoers a good time.

Inside there was a swirl of bodies, people talking idly beneath a massive crystal chandelier that dominated a wood-paneled foyer. More guests spilled into a large receiving area toward the rear. Waiters in white tuxedo jackets circulated with trays of hors d'œuvre and wine. One came close and Cooper snagged a glass from him. He turned down the hors d'œuvre, which looked unfamiliar and smelled funny.

He was not surprised that he didn't recognize anyone. He didn't even see Ruíz among the guests, though they were strung out between two rooms, with more deeper in a wide corridor that led into the guts of the house. Tendrils of smoke crawled up from cigarettes and clouded around the ceiling. Occasionally someone would laugh loudly enough to break through the ongoing murmur.

Cooper did even know what Rafa Madrigal looked like and hoped he wouldn't come face to face with the man. There were many lovely young women there, and Cooper looked from one face to the next hoping he would spot Lorena. She would tell him who was who and guide him to the right place in the party. These were her people.

Exploring more deeply led Cooper to a door to the outside. An immense tiled patio where gaslights and torches lit a burgeoning crowd of partygoers, some of whom filed in from a different set of doors, dominated the rear of the house. A large, twin-tiered fountain stood at the center of the patio. Tables were set for dinner and scattered around the space. People milled with their glasses and Cooper slipped in among them.

At first he thought he was the only Anglo on the guest list, but before long he found a clutch of Americans speaking English to a small crowd of appreciative Mexicans. They were talking about the *maquiladoras*, about productivity and wages. That didn't interest Cooper and he moved on.

A woman crossed his path. He guessed she was in her late forties and trying to be younger. Her dress was tight over propped up breasts. "Where have you been hiding?" she asked Cooper.

"I just got here."

"Well, dear, you're behind in your drinking already."

Cooper smiled politely and moved away from the woman. She didn't follow. He made his way to the fountain and lingered there. When another waiter came by he exchanged his empty glass for a full one. If he were behind in his drinking, then he would have to make up for it.

He wouldn't become drunk. That was unacceptable. He would, however, gain that pleasant softness around the edges that hinted at drunkenness coming on. Somewhere he figured he would find a bar and there he would have something stronger than sparkling wine. Perhaps he would even drink a finger or two of Canadian Club as an offering to the spirit of Bingham.

Cooper jostled a woman by accident. "Oh, excuse me," he said and then looked into her face.

Señora Ruíz looked at him and through him. They were face to face and Cooper froze expecting her eyes to focus on him, but they didn't. "Watch where you're going," she said.

"I'll do that. So sorry, señora."

They parted and Cooper's heart settled. His gaze passed idly over the party, but he didn't see Lorena until she was practically close enough to touch. It was hard to believe he'd missed her: she wore a black dress and a necklace of pearls and her hair was up. She had pearl earrings, as well. Her face was made up and it added age to her in a good way.

"Hello, Cooper," she said.

"Hello," Cooper said, and when she offered her hand he took it.

"Have you been here very long?"

"No, not long."

"That's good. Señor Madrigal's parties go on for a long time. If you come too early, you might not make it until the end."

"I'll have to thank him for the invitation."

Lorena nodded. When she drank from her glass of wine she left a trace of red lipstick on the crystal. "I know his son, Sebastián. He was the one who invited you."

"Then I'll thank him, then."

"Better you don't speak to him at all. He doesn't much care for Americans."

"I saw your mother."

"Did she see you?"

"Kind of."

"Better if she doesn't recognize you, don't you think?"

"It seems like I don't have any friends here at all."

"Let's go make you some."

She led him away from the fountain and into the sea of people spilling onto the patio. Cooper trailed a step behind her, mindful of the way she looked tonight and of how he looked with her: a beautiful girl stringing along a man more than twenty years her senior.

The first person he met was the son of a businessman who did work with Rafa Madrigal. From there they passed into the circle of the daughter of a wealthy landowner from the south of Mexico. Lorena introduced him to a young couple involved in the *maquiladoras* as administrators.

Once they passed very close to the cluster of people around her father. Cooper turned his face but kept his eye on the man, but neither Ruíz nor any of those with him even noticed he was there. Another time he saw Rafa Madrigal himself: a tall, almost noble-looking man with a straight back and the bearing of a prince.

The people Lorena knew were all young, none of them older than twenty-five. The apprentice bullfighter from Mexico City. The journalism student whose father was involved in bottled water. They were all unfailingly polite, well groomed and friendly so long as Lorena was around. If she drifted too far from them, an unseen veil would pass between Cooper and the person he was talking to. The first time he thought it was his imagination, but after the third he knew it was because they were only humoring him.

Cooper wasn't poor. He did well enough to drive the best cars, wear his tailored suits from Garza and travel when and where he wished. Even when he wasn't living on the ticket of someone like Barriga he was doing well. But the guests of Rafa Madrigal were another type entirely; they lived money and passed it through their systems like air or water. Just from the way they spoke to one another he knew they recognized their own kind instinctively.

He drank more than he should and the sour feeling in his stomach intensified. He met a young man just out of university in America, living on his parents' largesse. He talked to a stockbroker who worked at the BMV in Ciudad de México. Lorena spent some time chatting idly with a girl headed off on a summer trip around Europe. Cooper just smiled and nodded and spoke when he should. He did not feel a part of the conversations even when Lorena tried to draw him in. He could tell the others were just as well to leave it that way.

Eventually they passed off the patio and into the house. Cooper's head was fuzzier than he liked by then and he didn't remember stepping across the threshold in the half-lit interior of a side hallway. When Lorena stood on her toes to kiss him, he grounded and put his hands on her body to pull her close.

She slipped away from him and took one of his hands in her own. "Come with me," she said.

They went up a set of stairs lit by a lone bulb on the second floor, then down a passage that was almost completely dark. When Lorena stopped at a door it looked the same as all the others. Cooper was unsure where he was in relation to the entranceway and foyer, the patio and the guests. Lorena pushed the door open.

Flickering light spilled in through tall windows with open curtains. The room was broad and decorated in a feminine style. The bed was a four-poster with drapes tied to each. A wardrobe and a full-length mirror stood in the corner. There was a writing desk and a small, straight-backed chair. A dresser also had a mirror on it and Cooper caught a glimpse of himself.

Cooper reached for her and they kissed again. Lorena's tongue touched his and then she pulled his lower lip between gentle teeth. She was hot underneath Cooper's hands, the dress like some filmy layer that could be stripped away by applying only a little pressure. Her breasts were small and high. He touched one, tried to slip it free of her dress, but she stopped him.

"It's eleven o'clock," she told him when they stopped to breathe. Her voice was low and she avoided his mouth when he went to kiss her again. "Be here at midnight. This room."

"What do you mean?" Cooper whispered back. There were no sounds of the party nearby. The hallway was silent. He didn't know who might overhear them. "Whose room is this?"

"No one's," Lorena replied.

"You want me to stay here an hour?"

"Will you?"

This time when Cooper tried to kiss her she let him. He loved the smell of her, the softness of her. He wanted to tangle his fingers in her hair but he knew that he couldn't spoil her for the party. His erection pulsed.

"Will you?" Lorena asked him again.

"I will."

"Then stay here," she said and pulled away from him.

Immediately Cooper wanted to draw her back into his embrace, to kiss and touch her again, but she was at the door of the room and pausing to be certain her dress was arranged and her hair neat. She used the little mirror on the dresser to check her makeup.

"Don't be late," Cooper said.

"I won't be."

When she was gone Cooper was unsure about what to do. He paced the little room a few times and then looked out the window. He saw the partygoers down below, scattered thickly across the patio. The fountain was almost centered in his view and the people circulated around it in slow curls that even they probably did not recognize.

He drifted to the bed. It was piled high at the head with decorative pillows in ornate cases. The quilt cover looked as though it was crafted by hand. Everything seemed laid out just so, as if no person used this room for anything, or hadn't for a long time. The effect put him in the mind of a hotel room, always waiting but never personal.

When he was tired of standing he took to the bed. His feet were sore. There were still forty minutes to kill before Lorena would return. Cooper lay back and allowed himself to think of how he would touch Lorena when she returned, how she would make familiar sounds that were also new, how she would taste.

The alcohol made him drift and once he caught himself falling asleep. After that he stood despite the discomfort in his feet and watched the party from his remove. He looked for Lorena but didn't see her.

29.

The last ten minutes were the hardest. Cooper licked his lips, thirsty for another drink even though his edges were soft and foggy and he didn't want more. The party went on below him as if he had never been there at all. He wondered if anyone noticed one way or another that he had been there or that he had gone. Once he thought he spotted Ruíz among a group of men talking loudly and smoking cigars, but it wasn't him.

Lorena didn't come at midnight. He waited five minutes feeling anxious and stupid. He considered just leaving the room, leaving the party, and forgetting that he ever entertained the idea of Lorena beneath him on this bed. Then he barely caught her voice, talking down the hallway more loudly than he expected.

A tremor built up behind his knees. Cooper clamped down on it. He heard her again, speaking loudly. He didn't understand why she would do that until he heard the murmur of a man's voice speaking back to her.

Wakefulness pushed back the fog. He looked around the room quickly. There was room enough in the space behind the full-length mirror, hard up against the wardrobe. He moved there, pressed himself until his back was tight against the wall.

The door opened.

"You are so beautiful," said the man.

Cooper heard kissing, and the brushing sound of cloth on cloth. The door closed and footsteps moved farther into the room. Cooper saw the edge of them just visible around the curve of the mirror. When they made another step, he saw Lorena and then the back of a graying man's head eclipsed her face.

"So beautiful," said the man.

Cooper didn't breathe. They went to the bed. He shifted his position enough to see Lorena pushed back against the quilted bedcover and her leg in the air as the man fumbled with his pants in the darkness. Lorena's shoe was off and her toes pointed at the ceiling.

The pushing and moaning followed. The bed-frame creaked. On his right hand, the flickering lights from outside and the murmur of voices turned up against the night. His left hand touching the wall, sweating. More sweat on his face. He didn't understand why his fingers were trembling.

He could see Lorena watching the window. Her eyes were dead. She made no sound. And the moving, grunting shape of the man atop her, grinding himself into her over and over again until he let go and the air went out of him slowly in a sigh that lasted half a minute.

The man pressed himself up from Lorena and Cooper saw Ruíz's face for the first time. Then he was struggling with his pants again, wandering the room like an invalid old man, muttering to himself things Cooper did not understand or didn't want to. He turned his gaze back on Lorena and watched her as her father dressed himself and made himself look presentable in the reflection of the full-length mirror.

"We should never have done it here," Ruíz admonished. "Never here. What if people see? They'll figure it out. We can't have that."

Lorena said nothing.

"I'll go downstairs to the party. Wait fifteen minutes. And make sure your dress is still pretty. They can't figure it out."

Ruíz went to the door and then he was gone. Cooper still didn't move. A heavy layer of silence descended over them. Cooper could not even hear Lorena breathing.

After a long time she sat up on the bed. She was still in her dress and she smoothed down the hem. When she turned her head to the side Cooper knew she was waiting for him to slide out into her field of vision and he did it, appearing from behind the tall mirror but still close to the wall. The wall was cool and solid.

"You saw it?" Lorena asked.

Cooper nodded first and then he cleared his throat. "I saw it."

She was a long time rising from the bed and when she put her shoes back on it seemed such a simple, trivial thing for her to do that Cooper's mind rejected it. He expected her to explode or cry out or come to him, but she did none of these things. Instead she looked in the little mirror on the dresser as she had before. When she turned to him her face was unreadable, but it had none of the light it held before.

"How long?" Cooper asked finally.

"Since I was twelve."

"Why?"

"He says it's because he believes I'm not his. He says my mother cheated on him and now he can't be sure if I'm his daughter or not. But he doesn't try to make sure. This is how he makes sure."

"But you—"

"I never encouraged him."

"No," Cooper said and he put his hands up to push the thought away. "No, that's not what I was going to say. I mean, how can you?"

"What choice do I have?" she asked in the same flat voice.

"You're seventeen. That's not too young to leave."

"To what? What money I have belongs to Papá."

"Your mother, then. She could—"

"My mother is addicted to my father's money and everything that comes with it."

"Does she know?"

"No. And I won't be the one to tell her."

Cooper moved to come closer to her, but she stepped back to keep the distance between them. "I wasn't going to do anything," Cooper said.

"I know you wouldn't." She gathered something from the floor. Cooper saw it was the little clutch purse she'd been carrying when she came into the room. It was the same color as her dress. When she looked at him again, her expression was softer. "I want to see you again. Away from here. Will you see me?"

"Of course."

"Then I'll send you word."

"Lorena," Cooper said.

She paused in the door of the room. The hallway was a rectangle of black behind her. "What?"

"Why did you show me this?"

She went. When she was gone, Cooper felt like he could breathe, truly breathe, again. The sweat was drying on his face though his palms were still wet. He couldn't bring himself to sit on the bed, which was rumpled from father rutting with daughter. Suddenly he felt nauseated, but he didn't throw up.

30.

He went back to his rented house and passed six days without hearing from Lorena. He wasn't even sure how she meant to get word to him, or if it had all been some kind of grotesque show meant to turn him away from her.

Cooper found he couldn't read or relax the way he'd hoped to. When he closed his eyes he saw Ruíz on top of his daughter, his hips plunging, and the dead expression of Lorena as he finished inside of her. Cooper had killed many men and he did not remember any of them as well as he remembered this.

When Marita made food for him, he ate it. When the sun went down, he went to bed. In the daytime he would occupy himself with swimming restlessly back and forth until he was exhausted from the endless repetition. Even medicating himself with the news was not enough. He started drinking from the selection at the house's bar. Several times he was drunk by noon and that made him ashamed.

He was in the library when he heard the rapping at the front door. There was the murmur of Marita's voice and the lower pitch of a man's. He heard the door close, felt the change in pressure in the room, and in a few moments Marita was there with a letter in a yellow envelope.

Cooper took the envelope and tore the end off. The letter inside was written in longhand. Lorena had beautiful script so light it lifted from the page.

It was only after he read the letter that he began to wonder how it made its way to his door. Lorena hadn't asked where he was staying and he'd not had the time to volunteer. And yet a messenger had come directly to him. The letter was dated that day.

Without a word to anyone else, he crept up to his bedroom and peered out the window. The sun shone on that side of the house, so he would be hidden from sight by the glare. He spent a long time looking left and right along the visible section of roadway, unsure of what he hoped to see, knowing he would know it when he saw it.

He went to the back of the house and took up station in the broad windows of the master suite. Beyond the low wall around the house were mesquite trees and hardy grasses, dirt the color of rust and sand. If someone was watching there, he did not see them.

A high window at the front of the house let light into a full bathroom for guests. Cooper stood in the tub barefoot and kept vigil from there for fifteen minutes. A child went by on a bicycle. Not a car drove past, nor did anyone or anything else stir out there beyond the wall.

He didn't know and not knowing tied him into tighter knots than before. This time he told Marita he didn't want any dinner at all that night and shooed both her and Aurelio out of the house before sunset. Alone in the house he was able to think more clearly, as if the other two provided some unconscious static that disturbed his rhythm.

Of the more than a week he had been there, he had been out of the house for just that night at Rafa Madrigal's home. If anyone had been watching before then, he was sure he would have seen them. They would have had to wait until he was gone and do their work quickly, but they also would have had to know he was there already.

The real estate broker was a link. He would have to check on her. Or perhaps someone had still been watching him after the business with Ruíz was completed. If that were the case, then he was stupid and he'd let them find him while he lazed away thinking he was safe alone.

Cooper prepared himself something cold from the refrigerator: a simple sandwich with meat and lettuce and a slice of tomato. He sat in the kitchen in the dark watching the dim kidney shape of the pool out in the shadows of the yard. A car went by and its lights cleared the rim of the wall and flashed across the room.

It took all his self-control to stay there. His bags were half-packed and he could be gone by the morning. He would stay in a hotel overnight; find something new in the morning. He would pay cash and no one would know his name.

But then Lorena wouldn't be able to find him again. And he wanted her to find him. That much he was certain of: that he wanted her to find him, but only her. If he wanted he would ask her how she did it, and if her father knew. Was Rudolfo the one who tracked him down? Would he find a camera watching him?

He stayed up very late, until his eyes were itchy with sleep, and he couldn't keep awake sitting in the dark any longer. He heard nothing and saw nothing and the whole world was asleep.

Lorena's letter asked him to meet her the next day.

31.

The morning was hot and as afternoon approached it grew hotter still. Cooper knew that he would never be able to wear a jacket and appear like any other man on the street, so he could not bring his gun to meet Lorena. He had only the dart-shaped knife, worn under the loose cloth of his sleeve, lurking.

As if to make up for the night before, Marita served Cooper a breakfast that rivaled anything he'd had at Ruíz's home. He was hungry for it, and ate with gusto, until his belly was stretched and he could eat no more. Then he retreated to the library and stared out the window until it was time to go.

He thought the weak link might be the car. He ran his hand up into the wheel wells and checked along the body for something attached that would send a signal back to his followers. Cooper didn't find anything, but that didn't mean it wasn't there. Driving with both hands on the steering wheel, he wondered if they were tracking him now. The idea made him sweat. He did not want to lose the car.

Lorena's summons brought him back into the city and the thick afternoon traffic. He barely noticed the police and army vehicles patrolling the streets, and suspected it was the same for most Juárenses, too. They were living with the violence and becoming part of it. Cooper was more concerned about the car, about invisible crosshairs falling down on the roof from high above, a satellite watching him. He gripped the steering wheel tighter and more tightly still.

The Universidad Autónoma de Ciudad Juárez was a campus of mixed structures. The main building was concrete and glass and bespoke modern Mexico, while others scattered nearby were constructed in the 1960s and 1970s and had a worn look of administrative buildings given long use. But there was new construction underway even now, and a crane flew a Mexican flag as it lifted a slab of concrete that would become a reinforced wall.

Cooper was looking for the medical school, but he parked well away from the campus and came back to it on foot. His suspicions about the car were growing and he did not want it near him for this.

The Auditorio Municipal was built adjoining the medical school. It was a lovely structure that, like the new buildings of the university, lacked the heavy, poured concrete sullenness of years past. It was airy and open and its glass flashed in the afternoon sun. Banners were set above the doors advertising *Aida*. Cooper had seen another sign on the road.

He bypassed the front entrances and swung around the building's far side. There were roll-up doors here and loading docks. One was open and a truck squatted in the full glare of the sun while men unpacked its contents.

One man sat watching the others, smoking a cigarette and seeming listless. Cooper approached him. "*Hola*," he said.

"*Hola*," the man returned.

"You are Cornelio?" Cooper asked.

"I am," the man replied. He dropped his cigarette on the ground and stepped on it. At the truck men were still unloading packages wrapped in loose plastic. The air smelled of dust and plaster. "You are Cooper?"

"Yes."

"*Vamos.*"

They left the workingmen behind and entered the building. It was cooler out of the sunlight even without air conditioning, but when they passed out of the loading dock and into a long corridor with a polished floor, the air was chill enough to raise the hairs on Cooper's arms.

The man called Cornelio walked in a relaxed way. He carried no gun. Cooper tried to remember if he'd seen the man before, but nothing came to mind. He would remember the man if he ever saw him again.

They stopped at a set of double doors. Cornelio pushed one ajar. "Through here," he said.

Cooper took the door from him. He started to say thank you, but the man went away quickly, back the way they'd come, and did not look back. It was dim and chill through the doorway.

On the other side Cooper's eyes had to adjust. Only a few lights were on and those were high above in a wild scaffolding of catwalks and pipes. A curtain fell like a heavy wall to his left. He was aware of the shapes of scenery collected in a mass through a vast space that was backstage. And in the center of this was Lorena, pale in the half-light.

"Hello, Cooper," she said.

He came close to her. The smell of her drifted and was taken up by his nose and he wanted to have more of it, taken from the surface of her skin. He stirred in his pants.

"Lorena," he said.

"I'm sorry I couldn't meet with you sooner. There are people watching me."

"There are people watching me, too," Cooper said.

A look of distress crossed her face. "Who?"

"Your people. Your father's people. The ones that told you how to find me."

If she meant to dissuade him, she didn't. She held her small purse closely, wrung between her hands like a rag. Her eyes were black, just like they had been on the night he saw her with her father. This didn't make him want to touch her any less.

"You know you never answered my question," Cooper said. "About why. Why did you show me what you showed me?"

"How could I tell you?"

"Why would you tell me?"

"Because you're a killer."

Cooper blinked and took a step back from her without meaning to. He felt exposed again, the way he felt driving the car *knowing* that this was how they were keeping track of him. Knowing that his secrets were under assault and he could do nothing except wait for the barriers to crack. Like now.

"How—?"

"I know my father's business well enough to know a killer when I see one. You are a killer. I could tell from the moment I saw you that you've taken men's lives. And that you were there to kill Papá."

"That was never for sure."

"But you would have?"

Cooper wiped his mouth with his hand. "Yes," he said.

Lorena moved closer and put out one hand to touch Cooper. He flinched at the first contact, but then let her lay her hand on his forearm. Her fingers were small and cold. It was too cold in here. "How could I tell you what I thought when I saw you?"

"What did you think?"

"That here was a man come to take my father's life."

"That didn't frighten you?"

She looked in Cooper's face. "My father has raped me hundreds of times since I was a little girl. What do you think frightens me any more?"

The image of the bedroom and Ruíz came unbidden once more and Cooper swallowed it back into his memory. He concentrated on the touch of her fingers and the sound of her voice. There was a tremor when she spoke. Cooper felt it in her hand, too.

"It's none of my business," Cooper said.

"You wanted me. You had to know."

"Is that what you do to everyone who wants you? Make them watch your father...."

Cooper let the sentence trail off. He didn't want to say the words *fucking you*, but they were the only ones that fit. He could not say *making love* because that would be mocking the act and he could not bring himself to mock what he had seen.

"You're the only one who knows."

"How can that be possible?"

"Do you think I want people to look at me knowing?" Lorena demanded, and she took her hand away from him and used it to cover her mouth. "Do you think that of me?"

"No. No, I don't."

It grew quiet and somewhere far away a door slammed shut and there was the sound of men talking loudly. For a moment Cooper was reminded of the party through glass as he stood in a guest bedroom of Rafa Madrigal. Then he was back with Lorena again.

"You're a killer," Lorena said.

"Yes, I am."

"I want you...," she said. "I want you to kill him."

The men spoke again and there was laughter. The door banged again. Silence.

"I don't kill people just because someone asks."

"You want money," Lorena said, not asking.

The cold backstage was getting to Cooper. He trembled, or maybe he trembled because his heart was beating too fast and what he was hearing was too much. In a way he was only hearing what he wanted to hear, what Barriga had never said to him. "Money," he said thickly.

"I can get you money."

"How?"

"There is way for me to get some. And when my father dies, I will have more."

"It's not that simple."

"Why not?" Lorena demanded and her eyes sparked in the dark. "You are a killer. Here's a man I want you to kill. I'll pay you. What else is there?"

"I don't know," Cooper admitted, "but there has to be more."

"More of what you've seen?"

"No, not more of that."

He turned away from her then and walked into the shadow of great hunk of scenery he couldn't recognize in the dimness. His mind was turning, his thoughts too quick and she was watching him, waiting for an answer he knew he would give her before he even had a single idea in his head. *Of course* he would kill Sandalio Ruíz. Of course he would do this because it was what he wanted to do all along.

Lorena was watching him. Cooper had the sense that she would watch him all day and into the night if she had to in order to get her reply. The vast black of the closed curtain seemed to swallow her up until she was just a white sliver against all that darkness.

"How much will you pay me?"

He had to play it out. The story must be told a certain way and no other would do. Cooper was assigned his role and Lorena hers. Now they were just actors and their subject was killing.

"I will pay you whatever Señor Barriga would pay."

"That's a lot of money. You said you didn't have much. Not enough to live on your own."

"That is relative. Haven't you noticed?" Lorena asked. "My family is rich."

"How would you want it done?"

"I don't understand."

"I don't do killings with pain," Cooper said. "I do clean hits. The client doesn't know what happened to him. I'll do it close up, but I won't make a mess out of it just because you want me to."

She put her hand over her mouth again. When she took it away she said, "You will do what you must do."

Cooper came closer to her by inches, stepping short as if he were fighting her gravity. When he was close enough he took her by the arms and pulled her next to him. She tilted her face up to his and they were kissing. He put his hands in her hair the way he wanted to and she pressed against him.

Lorena spoke to the hollow of his throat: "Please. Please do it."

"I will."

32.

He found his hands were shaking when he went away from her. Out of the shadows of the backstage and into the sunlight again, he was calmer, steadied by the heat and brightness. He didn't see the man who'd let him in when he passed through the loading dock again.

His car wasn't far, but Cooper didn't rush back to it. Instead he walked the campus, past quiet buildings hosting a few summer students, letting his mind settle and his thoughts come clearly.

It wasn't the killing. He had known from the start that he could do it. And there was something about being ready to kill a man that didn't go away, even when someone like Barriga said *no*. Lorena couldn't know that. She had to ask because she didn't know what it was like to be a hitter. That it was easier to agree than to disagree when it came to the matter of death.

Once, early on when he was just learning how to do it, he was asked to kill a man and he agreed for the right price. The woman who hired him changed her mind and then changed it again. She contacted Cooper over and over; worrying about details she had no cause to concern herself with. One day she would tell him she would pay him not to deliver the package and other days she would tell him to go ahead with it.

Cooper learned how to tune out the buyer. After the second reversal he stopped listening to the woman. He took her calls because he was foolish enough in those days to leave a point of contact open, but he didn't pay attention to what she had to say. Instead he planned out the hit and when the time came he did what he was paid to do.

She could have turned his head from it if he'd let her. The arguments against killing were as valid as the ones that brought her to him. But then Cooper realized that he *wanted* to make the delivery. He was primed for it, looking ahead to it and past it to the point when it would be accomplished and he could feel good about what he had done. All the talk was just noise and he couldn't let noise distract him.

A little square of trees cast shade over an empty bench outside a plain-faced building of white. Cooper stopped there for a while and let the memory unspool. Now he could have used a cigarette, but he had no cigarettes because he was sworn off them. A trash can nearby smelled of stale smoke and ash and there were spots on the concrete where butts had been crushed.

He stood up and turned back toward the car. He'd walked through half the campus, but he still knew the way. Out of the shade the sun hit him again but it was less welcome now. Cooper had started to sweat.

When he saw the first man he was unsurprised. He hadn't seen the man following him, but some part of him must have been aware. The man wore a suit jacket and tie despite the heat, but the clothes weren't fitted to him. Sunlight gleamed off dark aviators.

After he saw the first he saw the second, coming from almost the opposite direction, dressed much the same. Cooper didn't recognize their faces.

He kept walking straight as if he hadn't seen them, but he watched them closing on his left and right, keeping pace with him and picking up their step. They were set to trap him between them and building ahead. There was no one around.

"Hey," said the first man when he was close enough. "Hey, señor."

Cooper ignored the man. They were near to him now, but not so close that he could reach out and touch them. The second man was coming on faster than the first, throwing off the timing of their maneuver.

"Hey, I'm talking to you. Hey, asshole."

The second man moved in on Cooper's right and reached out a hand to grab him by the shoulder. They passed under a lip of shadow cast by a nearby building. For an instant Cooper's eyes were adjusting. He blinked and the second man was right on him.

Cooper turned and caught the second man by the wrist. He twisted and wrenched and the man's arm came down elbow-first. Cooper broke the joint with a rising knee.

The first man stopped calling and came on at a run. Cooper put the flat edge of his hand across the bridge of the man's nose and smashed it. He was still hanging on the second man's arm and the man was screaming high-pitched screams as bones ground together.

He stepped into the side of the screaming man's leg and cartilage in his knee gave away. Cooper let the man fall. He put a hand to his sleeve and the dart-knife was there. He spun around. The first man was running blood from his nostrils and had fingers to them, slick with red. He fumbled around under his jacket for a weapon, but he was off balance and his eyes were flushed with tears.

Cooper stabbed the man three times in the left side of the chest under his questing hand. The steel dart came away wet and the concrete was spotted with new blood that stained the cheap suit jacket and splattered on the man's legs. Another moment and the man crumpled in slow motion, still trying for his gun.

Cooper could have killed the second man, but he ran instead. He ran around the corner of the closest building and flat out for fifty yards along a broad sidewalk devoid of people. When he got to the street he found his car with a ticket tucked under the windshield wiper. His keys were in his hand and he was behind the wheel and the engine turned over and he was away from there. He left tire marks on the pavement as he went.

33.

    It troubled Cooper that he didn't know who the men were. He wasn't concerned with their faces, which could have been any face, or their clothes, which could have come from any rack. He wanted to know *why* and this was beyond him.

    He believed he would have seen them if they were following before he met with Lorena. They were not in the auditorium when he met with her, or anywhere around the loading dock. Somehow they had come from nowhere and this made him even more concerned.

    When he returned to the house he changed into jeans and a t-shirt and went out to the car. Under the carpeted liner in the trunk were a spare tire and a jack. He used the jack to raise the car. He had a little flashlight and lay down in the dirt to get underneath it.

    He spent thirty minutes looking at the guts of the car from underneath, poking his light into tight places and shadows. But he saw nothing there that shouldn't have been there, or at least he didn't recognize what he was looking for.

    With the wheels back on the ground he opened up the hood and did the same thing again. If it was there he knew he would have seen it, but he didn't see it and somehow he was unwilling to believe it wasn't there. They had to have a way to find him.

    His shirt had grit and oil on it when he went back inside. He had a headache coming on that a drink from the downstairs bar helped tamp down. Afterward he took a long shower and lay down naked on the bed in his room underneath the slowly turning ceiling fan to let the last water evaporate from his skin.

If they knew where his car was, then they knew where the house was. This was the only thing he knew for certain. But they hadn't shown themselves around here. Cooper refused to believe he wouldn't have noticed them; the roads were too quiet here for someone to linger.

He thought about swimming to move his body and still his mind. He thought about asking Marita for an early dinner. Instead he laid where he was, thinking of them and what they wanted. He lay there thinking about *why*.

It occurred to him that they weren't following him at all, that they were following Lorena. If she had known, then she would have said something to him. They were not safe meeting while there were eyes on them. Ruíz's eyes. Of course it could be nothing else.

Cooper wondered when Ruíz had first come to suspect. Did he know Lorena was coming to meet him, or could she have been meeting anyone? How closely was she watched? Why hadn't Cooper seen them before? Were these Rudolfo's men, blank-faced and badly dressed? How many times had they watched Cooper through the cameras on Ruíz's lawn? What word would they take back with them?

Suddenly he was not so certain of killing Ruíz. His work depended on discretion and if those were Ruíz's men then he would know Cooper for what he was. Maybe he had always known and had only been indulging Barriga's game. Cooper wasn't certain which was worse.

He would have to meet with Lorena again. This was because he needed to know the answers to certain questions and also because he simply wanted to. It would be foolish to meet too often, but they could afford one more time together to exchange information. And he could put his hands on her again.

His cock twitched just thinking about it. For a moment he wasn't thinking at all of the men in cheap suits but only of Lorena. The feel and smell of her. The touch of bodies. He wanted to fuck her so badly that perhaps fucking wouldn't be enough. He wanted to *have* her, even though the thought was foolish.

At last he dressed himself and wandered downstairs. He allowed himself another drink and then a third because it was getting on in the afternoon. Marita fixed him a sandwich and he ate it out on the pool deck staring at the blue water and for a while thinking nothing at all.

He had learned not to leave points of contact open, but now he needed one. The idea that Ruíz might be aware of them was problematic. He needed to know certain things or he couldn't be sure he could even deliver the package. What did they know and how had they learned it? How were they watching him?

Cooper decided that sometime in the next few days he would send a letter to Lorena. He couldn't know that her mail was left untouched, so he would be circumspect. The letter would be unsigned and the business of it vague enough to pass inspection. He would ask her for another get-together and he would warn her of watchers.

The hair prickled on the back of his neck and he looked around at the walls that enclosed the back lawn. He saw no one peering over and felt foolish for even thinking there might be someone there. He knew that tonight he would sleep badly because he couldn't be sure they weren't in the house, despite the alarm system. He would set a chair in front of his door and sleep with a gun to hand. It was the only way.

34.

"Señor Randolph? There's a telephone call for you."

Cooper was in the library of the rented house, not reading, just staring out the window. His mind was elsewhere, roving around the grounds and into the surrounding roads, still imagining who was out there and what they could see. If this kept up he would have to move again. It was already affecting his sleep.

"Who is it?"

"He didn't give his name."

He left the library behind and picked up the phone in the living room. "*Bueno*," Cooper said.

"Cooper. It's Barriga."

Cooper put his hand over the receiver and looked around reflexively. His stomach felt as though he'd swallowed something hard and cold. Marita moved to the next room and Cooper waited until she'd hung up the extension before he allowed himself to say anything.

"How did you get this number?" Cooper asked.

"My people have extensive contacts. You should know that by now."

"I didn't know they were watching me."

"We keep track of many things. It's good business."

Marita moved across the doorway in the next room, busy with something Cooper didn't know. He didn't know where

157

Aurelio was, but the man seemed to come and go according to his own schedule. The work got done, which was all Cooper could ask, but the irregularity made him nervous.

"What do you want?"

"It's not something I want, Cooper. It's something good for you. Information you need."

"Is that why you're giving it to me directly?"

"Exactly. And it's better the fewer who know where you are."

Cooper thought of the car, the armed men on the campus and the time he spent simply looking out the windows watching for the first sign of something unusual. With this call, Barriga opened the floodgates for more paranoia. He had the urge to put down the phone and walk out without collecting any of his things, just so he could be gone and no one would know where he went.

"What is it?"

"It's about the package you delivered in Texas."

Bingham. It had to be about him. It had been more than three years since Cooper had worked in Texas before Bingham. Nothing would come back to him after so long. "That was done according to specs," Cooper told Barriga.

"Apparently not."

"What are you talking about?" Cooper asked sharply.

Barriga was quiet on the other end, as if he was considering hanging up the phone without telling Cooper what he'd called to say. Finally he continued: "Somehow your name came up. We don't know how or why exactly, but there've been inquiries made about you. People are interested in discussing the delivery with you."

The cold, hard sensation was back, stronger than before. "I was completely discreet."

"I believe you. I'm only telling you what my people have heard; that certain parties have taken an interest in you related to the delivery. So far the questions they're asking haven't gotten much farther than Dallas, but these things have a way of spreading quickly."

"How long have they been asking?"

"A little more than a week."

"Do you know who's behind it?"

"We have a few names. But it's more than you could handle on your own. This many people talking can't be shut up."

Cooper held the receiver in the crook of his neck and shoulder. He patted his pockets down automatically, looking for a pack of cigarettes that was not there. The bar was across the room. He could see clean tumblers lined up waiting for a drink.

"Cooper, are you still there?"

"I'm still here."

"This is simply a courtesy call, Cooper. What you do with the information is, of course, entirely up to you. I've assured my people that whatever you do won't have repercussions for our organization. You're too professional for that."

"We should meet," Cooper said.

"That wouldn't be advisable."

"Damn it, you can't just drop this in my lap and expect me not to do anything about it."

"As I say, it's your choice what to do about it."

"That's not good enough."

"I don't understand."

Cooper's voice was raised, but he was too agitated to stop. He wasn't shouting, but he felt breathless anyway. "Everything on my end was handled correctly. If there's blowback it's because someone in your organization violated security."

"How many people do you think knew about the delivery?"

"I don't know. Enough."

"Then you think *I* had something to do with it?"

"No. I mean... no. I don't know who was responsible."

"If there's blowback, Cooper, it's something you'll have to handle on your own."

The men on the campus had to be a part of this. Things Cooper hadn't understood began to make more sense. He was exposed in Juárez. Word might have already gotten back to Texas about where he was, where he was living, what he was doing. Again there was the urge to put down the phone and flee, but he knew as soon as he thought it that he wouldn't; Lorena would not know where to find him, and Ruíz wouldn't die the way he had to.

"I'll take care of it, then," Cooper said. His voice was even again, though his mind was still crackling. He licked his lips.

"That's nothing less than I expected."

"Will your people want to know when it's settled?"

"That would be the courteous thing to do. We're exposed on this with you. If someone has your name, they might know you've done work with us before. It could make for embarrassing connections."

"I'll take care of it," Cooper repeated.

"Then we have nothing else to talk about."

"No."

"Good-bye, Cooper. Good luck."

The line went dead. Cooper held the quiet receiver against his ear for a long minute until the connection reset and he heard a dial tone.

"Fuck," he said. He hung up the phone and went to the bar for a drink. His hands were trembling and the liquor made them stop. There was the clink of dishes from the kitchen. Cooper's face was sweaty despite the cool in the house. "Fuck!"

35.

With the door locked and the chair in place, Cooper went over his weapons. He had no need to, but he oiled his pistol and the rifle, cleaning them carefully with a wire brush. The process of doing this soothed him and he was able to relax for the first time in days. It was almost time to send his letter to Lorena and the nearness of it made his fingertips tingle.

When he was done with the guns he packed them away. Marita came in each day to make his bed and in the evening to turn down the sheets before leaving with Aurelio, but she had shown no curiosity about Cooper's things. Even so, he couldn't afford to be careless with his weapons. This discipline was the only thing he didn't feel was slipping.

There was a desk in the library with stationary and pens, but Cooper chose to do his writing at the small desk in his room. He brought up writing materials and, with the door still secured, drafted a letter to Lorena. He was, as he planned, circumspect about his business, but tried to convey the need to meet again and discuss details.

He didn't know if the letter would reach Lorena without passing through someone else's hands. After he was done with the first draft of the letter he marked it up with his pen and wrote another, tighter version. The first copy he burned in an ashtray by the bed.

With the letter finished, he let himself out the bedroom and went downstairs. He had no stamps, so he asked Marita to stamp it and send it out in the next day's mail. It felt strange letting it go like that.

He had nothing left to do except wait. He was drinking too much and too often from the bar and spending more time tanning by the pool than keeping his mind sharp with reading or puzzles in the newspaper. It eventually occurred to him that staying in Juárez had been a mistake from the beginning. He should be back in Monterrey in his own apartment living life on his own time. He would be better prepared to deal with the Texas situation if he was on familiar ground.

Daily he took up sentry at different windows on the second floor and watched for suspect activity. A part of him felt foolish for doing it because any watcher worth the name would be smarter than to be seen. As he planned, he slept each night with his hand resting on his pistol and only put the weapon away during the day.

After the third day waiting for a reply he began to wonder if the letter had gotten through at all. He wished for some better, more direct way to contact Lorena, but calling her on the telephone was out of the question. Even so, by the fifth day he'd begun to reconsider.

When the letter came there was only one page of onionskin paper inside, setting a date and a place. They would meet at the Catedral de Ciudad Juárez in a week.

It seemed forever to wait. Cooper fell into the orbit of the downstairs bar and drank to make the hours pass. When he forced himself to read something from the library he forgot the words as soon as his eye passed over them. He took long naps in his secured room, sometimes sleeping through lunch and finding the cold food saved for him under plastic on the kitchen counter.

He wondered what Marita and Aurelio thought of him. He felt himself going soft from bad diet and lack of exercise. Time in the pool didn't seem to help. They said nothing about it, but sometimes Cooper thought he could see something in their eyes akin to pity for the lonely American who had nowhere to go and no one to see.

Meanwhile the Texas problem wasn't going away. He was aware of the passing of every car whenever he ventured outside. He heard the engines cruise past the wall and listened for any sign that they were slowing or had stopped. A part of him expected the men in suit jackets, the ones he'd finished in the city, to reappear with automatic weapons and cut him to pieces by the side of the pool.

Looking at himself in the mirror, Cooper saw he needed a haircut, but a little gel swept the hair away from his face and into some semblance of order. His face seemed puffy around the eyes from too much drink and sleep, or maybe it was just his imagination. Whatever the case, on the last two days of the week he forced himself to stay away from the bar and kept himself awake all day. He slept better at night and his stomach, which had started to turn sour every night after dinner, settled down.

On the day he put on a white linen suit with a pale yellow shirt and dark tie. He was sure to carry his pistol in a waistband holster. Outside around the pool deck Aurelio was trimming grass. Cooper told Marita he would be out for lunch, but back in time for dinner and that she shouldn't make him anything for either; he would take care of himself. Without drinking he felt clearer, less foggy, and he swore to himself he wouldn't let his discipline slide like that again.

He was aware of the Mercedes when he drove into the city. Even now he was unsure if the car was bugged, if someone was tracking his movements and hadn't chosen to strike at the house because of some unknowable agenda.

The cathedral in the heart of downtown, the area called El Centro. Buildings clustered together more and more thickly and traffic congealed until Cooper was bumper to bumper with a truck in front of him and an old Ford behind. Heat lifted off the slowly moving cars in curling waves. Cooper drove with the radio off, but the street sounds didn't penetrate the cabin; he moved in silence.

Eventually the twin bell-towers of the cathedral hove into view. Cooper found a space half a block past it and slotted the car against the curb. The meter was old and rusted and somewhen a car or truck had run into it, leaving the stem creased. The concrete around the base was broken and the whole sidewalk was decaying into uneven squares of cracking cement.

He crossed the street and looked both ways for any sign of followers. When he came to the cathedral he went beyond it, turned at the next corner and came back up on the other side of the block, still checking for someone dogging his footsteps. There was no one.

The cathedral itself was a mixture of old and new. The façade was of the old style, with rough stone and pillars, and rose windows. The body of the place was decidedly more modern, boxy and marked from end to end by stained glass. It was not a beautiful structure.

Cooper went in by the front doors. Inside the entrance it was markedly cooler than outside, even though the doors were open. Even with his sunglasses off it seemed dim, but eventually Cooper's eyes adjusted and he could see.

It was noon and there were services at noon. Cooper went through the inner doors and into the cavernous interior of the cathedral. The voice of the priest at the far end of the open space echoed over the heads of twenty or thirty parishioners gathered to celebrate Mass.

On both sides there were prayer benches and rows of candles for lighting, a metal box welded at the end of the frame to accept donations. Cooper passed right, headed toward a three-booth confessional along the wall. His eyes were on the pews and when he came around a massive square pillar he saw her waiting for him in a seat three rows from the back.

He didn't sit next to her, but came up behind her and sat just to one side. Lorena was dressed in dark clothes and she wore a small hat for decorum's sake. When Cooper sat down she didn't look back at him, but kept her eyes forward on the distant celebrants.

"I'm here," Cooper said.

"I'm glad," Lorena replied without turning to him.

"We have a lot to talk about. I need to know more."

"When you say you need to know more, is it because you have second thoughts?"

"No, I don't have second thoughts."

Lorena was quiet for a while. The parishioners stood and sat twice, moving like a tide as the words of the Eucharist blew over them. Cooper turned down the kneeler on the back of

Lorena's pew and got on his knees. He was close enough to put his lips on the back of her neck and he smelled her.

"You want to know how it can be done," Lorena said at last. "How you can kill him."

"That's one question. An important one."

"You say you will do it cleanly?"

"As cleanly as it can be done. Why?"

"He is my father," Lorena replied.

She didn't have to explain herself. Cooper understood what she meant because he had heard such things before. Even at the moment of planning someone's death there was still love, attachment, some vestige of what brought two people together before they were to be separated by violence. Even after what Ruíz had done, he was still her father and she did not want him to die with pain.

"A shot to the head is all it takes," Cooper told her. "I just need to know where and when I can deliver the package. That's all you need to do."

"You have seen our swimming pool," Lorena said. "You know it is exposed to the hills beyond our property."

Cooper was surprised. "Yes," he said.

"My father is a night swimmer. He doesn't like to go out in the heat of the day. You will be able to see him perfectly in the pool with the lights on. That's when you can... deliver the package."

"It has to be something he does regularly. I have to know he'll be there when I come, otherwise there's no point."

"He goes out every night between ten and eleven when the weather is good," Lorena said.

Cooper kept wondering when the congregation would sing, but there was no singing at this service. The priest continued his invocations and no one paid any mind to two people far back in the nave. No one had come in after Cooper and it was deathly still around them.

"Will you tell me when you're coming?" Lorena asked Cooper.

"It's better if you don't know. That way you'll be surprised the way you should be surprised. But it will be soon. As soon as I can arrange it."

"And you'll be able to kill him this way?"

"Yes."

"You've killed other men like that?"

"I have."

For the first time she turned around and looked at him directly. Her eyes were moist, but Cooper couldn't tell if she was happy or sad. He had his hand on the back of her pew and she put her hand over his. "Thank you," she said.

"We won't be able to meet for a while afterward," Cooper told her.

"No one will suspect you."

"I'd rather not take the chance. We'll wait a month, maybe two."

"You don't want to see me?"

"Yes, I do," Cooper said. "I'll contact you."

"Cooper," she said, "he hasn't ruined me."

"I never thought he had."

36.

Summer night came late. Cooper waited until it was fully dark before he approached the far edge of Los Campos. He drove the last half a mile without his headlights on, watching for other lights coming his way. Finally he pulled off the road and drove over rough ground until he was a hundred feet away, well back from where a random passerby would spot the vehicle. There were no trees to hide the car, just low brush that would have to be enough.

He brought the AR-30 out of the trunk where it lay on two thick woolen blankets and took the blankets, too. Afterwards he hiked fifty yards to the marching line of metal and bars that marked the beginning of private property. His clothes were black and he wore a knit cap that covered his hair.

The blankets went up and over the top of the rigid fence, covering the coils of barbed wire there. This was the wicked kind, the sort with blades instead of spurs, and he could still be cut right through the blankets if he wasn't careful. He put on leather gloves and then proceeded to climb the fence with the rifle on a sling over his shoulder.

At the top of the fence he tested the blankets and found a spot where the coil dipped in, not up. Taking it slowly, he pulled himself onto the top of the fence and for a moment he was balanced precariously with the sharp edge of a razor threatening to come through the blankets and snag his flesh.

He jumped from the fence and soaked up the landing with bent knees. The blankets he left in place for the return trip; no one was going to see them hanging there.

More brush and even some trees covered the ground between Cooper and Ruíz's home. He could see the haciendas standing out amongst the foliage like floating barges filled with lights, each in an island of darkness that marked their territory.

The night provided little respite from the day's heat. The ground had soaked up so much sun that now it was giving back into the cooler air. It was like passing over the surface of a pan set on a stove. Eventually the temperatures would equalize and then it would become surprisingly chill just ahead of another scorching day.

He moved quickly across the landscape because his eyes were adjusted to the night. He wasn't worried about snakes because they would be tucked away in their hiding holes until the sun came out to warm them again. Occasionally he heard the scampering of small animals and thought he caught the movement, but it was too fast and the night too deep for him to see.

Cooper oriented himself by the lay of the land. He knew a low ridge passed along the rear of Ruíz's property, so when he caught the leading edge of the fold in the earth he followed it along. Off in the distance there were flashes of dry lightning, but it was too far away for him to hear the thunder. Storms in the Juárez summer could be fast moving and ferocious, flooding gullies and drowning the unwary.

Eventually he spotted the oasis of light that had to be Ruíz's home. The ground was leading inexorably upward, the estate dropping off on his left. He didn't have to check his watch to know it was after ten and that time was wasting. As quickly as he moved, he was still falling behind his timetable and he didn't like it.

The rise swung around closer to Ruíz's hacienda and Cooper followed it until he saw the bright blue rectangle of the pool snugged in among broad-shouldered trees. What he didn't see was Ruíz, or any figure in the water, but he wasn't there yet.

Cooper found the spot he was looking for, a straight shot across terrain that fell away to the wall of the estate and beyond. The entire pool was visible from this point, and the table where he had passed all those mornings eating giant breakfasts prepared by Ruíz's people.

The windows of the house were all lit up and as he watched a shadow passed across the sheer curtains in one. He wondered if this was Lorena, waiting in her room for the gunshot that she knew would have to come. She didn't know Cooper would be here on this night, so she would have to wait every night wondering if that would be the right moment.

Had Ruíz raped her again? The thought intruded on Cooper and he pushed it away. He had other things on his mind and didn't need ugly ideas floating around where they would distract him.

He crouched near a cluster of bush sage, putting his weight on the balls of his feet. He wore heavy-duty boots, not light shoes. The soles crunched audibly in the dry earth.

The rifle came off his shoulder. Cooper put down a knee and held the weapon across his body, watching the tableau below without another movement or even a sound. The grounds of Ruíz's estate were utterly still now, without even the movement of shades across the windows.

Two long minutes passed. Cooper wondered if maybe he'd come too late. Perhaps Ruíz had not wanted to take a long dip in the pool and had already gone inside. This was a risk like every other risk. Maybe tonight would be the one night Ruíz chose not to swim at all. These were also thoughts Cooper could ill afford to entertain in the moment because he was waiting and ready for what came next.

A dog bark carried from across the flat below. Cooper turned his eyes away from the pool and toward the sound.

At first he didn't know them for what they were, but eventually he understood what he was seeing. They appeared like glow-bugs drifting among the scrub and trees, one here and one there, both fairly close and farther away. He saw several of them in the dark spaces between the illuminated haciendas. They were men with electric lanterns, patrolling the open ground.

The closest one to him was easily two hundred yards away, and it was too dark to see any shapes. The light was ghostly, bobbing with the rhythm of an invisible man's walk. But Cooper knew the man was leading a dog — maybe all of them were — and eventually his path was going to take him between Cooper and the wall of Ruíz's estate.

Movement brought Cooper back to the scene below. The rear door of the house opened, and a thick-waisted man stood silhouetted there. He had a towel draped over one arm that made him look like an overweight matador.

Ruíz crossed the open ground to the pool. Under the lights Cooper could see him clearly, dressed in a robe and wearing sandals. He put the towel on the same table where Cooper had sat and shed the robe onto the same chair. He kicked off the sandals.

Cooper raised the rifle and flipped up the plastic covers on the telescopic sight. Ruíz jumped into view under the lenses of the sight, close enough to touch. The crosshairs settled naturally on the crook of his shoulder and neck and followed him across the stone pool deck to the water. Ruíz dove in.

Another bark distracted Cooper. He looked up from the weapon and saw the bobbing light moving closer and faster than he anticipated. Suddenly Cooper felt cold despite the lingering heat leaching from the soil.

There was only one man with one dog. He had his pistol and a suppressor. If he had to, he could kill both at close range in silence. But there were others out there and they would come running at the sound of the AR-30, which was not silenced. Cooper saw at least six lights and there were probably more. Someone would have a vehicle capable of traveling off-road and the way back to the fence was long.

He looked back through the sight at Ruíz. The man used a breaststroke to carry himself along the length of the pool. He turned and pushed off with his legs and headed back the way he'd come. As Cooper expected, it was almost too easy to make the target, dark on light like a paper silhouette.

His finger never touched the trigger. Cooper was cognizant of the way the patrolling guard and his dog were coming closer every second. The man would have a radio that would transmit Cooper's location to every security guard in Los Campos. All of them were armed with rifles. Cooper knew that. Maybe they wouldn't see him in the dark, but they would find him quickly enough with their animals.

Ruíz reached the opposite end of the pool. He turned and pushed off lazily. Cooper flipped the covers closed on the sight. He slung the rifle.

A part of him ranted at the back of his brain about the shot. Another part of him counseled him to go. He wanted to listen to them both. One shot and it would be done, but he would be in a race to the fence and beyond. If he turned away he would have to find some new approach and there was no guarantee it would be any safer.

He started his retreat long before the guard and his dog passed between his shooting perch and the estate. One time Cooper looked back and saw that Ruíz was out of the pool and headed back to the house. The time was past.

The landscape ahead of him was unlighted by any man on patrol. Cooper retraced his steps, but slipped once on an outcropping of loose shale. The moon was coming up, more brightly than Cooper anticipated. He would have been trapped under a moon like that one if someone had been looking for him. Without a cloud in the sky, the half-moon shone as brightly as a little sun.

At the fence he was careful on the climb over. When he was on the safe side he retrieved his blankets, which he used to wrap the rifle. He stowed both in the trunk. Back in the car, he allowed himself a long series of slow breaths to still the heart and the mind. He was away from Ruíz and away from the men with guns and dogs. They had never known he was there.

Without the headlights on he drove back to the road and turned the car back toward Juárez. Already he was looking ahead to the next thing. He knew he would have to be in touch with Lorena, but she would have to be the first one to reach out.

That was the way they'd planned it. She could wait a day, a week or a month, but he hoped that it wouldn't be so long.

Cooper wondered if she had been able to feel him when he was so close. He fancied that he could feel her, lingering inside the house waiting for him to kill her father. He imagined he could feel her now, thinking of him and wondering where he was or what he was doing. He had the same thoughts of her.

She would call him. She had his number, had memorized it before she left the Catedral de Ciudad Juárez. Cooper instructed her to buy a throwaway phone, one that was prepaid, one that couldn't be traced back to her unless she tried to refill it. He was sure she understood what to do.

When he was far enough away that he felt safe, he turned on the headlights and flooded the road ahead with light. He watched where he was going, but his mind was elsewhere, staring down into the blue pool at Ruíz.

37.

He waited for her call. It was days.

In the time he waited he wanted to do a lot of things he would not allow. He wanted to drink his time away. He wanted to prowl the house at all hours of the day and night. He wanted to sleep until the clock turned around on its dial and the idle time passed.

He second-guessed himself endlessly. There was no reason for him to fear the men with dogs. It would have been a single shot and hard to pinpoint exactly in that much open space in the darkness. Maybe, if he were unlucky, the muzzle flare from his rifle would have given his position away. It was impossible to know for certain and the lack of *knowing* scratched away at him until his mind was raw.

It was always possible to go back. He had gone in once and there was nothing stopping him from going in again. He could take the risks he hadn't before and hope for the best outcome, but that wasn't the way he worked; he was not about foolish chances, but playing to an advantage. If Ruíz was going to die, it would not be that way.

Cooper was just coming into the house through the kitchen when he heard Marita's voice carry from the front and then the thump of the front door closing. He found her in the living room picking up a dirty coffee cup and saucer. "What was that?" he asked.

"Oh, nothing, Señor Randolph. A man selling door to door."

Cooper looked toward the foyer. The door had a little window in the center where a peephole would go. The afternoon sun angled through it. "What was he selling?"

"I'm not sure. But as soon as he asked for the lady of the house I knew he was a salesman."

He left Marita alone and went to the front door. He peered through the little window and saw the front step and the stone walk to the wall and the gate. There was no one around and no vehicle on the street beyond. His hand was on the doorknob, but he didn't turn it.

When he came back to the living room Marita was gone. Cooper idled by the bar for a few moments, but the urge passed quickly. He had finished the only bottles of good stuff there, anyway, and hadn't sent Marita out to get more. What was left was the kind of thing he'd serve guests or people he wasn't trying to impress. After this was over, he'd drink plenty and without guilt.

The phone rang when he was almost on top of it and he flinched. He answered.

"He's not dead," Lorena said to him.

The connection was not good, but he could tell she was outside by the sound. It was windy where she was, as it had been windy over Juárez for several days. More storms threatened, though none had come crashing in yet.

"There's a problem," Cooper told her and then he explained the rest. It made more sense to him now, coming out of his mouth, than it had in the echo chamber of his mind. Before he kept coming back to his decision again and again until no decision seemed right. Telling Lorena was like setting it in stone.

"You're saying it can't be done?"

"I'm saying it can't be done *that way*," Cooper replied, and then he looked both directions to ensure he was still alone. It occurred to him briefly that Marita might pick up the extension, but she hadn't. They were as secure as they could be. "I didn't say it couldn't be done."

"What should I do?"

He didn't like the sound of her voice. He wondered if Ruíz had been at her again and for the first time there was anger mixed with his disgust. A part of him was angry with her for letting it happen. Cooper tried to let that go.

"I need access to the client. Better access."

"There is nothing better here."

"Then somewhere else."

Lorena fell silent. The wind warbled across the mouthpiece of her cheap, throwaway phone. Finally she said, "We have a house. Another house. North of Chihuahua. On a ranch my father owns."

"Why would he go there?"

"If I asked him to. It's... special to us."

Cooper swallowed something unpleasant.

"I can ask him to go. It would be for a couple of days. We could make arrangements for you."

"What about security?"

"It's not the same there. The house is small. He never brings more than one guard. Rudolfo. You know him."

"I know him."

"If I can convince him to go, will you come?"

Cooper wanted to say no, but his answer was already decided. Speaking it was almost unnecessary. But he knew Lorena had to hear it because the fear was in her voice. Not a fear of her father dying, but a fear of him *not* dying when his death was something she wanted more than anything.

"Will you come?"

"I'll come. But I need things from you. A location to start. Where is this place? When will you be there? And I have questions about the house."

"I'll tell you everything," she said. "Whatever you want to know."

"How many minutes do you have left on your phone? Are you somewhere you won't be heard?"

"I'm in a safe place."

"Wait."

Cooper went from the living room into the library and picked up the extension, and then he went back to the living room to hang up the phone. In the big desk in the library he found a pad of paper and some pens. He sat by the window and took the phone up again.

"Are you still there?"

"I am."

"I'm going to ask you questions and I need answers for all of them. If you don't know, then don't lie. It's better for me if you tell me the truth. Do you understand?"

"I understand," Lorena said.

"We'll start with the house. Where is it exactly and how do I get there?"

They were on the phone for almost an hour. He asked questions and she answered them. Cooper filled six pages on the pad and when he was done they hung up without saying goodbye.

38.

He told Marita that he would be gone for a day. Aurelio didn't seem to care one way or the other.

Cooper didn't even bother to pack a bag. He left Juárez heading south. The land there was blasted dry and the color of chalk, barely populated with green here and there to mark the passage of underground water. Little by little it grew hillier and finally he found the turnoff from the main road.

The car's wheels kicked up dry flakes of dust on a partly graveled road up to a functional iron gate held shut with a chain and a padlock. The fence that headed off into the distance on both sides of the road was simple barbed wire.

The sun frowned on Cooper when he got out of the car. The ground reflected a baking heat. If he touched the top of the car he would certainly burn his hand.

He climbed over the gate and stood for a little while in the quiet. Not even insects stirred during the worst of the day and the gate was set far enough back from the road that even a passing car would make no sound. A lone mesquite tree struggled out of the earth a few yards away and provided the only shade.

Cooper followed the road up a slow incline and onto a flat that extended two hundred yards or more. It was up there that he found the stone well and not far beyond it the house.

Compared to the hacienda in Juárez this house was nothing. It was one floor and broad, but not so sprawling as Cooper expected. The walls were brick and painted white with red shutters. An open car park squatted to one side of the house, not even a garage. Some of the shutters were open, but most were closed. Dirt crunched underfoot as Cooper approached.

A stubborn tree grew out front with branches spread widely enough to allow a handful of grass to grow. To Cooper the place looked sun-blasted and painfully dry and he had no idea why anyone would want to come there.

He looked through the few open windows and saw a house waiting for life. The furniture was uncovered, the rooms absolutely still. Cooper walked around the entire place counting steps. He noted where the doors were. A wide back porch was fully shaded by corrugated aluminum. Cooper let the sweat cool from him there.

Lorena called this place a ranch, but Cooper saw no sign of animals. Even plants struggled here so there could be no farming, either. There was only this house, dropped in the center of a crumbling rocky plateau, simply waiting.

The house had no security system. Cooper picked the lock on the back door and went inside. The air smelled stale. He left the door open and hot air followed him in.

Inside were four bedrooms, a kitchen, a living room, a study and a dining room. There was an impersonal atmosphere to the place that even pictures on the walls and books on the shelves could not dismiss. Cooper did not feel as if he was in someone's home. This was just a place.

The shutters on the master bedroom's windows were shut and the room was black. He turned on a bedside lamp and then sat on the edge of the bed. Out of curiosity he checked the drawer in the bed-stand, but it was empty. A part of him half expected to find a Gideon Bible.

He was tired from the drive, but he wouldn't sleep here. He didn't even lie back on the bed though the mattress was soft enough. When he got up he straightened the wrinkles on the bedspread.

First he walked the perimeter of the room and then he noted the angle of the doorway to the bed, the relationship to the windows. He switched all the lights on and then shut them off in different patterns, always watching the bed from the door. Then he turned them all off and stood in the shadows until his eyes adjusted and the bed was a black square. He could do it this way, too.

In the kitchen he looked in the refrigerator. It was empty. He got down a glass from a cabinet near the sink and poured himself water from the tap. It was a weak stream and the well water tasted gritty. When he was finished, he wiped the glass with a dishtowel and put it back where he got it.

Three of the bedrooms, including the master bedroom, were clustered at one end of the house. The fourth was at the far end, isolated from everything, accessible through the study. A simple double bed sat in the corner, made up like a military man's rack. There was a crucifix on the wall over the bed and a prayer candle on the top of the room's chest of drawers. A tiny bathroom stood off to one side.

Cooper checked the door. It didn't lock.

He went outside and put on sunglasses. The glare was punishing and it took some time before his eyes grew used to it again. He relocked the back door and headed back down the gravel road to the gate and the parked car.

From the road the house was invisible. The rise looked like a naked bulge of white stone and dirt. At night it would be impossible to even see lights.

Cooper started the car and drove back the way he came.

39.

Lorena called him three days later.

"Saturday," she said and then she hung up.

40.

He set out in the afternoon, retracing his path southward away from Juárez. He listened to Bach on the sound system and his hands were totally still. His mind roved, but only so far as the night and no further.

The rifle was packed away in the back of the car but there would be no need for it.

The drive timed out so that it was past eleven by the time he arrived at the turnoff. The sun was down, without even the last bit of glow on the horizon, and the stars were coming out. On this night there was no moon at all.

Cooper drove the last part of the way with the headlights off and stopped just where he had stopped on his last trip to this place. The chain was still wrapped around the gatepost, but when he got out of the car he saw that the padlock had been removed and hooked on a rusty nail.

He looked up into the sky and found it infinite and full of stars. Away from the cities the sky could turn wholly black and the spread of the Milky Way was vast and bright. It was possible to see his way without moonlight, the ground illuminated by the silver of the stars themselves.

The gate made a little noise as it opened and then swung shut. Cooper was careful to secure it with the chain before turning away. He looked up the rise and saw that he was right: the house didn't show itself at all.

He climbed the track to the flat and there it was, lit front and back. The shutters on all the windows had been opened, but not all the lights had been switched on. There was the cluster of outdoor lamps in the fore-corner of the house and a matching one on the far side. In the car park there were two vehicles.

Cooper circled at the point where light turned to shadow. He saw no one through the lit windows until finally he caught a glimpse of someone moving in a hallway. It was too fleeting for him to know who it was.

When he came to the back of the house he crouched down and waited. There were too many lights on and the night was still early. At least now there was the sound of little insects making music. He was not alone.

Time passed but Cooper didn't check his watch. Eventually he saw the lights in two rooms go out. In another fifteen minutes a third went black. Through the glass of the back door he saw a man walking from right to left and the glow of a cigarette.

He waited until even the bugs had gone still.

When he rose his knees creaked and Cooper knew he was getting older. He stole onto the poured concrete porch, put his hand on the knob of the back door and tested it once. It was locked.

Passing the lock was easy. He was inside now and smelled the odor of smoke going stale in the darkness.

Cooper counted steps in the darkness. He went from the dining room to the living room to the study. No sound came from anywhere and even his footsteps were silent.

The sound suppressor was already threaded to the barrel of his pistol. He held the weapon in his hand lightly, as if he was afraid to crush it, and went the last few steps to the closed bedroom door.

Rudolfo slept without snoring. Cooper swung the door wide and for a moment he was framed in the open doorway, shadow on shadow. A drift of starlight passed through the window over Rudolfo's bed. The man breathed slowly.

Cooper shot the man twice in the head. Rudolfo seizured once, his hand scrabbling against the wall beside the bed, and then he was still. The room seemed emptier.

Back the way he came. Cooper paused in the living room among sentinel furniture. He thought he heard something, but the sound didn't come again. He crept down the long hallway to the last three bedrooms. Here it was absolutely dark because there was no window, no lamp. Cooper moved with his fingertips brushing the wall ahead of him.

Now he heard it: short moans that came and went, breathless. When he came to the door to the master bedroom they were clearer and constant and Cooper did not have to guess what they were.

Light spilled underneath the door. He eased it open and more light came into the hallway, blinding Cooper for the seconds it took for his eyes to adjust. He saw movement first, and then shapes and then the pistoning buttocks of a man between Lorena's spread legs.

Cooper rose up. Ruíz was oblivious, rutting, and sweaty. Cooper came closer and then he saw Lorena's face. Her eyes were screwed shut and the sounds that came from her were ones she could not help.

"Señor Ruíz," Cooper said.

The man didn't respond. His hair was in disarray as he lunged into his daughter. His sounds were raspy, wanting. The whole bed shook.

"Señor Ruíz!"

Cooper took the man by the shoulder and hauled him back. The man separated from Lorena and stumbled over his own feet, crashing backward onto the carpet with his cock jutting out. Cooper kicked Ruíz in the side once and then again. Ruíz made squealing noises.

The man put his hands up. When he looked through his fingers Cooper saw the recognition come.

"What do you want?!?"

The first bullet passed through Ruíz's palm and punched into the man's neck. The second hit him in the mouth. The third crashed into Ruíz's face at the side of his nose. The gun made almost no sound.

Lorena was also silent, and all Cooper could hear was the roughness of his own breath.

41.

"What will you do?" Cooper asked her.

She was still naked. When her father was dead she left the bed and went to a vanity near the window. The shutters were open, but it was totally black beyond the glass. She looked at herself in the mirror and at Cooper reflected there, too. He still held the gun.

"The police will have to come," Lorena said. "That will happen first."

"What will you tell them?"

"What we agreed. That I was asleep in my bedroom when it happened. That I found my father dead in the morning. That I heard nothing and saw nothing."

"They'll wonder why you aren't dead, too."

Lorena met his gaze in the mirror. "How would I know why a killer does things?"

Cooper approached her from behind. He realized he was still holding the gun and he put it away. He put his hand on her shoulder. "If it was me, I would have killed you, too."

"Then I'm glad it wasn't you."

He touched her neck and her hair. She smelled sweetly despite everything. In the mirror the body of her father was hidden behind the bed. Cooper touched her softly.

"Not here," she said.

Lorena led him from the room into another bedroom. She lay back for him there and he stripped off his clothes in the dark.

There was no need to prepare her and he was ready. He kissed her as he pushed into her and she raised her knees.

Cooper wanted to take his time, but he was urgent with her and she complied. He entwined his fingers in her hair and held her head against the mattress and fucked her as if he never fucked in his life. When he came inside of her she drew him to her and she kissed his forehead when he fell atop her at last.

He rolled away from her onto his back. She lay beside him a little while and then straddled him. Cooper felt his semen dripping from her. She settled onto him. This time it was slower and he suckled her breasts when she leaned over him. He came again.

This time she lay in the crook of his arm. The still air wicked away their sweat and Cooper was chilled. He felt her breathing against him.

"I will have to be with my mother for a time," Lorena said at last. "But when that time is over, I want to go away from here."

"Where?"

"When I was younger, my parents took me to Palmilla. I loved it there. The sand and beaches. I loved to swim in the ocean."

"Palmilla," Cooper said.

"Yes. I think I will go there."

Cooper tried, but he couldn't think beyond this room. He imagined the gun was still warm, like the body in the next room.

"If I go there, will you come to me?"

"Is that what you want?"

"Yes."

"Then I'll come."

"I'll call you the way you taught me."

"No, don't call me again."

"Why not?"

"There are going to be enough questions. Don't call me. I'll come to you, but don't call me."

"How will you find me?"

"I will."

Cooper got up and found his clothes. He put them on in silence. The shutters were still closed here and he could barely make out Lorena's form in the dark. He felt slow, sluggish. The room was full of her smell.

"Do you have to go now?"

"I have to be gone before dawn."

"I don't want to be alone now."

"Well, you have to be," Cooper said more harshly than he intended. "That's just what you have to do."

"Cooper?"

"Yes?"

"You aren't lying to me, are you? You will come?"

"I promise."

He left her then. A kind of morbid curiosity drew him back to the master bedroom and Ruíz's corpse. The man's head had been leaking and the carpet around his skull was haloed with blood. His penis was finally shriveled.

Cooper went out by the back door and circled the house in full view of the lights. He didn't look back to see if Lorena was watching him from an un-shuttered window. The house retreated behind him and when he finally did turn it was almost hidden from view.

His hands were shaky. His hands hadn't been shaky for a long time. When he got behind the wheel of the car he steadied them on the steering wheel for a long minute before starting the engine.

At the road he turned himself back toward Juárez and put the rest of it behind him.

42.

He saw the flashes of lightning long before the first droplets of water hit the windshield. The weather went from dry and calm to torrential in a matter of minutes, turning the gullies off the shoulders of the road into rushing, muddy rivers. Cooper put the wipers on high and turned on his brights.

The morning sun was up, but shrouded in thick clouds. Thunder boomed a split second after lightning forked the sky, the great storm straddling Juárez. There were few streetlights and those he saw were almost swallowed up by the downpour.

Cooper was close to the house. He made the rest of the way almost by instinct. What tired he felt was washed away by the storm. He was pleased to see the familiar walls and the light by the gate.

He parked the car and rushed from it to the side door of the house. He let himself in with his key.

The kitchen was still and empty where he expected Marita to be. There was no sign of Aurelio anywhere. Outside on the back lawn the trees were thrashing in the storm winds and their leaves fell into the pool. Rainwater lashed the broad windows of the kitchen.

He stopped to look in the refrigerator for something to eat. He hadn't put something in his stomach for twenty-four hours. The wire was almost around his throat before he had a chance to realize it was there.

Cooper jammed his hand into the gap between the wire and his neck. The slack snapped up and a line of pain cut through the blade of his palm and into the flesh. Cooper staggered back away from the refrigerator and the man with the wire fell with him.

They collided with the kitchen island. Cooper drove his free arm backward and his elbow found ribs. The man behind him grunted, but the pressure didn't go away. Blood poured down the side of Cooper's hand.

Together they spun, crashing a butcher's block and a ceramic cock filled with wooden spoons to the floor, until they came up against the cooking range. Cooper stomped the man's arch and finally the wire slackened. He wrenched himself out of the hold. The bloody wire fell to the floor.

Cooper didn't recognize the man but he didn't expect to. The man drew a knife with a broad blade. He slashed Cooper across the arm and drew blood.

He didn't have the little dart-shaped knife. He passed on the inside of the man's guard, grabbed a wrist and turned. The knife came in again and missed. Cooper drove the man belly-first into the kitchen island, put a foot to the back of his knee, drove down with all his strength.

The man tried to come up with the knife. Cooper fell on top of him and they struggled for it. The blade came around slowly, levering against Cooper's grip, and the edge brushed the flesh under his eye. He felt heat and wetness on his cheek.

Two sharp blows to the ribs and the man curled up. Cooper slammed his knife hand against the floor until the tip of the blade snapped off. The man let it go and they were scrabbling in the shadow of the refrigerator as Cooper's blood wet the floor.

Cooper gouged his thumb into the man's eye while the man tried to leverage a hold on the back of his neck. Cooper pushed until he felt something rupture. The man screamed a high-pitched scream. Cooper punched him in the throat and it was quiet again.

The man was kicking. Cooper got his hands under the man's chin and squeezed. There was blood and fluid on the man's face and one of his eyes lolled free on a tatter of red flesh. His face purpled. He scratched at Cooper's eyes.

Cooper bore down with both arms. He didn't slacken his grip. The man flopped underneath him, then went still and died. Cooper fell on top of him.

The knife wounds on his arm and face were burning. Finding his feet was difficult, but he made his way to the sink and cupped two handfuls of water into his mouth. Thunder crashed outside.

He bound his arm with a kitchen towel and then he spent a minute emptying the dead man's pockets. He found a car key, a second knife and a receipt from a restaurant. The man carried no wallet and no identification. He also had no gun.

A round struck the stainless-steel side of the refrigerator less than six inches from Cooper, and a second slammed into his back. The shots were silenced.

Cooper went over the edge of the kitchen island and crashed onto the tile floor. The second man was a flicker of movement in the doorway to the next room and a final shot spiderwebbed the window above Cooper's head.

The wound in his back stabbed him as he crawled behind the island. He still had his pistol. Blood smeared on the grips when he drew it.

For a moment there was nothing but the rain and then the scuttle of shoes. Cooper tried to listen over the sound of his own panting in his ears. Moving was excruciating. He edged his way to the corner of the island and dared a look.

Two shots ripped the wood in front of Cooper's face and sprayed splinters into his eyes. He flinched but he was shooting, too, at the man he saw in motion just beyond the kitchen. There was a short, sharp bark of pain and then more silence.

Cooper levered himself onto his feet, coming up slowly from behind the island. The pistol stayed up, though his hand wavered. He took first one step toward the door to the next room and then a second and a third.

He found the man in the living room within an arm's length of the bar. The man bled out from the neck and blood surrounded him. His silenced Beretta was three feet away, abandoned.

Thunder boomed once again and the house lights flickered. Cooper went to the downstairs restroom.

Stripping off his shirt was hard. He could barely move his left arm from the pain in his back. Every time Cooper breathed he felt the spike of agony.

His face was a half-covered in blood from the cut on his cheek. He tried to wash his wounds out and reach under his left arm to stanch the flow from the bullet injury. He knew he would need a doctor.

Out of the bathroom he staggered to the couch. He sat there bleeding for a while until the crawling pain in his shoulder made it impossible to be still. There was less blood than he expected and maybe it was slowing on its own.

The house was covered in his prints. He could not think of anything he hadn't touched in his time there. Marita and Aurelio were late, but they couldn't be kept away forever.

His go-bag was in the closet upstairs. Cooper found a new shirt to wear and promptly bled through it. He ventured out into the rain to the shed where Aurelio kept his landscaping gear. When he was done he returned with a five-gallon container half-full of gasoline.

The kitchen was the easiest to soak down and the living room the next. He was sure to splash the dead bodies heavily. He snuffed the pilot lights in the kitchen and turned the gas on full.

He used matches from the cupboard to start the fire and waited until it was too hot to face the flames before he left the house and made his way back to the car. There was fire in the upstairs windows by the time he managed to back the car out of the driveway and onto the road. The blaze would gut the house and the rain would leave the shell standing.

Cooper drove.

43.

"Who is this?"

"My name is Amador."

"My name is Cooper. We met in Ciudad Juárez."

"I remember you, Señor Townsend."

"I need something."

"I'm just a contact, Señor Townsend."

"Tell Barriga I need to find a safe doctor."

"Señor Townsend—"

"Just tell him. And call me back at this number."

"I'll see what can be done for you."

44.

He drove south again, but he wasn't headed back to Ruíz's ranch hideaway. He passed the road that led there and kept on going until he reached the city of Chihuahua. It was a smaller place than Ciudad Juárez, but more open. There were more wrinkles to the terrain and a mountain and though it was dry there and was greener than anywhere along the border with the United States.

Directions had been given and Cooper followed them. Eventually he came to a place where the old buildings were close together and knitted to one another by electrical lines that tangled overhead. The car was out of place on the street. On the drive blood had leaked onto the front seat and made the backrest wet.

This time when he parked the car he left all the doors unlocked and took the key from his ring to leave behind in the ignition. From the trunk he grabbed his go-bag and the case for his rifle. With luck the car would be gone inside a few hours. It hurt to leave it, but he couldn't be sure they weren't using it to follow him. Just because he found nothing during his inspection didn't mean something wasn't there. Besides, he was insured against theft.

He took back stairs to an upper-floor apartment. The nameplate by the mailbox said *Dr. Francisco Gutierrez*. Cooper rapped on the door three times and waited. It was mid-morning.

The man came to the door. He was older, wore glasses and had black hair heavily streaked with white. When he saw Cooper on his step he did not have to ask why he'd come; Barriga's people would have sent word. The doctor was waiting for him.

They went to the kitchen, where Cooper took his shirt off and let Gutierrez examine him. The room was small, but it was kept neat and clean. A cat-shaped clock with moving eyes tick-tocked by the doorway to the dining room. Cooper thought he heard someone else moving out that way, but he couldn't be sure and anyway he was in no shape to do anything about it.

He felt trodden on and horribly tired. Cooper couldn't be sure how much of it was loss of blood and how much was simple exhaustion. He hadn't slept for a long time and didn't foresee a time when he would be able to sleep.

"You're lucky," the doctor told him after a while. "The bullet struck your shoulder blade and deflected. The bone may be cracked. Move your arm for me."

Doing that was torture, but Cooper was able to make a full rotation of his arm once and then a second time. The third time he didn't need assistance, though the pain was still there.

"The wound will need stitches. And you'll have to take antibiotics to prevent an infection," Dr. Gutierrez told him.

"I can do that," Cooper said.

"And you will need rest. You've been bleeding a great deal. That takes time to recover from."

"I understand."

"Try to relax. This will take a little while."

Cooper did that. The pain from the stitching needle was no worse than the pain he already felt, just pinpricks among the broader ache. He watched the cat clock and its moving eyes, letting them hypnotize him. The time meant nothing and passed without notice. Cooper was only interested in the eyes.

When the doctor was done, Cooper swam up out of his own mind back to the kitchen. The doctor had soaked several pieces of gauze with Cooper's blood. The wound felt tight, pulling slightly when he moved. He would have to be careful with them, and the doctor said the same.

"It will be some time before the stitches can come out. You'll need a doctor to do that; you can't do it yourself. But wait until the flesh has had plenty of time to heal. If you have the stitches removed too soon, the wound will reopen."

Dr. Gutierrez did not say that he would follow up with Cooper because he would not. He was a safe doctor, but he could only be used once. After this Cooper would be on his own. He would have to find a doctor he could bribe with the money in his go-bag, or from his savings if he was able to get back to Monterrey and his life.

"Thank you," Cooper told the doctor.

"I will go to the *farmacia* and get the prescriptions you will need. You can wait in the living room and rest. The couch is comfortable."

"Thank you," Cooper said again.

The couch was short and brown, but it was as soft as promised. Cooper had to lie on his side to keep the wet stitches from sticking to the upholstery. His go-bag had a change of clothes in it and before he left here he would get into fresh slacks and shirt.

He lay opposite a gray-faced television reflecting light from the front windows. Cooper didn't want to fall asleep here, in a strange place, but he did anyway and slept a fitful twenty minutes before opening his eyes again. The reflection hadn't moved and the television was still sentinel.

The doctor hadn't returned. Cooper didn't know how long he'd be. He thought about sitting up, but he wasn't ready yet. Tiredness pressed on him.

Now he could think about the men in the house. They hadn't spoken to him, or he to them. He wanted to know where they'd come from, how they'd known where to find him and where they would look for him next if he hadn't come back to the house.

He shouldn't be alive. This much he knew for certain. He had walked into the house before they were ready to set up for him, and that was the only thing that saved his life. One could have strangled the life out of him while the other put a gun in his gut and pulled the trigger. Either way he would be dead.

It occurred to him that Ruíz might have sent the men before his death. A letter intercepted or a telephone call overheard would be enough. This didn't answer the *how* of how Cooper had been found, but that didn't matter anymore; he had been found and the men had tried to kill him.

The other possibility was Texas. Cooper didn't know Bingham any better than he'd had to know the man, but he wouldn't have expected his death to raise so many red flags. Bingham seemed like a businessman with cheap tastes and a dick that went where it wanted. Cooper didn't ask why Barriga's people would bother with a man like Bingham or what kind of people Bingham had behind him. Those questions weren't important enough to consider. There was only the client and the package and what it took to bring the two together.

His incuriosity was usually an asset. Now it could place him in extreme peril. It occurred to Cooper that he had no way to contact Bingham's people if there was deal to be made. If he could make contact with them it would only be via Barriga's organization, and it was unlikely they'd want to put themselves out in that way. Getting the safe doctor was an unexpected generosity.

"I've done enough for you," Cooper murmured aloud.

He had done plenty for them. They owed him something more than money could offset. Barriga had relied on him enough to bring him aboard for his adventure with Ruíz. Not just anyone would have hired on and then walked away the way Cooper had. There was trust. Trust was worth something.

At first he didn't hear his phone ringing. It was in the other room with his discarded shirt. He rose from the couch and went to the kitchen.

"*Bueno.*"

"Cooper."

"Señor Barriga."

"You've seen our doctor?"

"I have. I'm with him now."

"He's a very good doctor. One of the best we have. You're lucky to see him."

"I feel lucky."

"You know I don't like being contacted directly."

"There was no other way."

Barriga exhaled into the phone. He was quiet for a moment. "There are people in my organization that aren't pleased with this. The whole situation in Texas."

"That hit couldn't have been cleaner," Cooper said. "I don't know how my name got put into the mix."

"But it's in the mix, Cooper. At the very least someone knows you're associated with us. They may be looking down a number of avenues, but it's *your* name that came to the top. That makes certain people very nervous."

"I told you before: I'm taking care of it."

"It doesn't seem like you're taking care of anything."

"This is just a bad turn."

"A bad turn."

"Yes."

There was more silence on the line.

"I know this is a problem," Cooper said to break the quiet.

"I'm glad you do. You've involved us. If this becomes *our* problem, then I won't be able to help you anymore. Do you understand?"

"I do."

"Tell Dr. Gutierrez thank you from me," Barriga said and disconnected.

Cooper stood in the kitchen. His old shirt was wadded up and cast aside in one of the kitchen chairs, looking like a rag used to clean up a boxing ring. His go-bag was in the corner. He picked it up and brought it back into the living room with him.

Stripping down in front of the blank television, Cooper saw he was bruised on the ribs and legs. He hadn't felt these, but they were large and purple welts that would spread under the skin as they healed and shade into brown and gold.

The clothes in his go-bag were wrinkled, but they were clean and that was good enough. He had blood on one of his shoes, but there was nothing he could do about that. The leather was dark and perhaps no one would notice.

Cooper checked his weapons. He couldn't hide the pistol and a silencer under the new shirt. He unscrewed the silencer and put it into the bag. The gun fit in his waistband now. The dart-shaped knife fit on his forearm, hidden by the loose cloth of his sleeve.

It was probably his imagination, but his arm moved better now than it had before. He still felt the tightness of the new suturing, but he no longer felt as if he was bleeding out by inches.

He thought about leaving before the doctor came back, but it was a foolish thing and he dismissed it. From here he had to obtain a new car, one that wouldn't be traced by the ones keeping watch over him. Out of Juárez he felt a little safer, but so long as he was being sought he could not relax. He had to make himself as small a target as possible.

Finally Dr. Gutierrez arrived with the medicines. There were three different medications he had to take, including one for pain. "The tissue will likely become inflamed," the doctor told him. "This will help."

When they were finished, Cooper offered Gutierrez some of the money from his go-bag. The doctor turned it down. There followed an awkward moment with Cooper still holding the money out and the doctor turning away from it. Eventually Cooper put the cash away. He asked Dr. Gutierrez to call him a taxi.

The taxi took almost an hour to arrive. During that time Cooper sat stiffly on the couch, Dr. Gutierrez watching him. They had nothing else to say to each other, but were forced into their respective company. Cooper noticed how perfectly kept the apartment was, and surmised that the doctor lived alone.

It was a relief when the cab came. Cooper bid Dr. Gutierrez good-bye and left by the same stairs that brought him in. He asked the taxi driver to take him somewhere he could buy a cheap car.

A twenty-minute ride later, the taxi dropped Cooper off at the crowded lot of a mechanic's shop. Cars were parked at odd angles, paired up or in clumps like bacteria growing in a dish. There was hardly a clear space to move, let alone to drive. The garage-bay doors were rusted around their Plexiglas windows.

Cooper found the office. It was as crowded as the lot, with a counter and a desk behind it, both overstuffed with papers and folders and other rubbish. A radio played in the corner and a man in a mechanic's coveralls ate from the contents of a lunch bag spread over the desk.

"Hello," Cooper said, "I was told there were cars for sale here."

"There are," the mechanic said. "We take cash only."

"I have cash if you have a car for me."

"How much cash do you have?"

"How much do your cars cost?"

"Take a look around outside. If you see something you like, come back to me. I will make you a fair price."

Cooper went away from the office and went back into the midday sun. Some of the cars were rusting into hulks, while others were just worn down. He was primarily interested in something that would run reliably, not so much about condition. Many of the cars were unlocked and he took the time to look under their hoods until he found a little Ford Escort that didn't seem too old or too worn out.

The mechanic was still eating when Cooper returned. "Did you find something?" the man asked.

"I did. The Escort. The blue one."

"That's a good car."

"I'll bet."

"I can let you have that car for 6,000 pesos."

Cooper looked back out at the car oxidizing under the sun. "I have 4,000 if you'll tune it up today."

"Four thousand?"

"That's right."

"I can do that."

The mechanic got up from his desk and the two shook hands on the deal. It surprised Cooper when the man got right to work on the car, slowly extricating it from the knot of cars on the lot and finally guiding it into one of the repair bays. The tune up took the better part of two hours, which Cooper spent listening idly to the radio and staring out the windows of the office. He may have dozed with his eyes open.

He paid the mechanic 4,000 pesos in cash. The fuel tank on the Escort was half-empty and the engine idled roughly, but the car worked. That was enough. Cooper left the lot never learning the mechanic's name. They did not even bother with formalities like signing over a title; such things were optional when cash was on the table.

Cooper's first instinct was to leave Chihuahua and head for Monterrey. It would be safer on his home ground. Another wave of tiredness hit him and he knew he could not make the drive without endangering himself more than he would by just staying in the city.

The first motel he found had an hourly rate. He paid for three in advance and went up to the room on the second floor.

His back wound felt hot and he found his shirt sticking wetly to the wound. It wasn't blood seeping from it, but some clear serum. When he lay down on his side in the hot little room without air conditioning he kept his shirt off. His pistol he put in front of him and rested his hand on it.

Sleep came more easily than he expected or even wanted. He opened up his eyes four hours later with the hotel manager rapping on the door, looking for more money. Cooper answered and paid the man for three more hours and then locked the door behind him.

He washed his face in a stained sink and ran wet fingers through his hair. It was a hotbox in the room, but he didn't open the windows. Looking at himself in the mirror, he saw the flesh around the cut on his face was ever so slightly puffy. He took his first dose of antibiotics and pain pills.

Cooper decided to wait until dark to leave the city. He would drive through the night in his anonymous little Escort. No one would be looking for his car and they had no idea of where he might be going. The fire would confuse people for a while, because they wouldn't know if one of the charred bodies in the house in Juárez was the man who'd rented the place. They did not even know his real name and references no one bothered to check before — when there was still more cash on the table — would turn out to be less than worthless.

He contemplated more sleep, struggled with the idea of staying awake for the next three hours just mulling over everything he knew so far and what he didn't. Sleep was the better option. This time he did not overstay his payment and he was out the door and on his way before the manager came to call again.

45.

Driving around the block six times revealed no one on his tail. He had been clean all the way from Chihuahua. The Escort was old and ran erratically despite the tune-up, but it was anonymous and that was all Cooper asked of it.

He parked fifty yards from the front of his apartment building and sat for an hour, just watching. Cars and people came and went. It was the middle of the day. He didn't see one pedestrian whose face repeated itself, and no one lingered in the vehicles parked opposite the building.

When he left the car he also left the go-bag and the rifle case. He wanted to be able to move if he had to, his hands free. His pistol was under his shirt, the knife in place. Whatever else, he wasn't defenseless and if caught out on the street and unable to run, he could make an accounting of himself.

The doorman knew him on sight and let Cooper in. At the elevators Cooper stood with his back to the doors and watched out for anyone who might follow or be too curious for too long. There was no one.

His apartment smelled fresh. The cleaners had been in recently, but Cooper didn't know when. He wasn't even sure what day it was anymore. The keys to the apartment and the Escort went on the glass coffee table. Out of habit he switched the television on to the news and turned the sound down to a whisper.

There was food in the refrigerator but it was no good anymore. Cooper poured himself a glass of water, drank it and found himself thirst for another. He drank five glasses, one after the other. The news was a blank to him; he saw it but didn't see it.

The shirt stuck to his stitches when he pulled it off, but he hadn't bled through the cloth. Cooper stripped in the bedroom, went to the bathroom and took a shower that lasted half an hour. He toweled himself down carefully. After that he put on underpants and a t-shirt and crawled under the covers of his bed to sleep for a long time.

It was still night when he woke up. The clock by the bed called it three in the morning. His mouth tasted bad so he brushed and flossed in front of the big mirror in his bathroom. The cut on his face made him look as through he had a dueling scar, and maybe that was true.

He put on his robe, found food in the freezer that was still edible and prepared himself something simple from found ingredients. He poured himself a drink from his own bar and relaxed on his own couch and let the light and colors of the news spill over him. He was still uninterested in anything it had to say.

He was aware of the friendly stillness of the apartment. It was not so large or ostentatious as the house in Juárez, but it belonged to him. He would miss having someone fix his meals and make his bed. It was safe here because no one knew where he went between deliveries and no one could have followed him in his flight from Chihuahua. For the first time in too long he didn't feel he had to watch out the window for someone out of place.

It was still before dawn and the city were shining outside his window. His apartment had a western exposure so morning came late.

His body didn't want to sleep anymore, but he lay on the bed in his robe until the sky was bright outside. He used the time to think.

The problem now was Texas. Bingham's people. They were looking for him, and after the situation in Juárez they might be inclined to think they had the right man for Bingham's murder. Maybe they had already made that decision. Or maybe they were simply removing anyone who might have delivered the package. It was cheap enough to do the latter.

Whether they were taking out everyone associated with Barriga's people or not, Cooper could not operate. They were on his scent. No one could find him here, but they didn't have to; sooner or later he'd have to move and then they would zero in on him. Until this was settled, he couldn't take another job.

He needed Barriga. Barriga worked on the level of these people and he would know what Cooper needed to know. He would have the contacts, or be able to push Cooper in the right direction. Cooper had already leaned on Barriga once, and doing it twice wasn't wise. There was no other choice.

This time when he called the contact number he didn't reach Amador or any other human being. It was a simple voice mail message that recited the number and nothing else. Cooper left a number and hung up without giving his name. They would know his voice.

On the television there was a commercial showing a sandy beach and a palm tree. Cooper thought of Palmilla, on the southernmost tip of Baja California Sur. He didn't know when Lorena would be there, but she would be there soon. Briefly Cooper imagined the pleasant burn of sand, salt winds off the Pacific and touching her, but only briefly. He couldn't go there without first dealing with Texas.

He had no idea how long it would be before he was contacted. He brought his go-bag and the rifle case in from the car. The go-bag he restocked with what he could; cash would have to come later. The rifle went back into the gun safe.

Cooper shaved and put a new bandage on his face. He dressed in clean, pressed clothes. And then there was nothing else to do. He sat down in front of the television, turned up the sound and waited.

46.

The call took four hours to come and Cooper didn't recognize the voice of the man who called. More than likely he would never see or hear from Amador again.

"You wish to meet with Señor Barriga in person?" the man on the other end of the line asked.

"I do."

"Señor Barriga's schedule is busy."

"He'll want to meet with me."

"That remains to be seen."

The call ended and Cooper waited another two hours before another one came. This time the voice was different again.

"Señor Barriga accepts your invitation to meet."

"Good. When?"

"Tomorrow evening. At the Presidente Monterrey."

"I know the place."

"He will meet you at Los Continentes at ten."

"I'll be there."

"Do not be late."

Cooper put away his phone and took a deep breath. As much as he wanted to pretend he wasn't worried, he was. Without Barriga it would be that much more difficult to deal with the Texas problem, and if Barriga had said *no* then Cooper would have had to feel his way into Bingham's organization. He did not want to do that. Such a thing exposed him and he was exposed enough already.

Now he had time to kill and only the television for company. In such a situation before he would have called Valencia and asked for someone to visit him, but he didn't have the urge. Even the thought of Olivia didn't move him. When he tried to imagine the woman he thought instead of Lorena.

He ate and he slept again and in the morning he went out for a breakfast to rival anything he'd been served at Ruíz's estate. He took out one of his suits to give it some air, found a book he'd already read once and tried to idle his mind until it was time to leave. By the time the sun went down he was more than ready to go. His stitched wound had begun to itch.

Instead of driving the filthy Escort to the hotel, Cooper called a car service. They provided a black Cadillac and a driver. It was comfortable, though the back seat smelled vaguely of cigarettes. Cooper tipped the man when they got there and made arrangements to be picked up in three hours.

He arrived at the restaurant at two minutes to ten o'clock. Barriga was already there, seated near a long bank of windows that opened onto the cityscape. He had a cocktail. After Cooper sat down he ordered something for himself and a glass of ice water.

"You were almost late," Barriga said. He surveyed the menu through reading glasses. They were delicate, but they made Barriga look older. The gray in his hair seemed to stand out more when he had them on.

"I like to be on time."

"A good habit."

Barriga showed no sign of continuing. Cooper took up his own menu and browsed. From what he was told, the tortilla soup was well worth trying. He would have a steak for dinner, cooked rare.

Eventually Barriga put away his glasses. He set the menu down and rested his hand atop it, as if pressing it to the table. His gaze was sharp. "I don't like what's happening, Cooper."

"I don't know what you mean."

"You know what I mean. The Texas business. I don't like how your name floated to the top. Out of all the names that they could have chosen, they settled on you. And now you come to me — *again* — to deal with the fallout from that situation."

Cooper was ready for this. He took some of his drink, let himself taste it and then swallowed deliberately. The pause was long. "I think we both know this is a problem I can't settle on my own."

"You said you were taking care of it."

"And I am. But it will go faster if I come to you."

"That's the part I don't like."

"You won't be exposed."

"That's the problem: I'm already exposed. My people are exposed. What happened at your house in Juárez? Exposure. There's no other way to look at it. You told me you could handle this, and I believed you."

"I will still handle it," Cooper stressed.

"But with my help."

"Yes."

"It doesn't occur to you that by helping you I reveal my people's complicity in the Bingham delivery?"

"I wouldn't have contacted you if it wasn't a problem."

The waitress came to take their orders. Cooper asked to have his drink freshened. They didn't talk for a while and Cooper watched businessmen in suits chat over expensive dinners their companies would pay for. He was aware of Barriga next to him, his mood unimproved, and after the appetizers came he continued.

"I need to know exactly who's contracting for me," Cooper said.

"What makes you think I can get that information?"

"Can't you?"

"Of course I can."

"Once I know who's on me I can make contact with that person."

"Not through us."

"No, not through your people. I have my own contacts."

"And what will you tell them?" Barriga asked.

"I'll make them believe I wasn't involved in the delivery."

Barriga smiled a little for the first time since they sat down together. "You'll make them believe that," he said.

"Yes."

"How?"

"It doesn't matter how. The point is I'll do it on my own. You just have to point me in the right direction."

Barriga looked at Cooper for a long time. His eyes glittered. The smile faded. "After this there will be no more favors, Cooper," he said. "After this you really will be on your own."

"I understand that."

"I hope you do."

Cooper turned his attention to his soup. It was already growing cool, but it tasted fresh and spicy and he liked it. Barriga ate a large salad with a fried egg on top. They were quiet again.

"There is one more thing," Barriga said after a while.

"What is it?"

"Ruíz."

Cooper swallowed. A tingle started at the small of his back and traveled forward into his stomach. His face was stoic. "What about him?"

"He was hit."

"When?"

"Not too many days ago. It would have been when you had to leave Juárez."

"I didn't have anything to do with it."

"That's good. My people, they wanted me to ask you about it. The delivery was very much like one of yours. Very clean. I told them it couldn't have been you. For one, you knew he was to be left alone. For another, the daughter survived."

"She was hit?"

"No. She was sleeping in the next room and never heard a thing."

"Lucky."

Barriga nodded over his salad, slowly. "Very lucky."

47.

His online bank statement showed a deposit. The amount was the agreed-upon sum. Lorena had paid him.

Cooper was less happy about this than he might have been. It occurred to him that it might have been wiser to find some other point of payment for what was done. Someone with an interest and enough resources could trace a transaction like that one. Cooper was unsure if Barriga's people were that kind.

Of course he'd known they would be upset. Whatever Barriga and Ruíz had discussed, the parley had resulted in a reprieve. He was useful to Barriga's people somehow and now he was dead. They would want to know who did it, the same way Bingham's organization wanted to know who finished him.

The smartest thing to do would be to walk away from it. He had more important things to deal with in the Texas problem. Lorena would be in Palmilla soon. She would expect him. That didn't mean he'd have to come. He could cut her off, change his number, and just disappear. It wasn't as if he hadn't done it before.

He considered calling Valencia and asking for Olivia. Being with Olivia again would clear his mind, perhaps, and he could think more clearly. She would be immediate, seductive, and he wouldn't have Lorena on his mind.

It wasn't immediately apparent to him *why* Lorena stayed with him. She was just a girl, not a woman. He could compare her to Olivia, with her full body and attitude of worldliness, and Lorena came up wanting in every way. But still he desired her, though he couldn't explain it. Nor could he ever explain it, because to explain it would be to reveal that they had been together.

Barriga's people would be watching. He knew it as certainly as he knew he would go to her anyway. Would they wait for an answer to their question? That he couldn't know for certain. Going to her was stupid, and yet he already saw himself with her again.

The money was in his account. They were linked now.

It took several days for Barriga's people to get back to him. The name they provided was Swenson. Cooper made a note of all the relevant information and when he had memorized it he burned the note. Now he knew the point of contact and the next part could happen. He would expose himself still further.

He put in a call to San Antonio on the other side of the border, and left a message with a man named Fernando Cajigas. The message was circumspect. He would wait until they were face to face to tell Cajigas everything he needed to know.

In the meanwhile he prepared himself for time away from Monterrey. He had two suits sent out for cleaning and packed fresh shirts. The wound on his back was healing, but slowly. It was awkward, but he managed to put a gauze pad over the stitches and this seemed to help. The wound still seeped sometimes and once he woke in the night to find himself stuck to the sheets.

His arm still didn't move as freely as it should. This could be a problem, but it was one he couldn't avoid. For the first time since he killed Ruíz he cleaned his pistol. He found flecks of blood on the slide.

He felt nothing one way or the other about Ruíz death. He was glad it was done, but that was a different thing. It was good to have done it for many reasons and he could be happy that he'd performed correctly.

He tried not to think about why he did it. The reason for delivering a package to the client was never important. Cooper felt it was enough to know that someone wanted someone else dead and the rest was less of a pressing matter. He was a facilitator, not a judge. But he could not help but judge Ruíz for what he'd done.

Cooper didn't understand it, but he'd never tried to understand such things before. He'd killed deviants and drug addicts and family men alike. Their personalities meant nothing to him. Their commitments meant nothing to him. The only thing that mattered was when and how the package could be delivered. Everything else would sort itself out.

Ruíz was sorted out now. And everything he'd done could be buried with him. Cooper imagined Ruíz's secrets vanishing under white sand and the crash of an incoming tide.

He would be in Texas soon. He would forget all about Ruíz.

48.

Five calls resolved the problem of his car. The insurance company saw to it that he received a loaner: a black C300 Mercedes. He was told that it could take as long as three months to qualify his claim. Long enough for the police to look for a car that had likely already been parted out, assuming they looked very hard at all. Mexico had greater problems than missing cars.

He left the Escort in its spot by the curb until finally one day it was gone, towed off by the city. It was fine that he would never see it again.

When the time came Cooper packed the car. He had his American passport with him and the weapons he hopefully would not need. And then he turned himself north toward the border and drove.

It had been a long time since he'd lived in the United States. He had settled in Monterrey long enough that it seemed like home to him more than any place he remembered north of the border. Once he'd lived in Texas for a little while, but he was born in the northeast, in Maryland, and grew up outside Washington DC.

His life before was closed to others and he rarely thought of it himself. Someone might have thought to analyze him by examining his childhood but they would find nothing there. Cooper had been an ordinary child. He wasn't the brightest or the fastest and he had no history of violence. Instead he was average in every way.

Cooper's father worked for the US government, for the Department of Energy. His mother was an attorney. Both of them worked long hours and Cooper spent much time in day care. He had friends and he played and it was not unusual. In school it was remarked upon how well he got along with others, but this was the only thing they remarked upon.

He graduated near the middle of his class. College came next. First a community college and then two years at the University of Maryland. His grades were adequate to his needs. Cooper was never on the Dean's List, but that didn't matter to him. Already he was changing, and his desires were different. He didn't seek out success by the same measures and he was happy to be ordinary in most things.

If there was anything about him that someone could point to, it was his clothing. Cooper didn't like cheap clothes and wore the best he could afford. Sometimes he would go without meals to afford the right shirt or the right pair of shoes. It was important to him to wear clothes that were fitted to him. While others wore t-shirts and jeans, he wore slacks and perfectly ironed cotton shirts. He loathed sneakers.

The women noticed him and this he liked. Cooper had no regular girl. In time all of them would come to dislike his quiet and his insularity and they would leave him. He wasn't cold to them, but he saw no reason to let them inside to see what he was thinking, what he was feeling. Those things belonged to him.

For the most part when they were with him they found him to be a gentleman. Cooper kept himself the way he kept his clothing. He wasn't a rude man. When he made love he always saw to the needs of his partner. He was not a selfish man. When it came time to hold each other in the darkness afterward, he did so without complaint.

After college he was unsure of himself for the first time. He considered going to law school like his mother and he worked as a paralegal while he made up his mind. If he hadn't, he would not have met Shattles and things would have been very different.

George Shattles was like Cooper. He kept himself well and he was careful not to be too much to anyone. His job was to watch and learn and take the information he gathered back to his clients. And sometimes he killed because killing was more lucrative than spying.

They met through the law office. Shattles saw that they were alike and they became close. The first package Cooper delivered was on Shattles' behalf. They were more alike then and Cooper learned.

It was Shattles who first told Cooper about Mexico. About the freedom and the women and the good life a man could have there. Shattles spent half the year in Mexico and one time he invited Cooper to come with him and see for himself. They spent a month on the sands at Mazatlán.

They both knew the time would come when Cooper wouldn't need Shattles anymore. They were careful never to speak of it, never to act on the knowledge, but it was coming nonetheless. When Cooper killed Shattles in Mexico City, he cried for the first and last time. Barriga's people were happy.

Cooper thought of Shattles sometimes when he listened to Bach. The Goldberg Variations had been Shattles' favorite and he listened to them often before delivering a package. He said

Bach helped clear the mind and steady the nerves. This was something Cooper came to believe, too.

He drove by night because he preferred the roads in the dark than by the day. It was a long drive from Monterrey to the border crossing at Nuevo Laredo. He listened to Bach and he remembered Shattles and he was not sad anymore for anything that had happened or what he done.

Again he found his mind drifting toward Lorena. At once the memory of fucking her was so vivid that he had to blink to keep himself on the road. He wondered how long it would be before he could fuck her again and if this time it would last longer than it had the first two times.

He drove toward Texas and thought of this. It was better than thinking of Shattles.

49.

Cooper did not like Nuevo Laredo. It reminded him too much of Tijuana in that it was full of tourist junk and lacked an identity of its own. It was a dirty city with broken streets and many bars and strip clubs. The brothels in Nuevo Laredo were sad places full of hollow-eyed women. The entire city reminded Cooper of the tourist district in Ciudad Juárez.

Nuevo Laredo was the kind of place for horny college students and idle shopping for cheap trinkets that were meant to represent Mexico. Straw sombreros and papier-mâché marionettes and plastic gewgaws. The crime here was not as bad as it was in places like Juárez, but it was getting there. The entire police force had been dismissed for corruption. The Army and the Federal Police took over.

Despite the early hour it was crowded at the border crossing. It was always the same: people wanted to get out of Mexico, but few wanted to get in. There were twice as many lanes headed into the United States than there were coming out. Only one booth was open now and traffic was backed up.

Cooper listened to his music and was in no hurry.

Eventually he was at the front of the line. He put down the window and presented his passport to the woman in the booth. She looked at his face and photo and then at the car.

"How long have you been in Mexico?" she asked him.

"Not long. A couple of months."

"You're a resident there?"

"That's right."

"Are you carrying any fruits, vegetables or any other items that you need to declare?"

"No."

A man in a Border Patrol uniform walked around the car with a mirror on a stick, reflecting under the edges of the vehicle. Cooper knew this was a waste of time; any smuggler worth the name wouldn't be so obvious.

"May we inspect the interior of your vehicle?"

"You may."

He stayed where he was while the same man looked in the trunk and under the seats. They asked him to pop the hood and they checked there, too. Finally they were done.

"Thank you for your time, sir," the woman in the booth said.

"Have a nice day," Cooper said.

The route to San Antonio was a straight one: 155 miles up I-35 almost directly north. Cooper stopped at a roadside diner to have a breakfast of waffles, sausage and eggs and plenty of coffee to keep him awake the rest of the way.

He was a little more than an hour away from the border when he saw a police car in his rear-view mirror. The cop came up behind him and flashed his lights and then turned on the bubble lights for him to pull over. Cooper obeyed.

The policeman was a tall man, but going to fat. He wore mirrored sunglasses.

Cooper put down the window. "Is there a problem, officer?" he asked.

"No problem," the policeman said. "Can I see your license? Do you have registration papers?"

"It's a rental, but I'll see."

The cars papers were in the glove box. Cooper turned them over, along with his driver's license. The policeman looked these over for a long time. "You're an American," he said at last.

"That's right."

"What are you doing with a Mexican driver's license?"

"I need it to drive in Mexico."

"Living down there, are you?"

"Yes."

"Listen, the reason I pulled you over is to search your vehicle."

"For what?"

"This route is popular with *coyotes*. It's nothing personal. Just a random stop. Could you open the trunk?"

Cooper did as he was asked. The policeman went around back to see no one was hiding there. When he came back, the policeman turned over Cooper's license and the car's registration papers.

"Nice car," the cop said.

"Thanks."

"I appreciate your time. Drive safely."

Cooper put the window back up again. He waited until the policeman had pulled out and around him and was on his way before he turned over the engine and pulled out himself.

They were foolish, stops like those, but Cooper understood why they were done. It was to give the impression that something constructive was happening along the border and on the way north. People in America wanted drugs intercepted and illegals apprehended and it didn't much matter to them how it was done. All they cared about was that policemen were making stops and asking questions and maybe once in a while someone was caught.

Cooper drove until he had to stop for fuel at a gas station off the highway. He bought another cup of coffee and finished it before he got back behind the wheel. The caffeine was deep in his system now, making his fingers tingle. When he got to San Antonio he would get a room and catch up on his sleep.

Eventually he came close enough to the city that he could see the tall buildings of downtown and the spire of the Tower of the Americas. Traffic was thick inside the outer loop because of an accident on the freeway. Cooper turned on a talk radio station and listened to a crazy man talk about the government for forty-five minutes. This was something he did not miss.

Finally he made it onto Dolorosa Street and cut through to the heart of the city. He passed the red granite courthouse and a quiet square of trees and stone outside the Main Plaza Building. The route took him across the San Antonio River once and then back again as he navigated to the Rivercenter, along the Riverwalk. He parked in the garage for the Marriott there and got out to stretch his legs.

He had time before his meeting with Cajigas. Time enough to check into the hotel and bring his bags up to the room himself. He had a bottle of water out of the minibar and then stretched out on the bed to rest his eyes. Cooper slept exactly fifty-five minutes and woke up feeling refreshed.

There was still time enough for him to shower and change his clothes, so he did. Then he went downstairs to the lobby and had one of the doormen grab a taxi for him. "Mi Tierra," he told the driver. He didn't have to add that it was on Produce Street.

The cab took him around to the restaurant and left him in the parking lot. Cooper tipped extra for the smooth ride.

Mi Tierra Cafe Y Panadería was a fixture in San Antonio: a twenty-four hour restaurant with good, cheap food and live music provided by roving groups of mariachis. It was popular with locals and some tourists who knew where to go. The bar was large.

Cajigas wasn't there yet. In the big foyer of the restaurant there were glass cases full of pastries and cookies and other Mexican treats. Cooper retreated to the bar for a drink even though it was early. The lights were turned comfortably low and for a while Cooper could relax.

He spotted Fernando Cajigas before the man saw him. Cajigas was small, but he dressed well and had a pleasant demeanor about him. Cooper took his second drink from the bar and met him in the lobby. They shook hands. It had been five years since they last met face-to-face.

"Let's get a table," Cooper said.

The restaurant meandered through the shells of two buildings. The hostess seated them away from other tables when Cooper asked her to. A waiter brought water, coffee and menus.

Cooper perused the menu and settled on the Chilaquiles Famosos. He was hungry this morning despite the breakfast of waffles he'd eaten on the near side of the border. The drink from the bar was empty and he helped himself to coffee from the pot.

"I did what you asked," Cajigas said.

"You were able to find him?"

"I did. It wasn't easy."

"You'll get paid."

"That's not the problem," Cajigas said. "I don't like putting myself out there so much, you know? This Swenson, he trades on a higher level. I had to make a lot of connections. They know me now."

Cooper added sugar and milk to his coffee. "They know you're not in with me. You're just the go-between. You don't have anything to worry about."

"If everything goes right."

"Everything will go right."

"That's what you say."

"That's what will happen," Cooper said.

The two men didn't talk for a while. The waiter came to take their orders. Cooper drank his coffee and watched the dining room. The morning rush was over and it was just a relative handful of people like himself, taking a late breakfast because he could. No one looked his way. There were no mariachis in the morning.

"I wish you hadn't called me," Cajigas said at last.

Cooper frowned. "Why are you so nervous? You never used to be."

"I don't know. I don't know why. It's the people. I don't like them."

"You don't have to."

The food came quickly. His breakfast was corn tortilla strips scrambled with eggs, topped with cheese and ranchero sauce and served alongside refried beans. It came with flour tortillas to sop the plate and a separate dish with pork tips in sauce. Cajigas had *huevos a la Mexicana*. They ate in silence.

"How is your wife?" Cooper asked after a long time. He didn't really care.

"We're divorced now. Two years. She has the children."

"That's too bad."

"Did you ever marry?"

"No," Cooper said. He was tired of this already. "When will I meet with Swenson?"

"Tomorrow night. At the Chart House."

"How many men will he bring?"

"I couldn't arrange a meeting alone. He'll bring someone."

"All right."

Cooper didn't know the place. If it were a restaurant like this one, the men who came with Swenson would be careful not to be seen. No one would hover over their table or linger by the exits. There would be two or three, but they would be at tables of their own, close enough to see, but not close enough to hear.

"Does he know why I want to meet?"

"He knows as much as you told me to say."

That was good enough. Cooper finished his meal. He had yet another cup of coffee. When he poured it his hands trembled a little. He would have to stop soon. Maybe he should stop now.

"You'll be paid when the meet is over," Cooper said. "Not before."

"I understand."

"Do they want you there?"

"No."

"Then we'll make arrangements to meet afterward. It can be here if you want."

"That's fine with me."

Cooper nodded. The waiter cruised past, watching their plates to see if they'd finished, and Cooper signaled for the check. Across the table Cajigas still seemed unsettled, but there was nothing Cooper could say that would make that go away. Now he just wanted Cajigas to be gone from him.

"I'll pay," Cooper said.

Cajigas got up from the table. "I'll be waiting for your call."

The man left and Cooper was alone. He looked at his coffee and decided not to drink it. When the check came he paid in cash for both meals and left a good tip. Out in the lobby he stopped to buy a *dulce de naranja*, a half an orange crystalized and chewy. He went out the back door of the restaurant and walked the quiet farmer's market where only a few stalls were open.

He thought of going to the restaurant tonight and seeing what there was to see, but he knew there was a limit to how much planning he could do ahead of the meeting. He decided instead to spend the day like a tourist and then rest himself overnight. This was something Shattles had taught him.

Cooper ate the candied orange outside a little stall selling religious icons carved out of soft wood. He pretended to browse while his mind was elsewhere and when he was done he went looking for a taxi to take him back to his hotel.

50.

Cooper walked the Riverwalk and looked into the little art galleries and boutique shops, but he didn't buy anything. Dinner was eaten by the water at a place called the Original Mexican Restaurant, which used to be called the Kangaroo Court the last time he'd been in San Antonio. The food was good, but unspectacular. He had a slice of cheesecake for dessert.

Back in the hotel room he turned on the news. It was different watching it in English, but it had the same tranquilizing effect; he fell asleep with it on and woke in the middle of the night lit by the bright colors of an infographic.

Downstairs in the lobby it was coffin-like. Cooper went out onto the street.

In Juárez he could not have walked the streets at night. Everywhere in the stillness there would come the crackling of gunfire. In the morning there would be bodies missing heads or arms or just the deep marks of mutilating blades. People were dying by the hundreds in Ciudad Juárez, but here it was quiet.

He wondered what would happen if the violence on the Mexican side of the border spilled over to peaceful places like this. When it wasn't safe for children to go to school or even to have a loud party for fear someone would silence it with automatic gunfire. Cooper thought it would be a national emergency. The military would be called out. Whole cities would be locked down day and night. There would be no measure too strict to employ.

But instead the killing stayed safely where it belonged. The cartels didn't export their violence the way they exported their drugs. Americans only paid for the wars, they didn't fight in them.

Walking now, passing from one puddle of light to the next beneath ornate street lamps, Cooper was reminded a little of Monterrey. The drug war was there, too, but not in the way of the border cities and towns. Cooper could go out in the night for food or drinks or to a nightclub if he wanted and not fear for his life. He felt safe there.

Safe. Cooper wondered where Lorena was at that moment. If she was still in the hacienda her father owned or if she had gone southwest to the peninsula where it was quiet. He wondered also what would happen when the cartel's war spread that far. The big tourist hotels would be empty because the Americans would stay away. There would be no fancy drinks served, nor barbecues on the beach.

Cooper stopped in front of a store that sold rare coins. The windows were made of heavy glass and still there was a metal mesh between him and the display. He looked at them idly and remembered that his father had an interest in coins, but never did much with it. His parents were somewhere now he didn't know. After Shattles he'd had no use for them anymore.

It occurred to Cooper that he had no real use for anyone anymore, and he couldn't remember when that had happened. Once he had assumed that one day he would find the woman who would look past his quiet and his privacy and would stay with him. That became more unlikely every year. He was happy instead to call Valencia and arrange for women like Olivia to see him. They didn't care that he didn't want to talk about himself or his work or anything important at all. They were like him.

Lorena was like him, too. She saw problems and then a way to a solution. Sometimes that meant that someone had to die, and she showed no compunction there, either. Her father was dead because she made the decision that he would be hit. Cooper hadn't made that decision for her; he'd simply carried out her will.

There was a bond that came from killing. Cooper and Shattles had it for a while. Cooper imagined that perhaps he and Lorena had it, too. He imagined that it was her finger on the trigger and not his. He imagined that they made love soaked in the blood of Sandalio Ruíz.

The imagining gave Cooper pause. He had thought of them together as making love and not fucking. Fucking he could understand because it was what he did with the women Valencia sent to him. It's what he'd done through high school and in the years when he worked with Shattles. Fucking was simple and when it was done it was done. But what did *making love* mean?

Traffic signals turned on empty intersections. On a stone bridge Cooper looked down on the river and saw it was black and oily. A man could fall into water like that and never come up again.

He had no way to contact her. They could be together eventually but not now. He could not go to her with Barriga's people watching him. And they were watching him somehow. They would know if he went to Palmilla too soon. They would know and they would come to understand quickly what this meant. Perhaps there might not be any time at all when it was safe to be with her again. That thought made him feel suddenly and inexplicably sad.

    Cooper wanted a cigarette to clear his mind. He walked back to the hotel and went up to his room. He sat in front of the news watching the ticker at the bottom of the screen scroll by in little info-bits that meant nothing to him anymore because he wasn't a part of this world, this American world. He was south of the border. He was with Lorena. He was a million miles away.

51.

The Tower of the Americas was 750 feet tall and had stood sentinel over downtown San Antonio since 1968. It was a poured concrete shaft topped by a big, round structure with windows on all sides. A glassed elevator traversed the distance from the ground to the peak. It cost money to ride the elevator.

Cooper ignored the gift shops and the café and went straight to the ticket booth selling rides to the top. He paid his money and stood in line with a handful of other people waiting for admission. When they went up he stood close to the glass and watched the ground fall away. The person next to him took a snapshot with a little digital camera.

The Chart House restaurant rotated to provide a full view of the city below. The hostess told Cooper to mind his step as they passed from the stationary center to the moving wheel of the restaurant itself. She gave him a table and cleared the extra places. She left two settings. Cooper carried a leather bag with him and put it on the seat beside his.

Cooper didn't ask how Swenson knew to find him. He did not like thinking about the implication. He saw the man enter the restaurant ring with a second man following close behind. The second man didn't stay after Swenson sat down. He gave Cooper one look and then retreated to the tower center.

Swenson was a surprisingly large man, heavy through the shoulders and carrying a little bit of a gut. His suit was well tailored and he had a fresh haircut. On his right hand he wore a class ring with a big gemstone set in the center. He'd gone to Texas State University. Swenson looked like the kind of man who played football.

They stared at each other for a while. Cooper had a drink of his water.

"I'm here," Swenson said.

"Thank you," Cooper said.

"We missed you in Juárez," the man said.

Finally Cooper had his answer. He did not know whether to feel good about it.

"I could have you hit before you leave here," Swenson added when Cooper said nothing. "Tell me why I shouldn't do that, Mr. Randolph."

So they didn't know his real last name. It was a little, but it was a comfort. "You represent people in Dallas?" Cooper asked.

"Yes. You know I do. We wouldn't be sitting here talking if I didn't."

"So what we discuss here is carried out at other levels."

"Maybe."

The waitress brought Cooper a drink from the bar. Swenson ordered a Tom Collins. When she had left them alone again, Cooper said, "I'm not taking responsibility for anything that was done to your man, Bingham."

"Of course you're not."

"I have questions."

"I'm not sure I'm in the mood to answer them, Mr. Randolph."

Cooper sipped his drink. He looked past Swenson to the other tables in sight and saw no one there who might be watching. A woman talked animatedly to a man who was probably her husband. Another couple sat quietly watching the city rotate beneath them. Cooper could see through tinted glass out onto the observation deck and tourists moving around.

"I want to know who gave you my name."

"Why would I want to tell you that?"

"Because it would make both of our lives easier."

"How so?"

"I could know who put me into the mix. You could know they're not to be trusted."

"I trust our source. Our source is reliable."

"How do you know?"

"I know."

The Tom Collins arrived. Swenson didn't touch it.

"As far as I'm concerned, Mr. Randolph, our source is absolutely correct. You did the job on Bingham. Interests opposed to ours paid you. You're here now to try and undo the knot you're tied up in."

Cooper nodded. "I'm here to cover myself, that's true. But only because your people are coming after me for something I didn't do."

"Prove it."

"You know I can't do that."

Swenson took up the Tom Collins and had a deep drink from it. He had anger lines on his face, not smile lines. His complexion pinked. "So we're back to the beginning, then," he said. "And I'm not in the mood to make deals."

"It's a good deal," Cooper said.

"What is it?"

Cooper put his hand on the leather case. "A payoff. I'll put my fee up against your claim on me. I can pay it in cash, right now. We walk away from the table getting what we want."

Swenson scowled and his lines deepened. "You think Rory Bingham was worth whatever you were paid?"

"I told you before: I wasn't paid to do the delivery on Bingham. This is my standard fee. If I had done it, this is what I would have gotten for the job. It's what I can offer. It's fair."

"Fair to whom?"

Cooper couldn't answer that question.

The waitress came back and they both ordered salads. With the waitress Swenson was charming. He smiled for her and spoke lightly. When he talked to Cooper his voice pitched lower and there was no shine in his eyes. "Let's say I take this offer to my people," Swenson said. "Let's say it's considered seriously.

Swenson sat back. He exhaled through his nose and watched Cooper.

"Do we have a deal?"

"I'll bring it to my people."

"You know how to contact me."

"We will."

With that Swenson dropped his napkin on his empty plate and pushed back from the table. When he stood up he seemed massive. He took one last look at Cooper and walked away.

52.

The next day Cooper went to the Alamo. He had never been before. When he had been new to the city he was surprised to learn that the building was right in the middle of everything, not set somewhere out in the country. It was possible to walk from his hotel to the front doors of the Alamo inside ten minutes.

He took the tour, which lasted half an hour. Cooper wasn't sure what he wanted from the Alamo, but he was disappointed in some small way by what he saw. The interior of the main structure wasn't that impressive, milling with schoolchildren and tourists. Out on the grounds there was just a low wall dividing them from the rest of the city, and live oak trees growing where they shouldn't, tearing up stonework. One day they would threaten the Alamo itself.

When he finished the tour he wandered along the buildings opposite for a while. There was a 3D show telling the story of the Alamo siege and an arcade. Lots of places to eat. Everywhere there were souvenirs to be bought, most with the image of the Alamo printed on them.

There was nothing else to do but wait. Swenson's people would make their decision in due time. Maybe it would come sooner, maybe later. And there was always the possibility that they would simply try to kill him before they made any decision at all.

Even when he was moving without any plan or course, he watched his tail. Sometimes he would double back on his path unexpectedly, hoping to surprise some follower and catch them flat-footed, but it never happened. Eventually he began to think that Cajigas had done right in brokering this little truce; they really weren't after him anymore.

His path took him into HemisFair Park. It was quiet and wooded here and there and not too many people joined him for the walk. He found a spot where water cascaded down from stainless steel frames that might have been some kind of artwork or just an excuse for children to get wet.

Cooper reached the Institute of Texan Cultures. It was a long, wide building shaped like the body of a boat. Down below the bridge to the entrance water flowed past granite blocks placed to look like outcroppings in a geometric river. He could have gone into the place but he wasn't interested in museums. He went back the way he came. Still no one was following him.

When he had lunch he considered again the difference between Mexican food and Tex-Mex. The latter was spicier, meatier and in a way more stripped down than the food gotten south of the border. Cooper liked it this way, but he also found himself missing the tastes and smells that had become familiar to him.

Of course it had been Shattles that turned him toward Mexico. Those times in Mazatlán and elsewhere. Shattles did not work in Mexico, but used it as his vacation spot. From the beginning Cooper was not so picky, especially since those who could afford to pay in Mexico were almost always wealthier than those Stateside. There was something about the Mexican rich that reminded Cooper of old-time nobility. They lived in baronial splendor like Sandalio Ruíz, spent money freely and when they were wronged they had no compunction about correcting the situation with murder.

Early on Cooper had come to terms with killing. He saw it as a task to be performed and nothing more. Maybe once he might have concerned himself briefly with the morality of what he was doing, but even that did not occupy him for very long. He was more engaged with the business of the hit than with the inevitable consequence.

After he'd eaten, Cooper went back to his hotel room to take a nap. He dozed for two hours, dimly aware of the television chattering away at low volume and making dream-pictures of men and women walking along a meandering path that might have been the Riverwalk, but was bizarrely in Juárez. He was looking for Lorena because she had arranged to meet him, but he couldn't remember where.

He awoke with a headache, got two pills from the minibar and washed them down with whiskey. It was too early for dinner and he'd had his fill of wandering for the day. Instead he went to the shops off the hotel lobby and bought shorts and a t-shirt with SAN ANTONIO emblazoned on both. Then he went to the gym.

The treadmill was something he could do without thinking and he set it to a slow jog. After a little while he was sweating and that was good. He kept on until he felt winded and his knees were starting to hurt, turned it down to a walk and let himself cool off.

A woman was in the gym with him, lifting weights on the all-in-one machine. She was pretty enough and Cooper considered striking up a conversation with her, but he didn't. He hadn't had much interest in sex since the night in Ruíz's ranch house, or at least not with other women. Getting back to Lorena was the thing he wanted most.

The hotel had a swimming pool adjoining the gym, but Cooper hadn't bought a bathing suit. Instead of dipping in he sat on one of the lounges and let the sun play over him. It was bright and they were at the top of the building so there was nothing but sky to see, and the spire of the Tower of the Americas. The elevator crawled up and down the structure steadily.

He wanted Cajigas to call, but willing it wouldn't make it happen. Again he wondered what Swenson would tell his people and what they were considering.

They would lose nothing by killing him. Even if he wasn't the one, he was one less operator working on the behalf of Barriga's organization. They would have to know by now that he'd done much work for Barriga. The same source that floated his name in connection with Bingham would know this, too.

Though the metrics worked against him, Cooper hoped the money would talk. Of course they wouldn't need the cash; they had enough money to hire the two men who came to kill him and could doubtless hire plenty more where the others had come from. The money was a gesture.

Money was the reason Cooper killed. Not the earning of it, but the cause. He'd long since gone away from the world where wives had their husbands killed for infidelities real or imagined, or husbands killed wives out passion they could not realize themselves. The packages Barriga wanted delivered were business-related. No one thought of them in emotional terms.

So it was money that would buy Cooper's way out of the crosshairs. They would take the money, he was sure, because it was a solid gesture. He wasn't claiming innocence, but he promised not to turn a profit. This was something they could understand. It was strictly a matter of accounting.

The woman from the gym changed from her sweats into a bikini and took a dip into the pool. The water was bright and filled with reflected light. Cooper watched her idly; saw how she tried to swim without getting her hair wet. He didn't understand that.

He decided he didn't like this hotel. It was too much like other hotels. It lacked the character of a place like the Hotel Lucerna in Ciudad Juárez. There was not the luxury of its rooms or the services. He felt like he was in a great block of rooms sealed together with cement and without much thought paid to who would be staying there or why. It felt like an airport hotel, and this made him think of Bingham.

Cooper didn't know who Bingham was to Swenson. Maybe he was just a name without a face. Cooper hadn't asked anything about Bingham's organization, he didn't know Bingham's people. He didn't even know what Bingham did. He was just another client for whom incuriosity was the norm.

They could kill Cooper here and no one would know. All those faceless doors huddled up against one another were sealed against penetration by anything. The cubicles of the rooms were tiny and airless. Cooper could end up on his face with his wallet taken and his pockets emptied and the police would think him just another tourist gotten unlucky. A year wouldn't go by before they forgot his name, and the room would have been rented out a hundred times.

He got up from the lounge and stretched his back. He was finished here.

53.

Cajigas got back in touch via text message. He set out a place and a time.

They met at a restaurant called Biga on the Banks at a table far back from the front. Cajigas ordered a half-bottle of wine for the table. He was sweaty. The temperature outside was over one hundred.

"They want another meeting," Cajigas said at last. "Tomorrow."

"Where?"

"The Mission San José."

"Why there?"

"Because it's quiet," Cajigas said, and both men understood.

Their wine came and the server poured a glass for each of them. Cooper was not a frequent wine drinker, but it was good enough for him. He drained his glass and checked his hands; they were steady.

"I tried," Cajigas told Cooper. "Everything I had to do, I did."

"I'm not blaming you," Cooper said.

"How much time do you think you have?"

"They could be looking for me now. Maybe they'll wait, but probably not."

"I didn't give you up."

"I know."

The restaurant was cool, but Cajigas was still sweating. Cooper looked toward the entrance of the restaurant. He saw a couple reading the menu outside. A copy lay on the table in front of him, though he hadn't touched it.

"What will you do?"

"I'll go back to Mexico," Cooper said simply. "What else is there to do?"

"They'll just follow you."

"They'll follow me wherever I go. In Mexico I have options."

Cajigas took up his menu. His hands trembled visibly. "We should eat," he said. "The food is good here. One last meal before you go."

Cooper looked back to the entrance. The couple was gone. A man in a suit jacket and tie stood there now, looking through the glass. When he saw Cooper watching him, he came through the door.

Cooper had his weapon out fast and was firing before Cajigas had a chance to drop his menu. His first shots were high and one hit a light fixture that exploded into a blossom of expanding sparks.

Sparks showered over him and the man pulled his gun. He fired back blindly. Cooper heard the bullets strike the curving wall to his right. Diners were screaming.

Cajigas scrambled to the floor beneath the table. Cooper was out of his seat now and moving backward. He shot the man in the arm and the chest as he retreated toward the rear of the restaurant. At the door to the kitchen he passed through with his eye still on the dining room and then he let the door swing shut in front of him.

The kitchen was large and had two aisles lined with rubber matting. A handful of Latino men in whites were working. They froze at the sight of Cooper and did nothing as he pushed past them.

He found the freezer door and then the back exit. A plastic bucket was wedged in the door to let out the heat. It was hotter in the kitchen than it was outside.

The back door opened onto a narrow notch that fed into a slanting alley that climbed up to street level. A stinking dumpster painted blue squatted at the end of the alley.

Cooper put away his gun and ran up the incline. He emerged on a corner he didn't recognize and whirled around to find some landmark to guide him. The Tower of the Americas jutted up over a building. He oriented himself by that, dashed across an intersection against the light and hurried along the sidewalk.

He didn't see anyone following him, but that didn't mean they weren't there. Cooper had no time to play tricks on a tail, and knew that doubling back or looping around would just make him more confused. Under the lip of a building he was out of the sun but he was perspiring heavily. The pits of his shirt were soaked.

Finding the hotel took the better part of twenty minutes. He cut through the Rivercenter Mall to get there, grabbed a back elevator and reached his floor. Now he slowed and stopped by a nook where the ice machine waited, humming.

His pistol was in his hand. Cooper wished for the suppressor, but it was packed away in his things. He edged up to the corner and leaned forward until one eye had a view of the long hallway. There was no one there.

Keeping his gun by his side, he advanced slowly up the hall. He walked deliberately so his footfalls made no sound on the carpet. When he reached his room he palmed the plastic key from his pocket and pressed himself against the wall by the door.

Cooper listened. Sunlight shone under the door and no shadow broke the light. Without peeling himself from the wall, Cooper fed the key into the lock. The sound of the latch was loud. He eased the door open.

The room was empty. Cooper checked the bathroom and the closet to be sure.

He gathered up his things: his garment bag and suitcase with the over-the-shoulder strap and also the leather case with the money inside. The gun he put away for now.

Quietly he opened the door again and sneaked glimpses left and right. He saw no one. Out in the hallway he hurried along to the main elevators, the ones that opened near the garage entrance. It seemed a long time before the car arrived.

Cooper was alone in the elevator. His reflection was in the brass fittings and he did not like the way he looked: flushed and damp with an expression that bespoke panic and not calm. He forced himself to breathe more evenly, willed his heartbeat to slow. The numbers on the floor indicator crawled down to one.

He was exposed in the lobby, but he had no time to scan the bodies moving there. He turned left and headed for the garage. He was another elevator ride away from his car.

The garage smelled of heat and oil. Somewhere a tire squeaked. Across a broad space where two more elevators emblazoned with huge, painted number ones. He pressed the call button a dozen times and noticed he was trembling. His breath was coming too fast again. This time he wasn't able to slow it down.

Cooper looked over his shoulder at the door to the hotel. No one else had come through. The elevator came and he rushed through the doors before they were completely open. He pressed three and jammed his finger on the door-close button.

This elevator was slow. "Come on," Cooper whispered out loud. "Come on, come on."

The doors opened in the clear. Cooper saw no one waiting, but he had no time to be thorough. He ran to the Mercedes, popped the locks and tossed his bags in the back seat. Behind the wheel he cranked the key and the engine came to life. He slammed the car into reverse.

The second car backed out of a space perpendicular to Cooper's. Fenders compacted against each other and the Mercedes stopped rolling. Cooper looked back through the rear window and saw men in motion before the glass imploded. He didn't hear the gunshots.

Cooper threw himself across the front seats and scrabbled at his gun. He got the passenger door open and crawled fast, dumping out into the space between cars. When he came up he was already shooting.

A man in sunglasses snapped around as the bullets struck him and then he went down to the concrete. Cooper cut left and ran, trailing rounds that spanged off the bodies of parked cars and spiderwebbed glass.

He dove behind the shelter of an SUV and uncovered himself once to fire back. Three men scattered when the shots rang out. Cooper missed all of them. The slide on his pistol locked open on an empty chamber. Cooper dropped the magazine and loaded a spare from a belt pouch. He had only the one extra magazine.

Pistols spat quiet bullets. They made a thumping noise when they sunk into the body of the SUV. The ramp to the next level down was across twenty feet of open ground. Cooper tensed himself.

He fired twice to put down their heads and sprinted for the ramp. They were up and firing and one slug tugged at Cooper's jacket as he ran. Now he was on the ramp, running at top speed, gaining momentum. The men were behind him now, but he didn't know if they were running or aiming at his back. No bullet struck him.

Cooper couldn't turn and he careened into the trunk of a parked car. He spared one look back to see two men dashing down after him. He squeezed off one round and ran again.

On the second ramp he nearly ran headlong into a car headed up. The driver saw his gun and stomped the brakes. Cooper kept going. He reached the parking attendants booth. He kept going. He was out on the street now. Someone shouted after him. He kept going. The men had to be just behind him, but there was no time to look. He kept going. At a corner he turned and kept going. He kept going until he was safe enough to put his pistol away. He kept going until the men were gone and he didn't know where he was.

He was still alive.

54.

He had only the things he carried with him in his pockets or under his clothes. What little cash he had was folded into his wallet and then there was the gun with a few bullets left and his knife.

Renting a car was not an option; he had only the credit cards issued in his name and no time to go fishing for a stolen one. They were looking for him, and so far they hadn't found out what he was called. They still knew him as "Mr. Randolph" and hopefully whatever source they had would not see fit to correct them.

In the end he bought a bus ticket to El Paso and waited four hours in the bus station for the motor coach to arrive and take passengers. He hadn't been on a bus in a long time and had forgotten the cramped, uncomfortable seats and the stale smell that was only partly masked by commercial cleaners.

Cooper took a seat near the back of the bus and didn't sit too close to the window. When they were in motion he could let his guard down a little bit, but he didn't like the idea of being spotted when the bus was still. He watched each of the passengers board with a close eye.

When there was no one else to get on he allowed himself to relax, but only a bit. When the bus driver took his place and they were underway, Cooper felt tension bleed from him such that he felt deflated, as though the pressure of fear was the only thing keeping him upright.

He watched the city go away and eventually they were in the rough country west of San Antonio. Cooper realized he'd been gripping the armrest so tightly that his fingers hurt and he relaxed his hand.

There were nine people on the bus besides him. They looked ordinary and showed no interest in him or one another. A woman pulled out a pair of knitting needles and something she was pulling together. A man read a paperback book. The sound of the engine was the only sound to be heard.

Cooper's plan was to reach El Paso and cross into Mexico from there. This would put him back in Juárez, but this time no one would know he was in the city. With access to his bank he could get more money, arrange for a new car and then he could go… somewhere. He hadn't thought it all through and trying to made his head hurt.

Monterrey would be the logical place to go. As far as he knew, they didn't know him there or have any idea where might live, but then he thought of the car.

The Mercedes he got from the insurance company was a loaner, a rental car paid for while his replacement car was arranged for. If they were smart, they would trace the VIN from that car back to the rental company it came from. That company would have his real name and also his address.

For the longest time Monterrey had been his safe haven. Now he could be heading directly into their hands by going there. Cooper pounded his fist on the thick glass next to his seat. He ground his teeth. This was not the way things were meant to go.

He could hope they weren't smart enough to take that step. But he knew he could hope all he wanted, but he must behave as if they had every advantage over him. If he believed they were left behind, they would be one step ahead. This was the way things worked.

If he didn't go to Monterrey then he had nowhere to go. The house in Juárez was burned out and he could not use the Randolph name there anymore. He could not take refuge among friends because he had no friends in that city. He had no friends even in his own city; he was cut off from the world outside because he had no need for it. Or at least he had no need before now.

So he would go to Monterrey. He would take every precaution and he wouldn't stay. He would make arrangements for things to be looked after while he was gone and then he would leave for a long time, maybe as long as a year. He wondered if he would even be able to stay in Mexico, or if that was closed to him, as well. He could head south, go to Costa Rica where it was beautiful and cheap and out of the way. Maybe he could start all over there and never come back to Mexico except to work.

There was also the possibility that he might not be able to work. A man burned could be an asset no one would touch. He had already tested the line of tolerance by contacting Barriga not once but twice and asking for help. He had no other buyers lined up, had become used to working for Barriga's people, and now he was damaged.

Going over the money in his head, Cooper figured he would be all right for a while. If he lived frugally he might be able to live ten years in a place like Costa Rica without having to work. But ten years was nothing. He would be almost fifty years old with no skills to trade except the ones he already possessed. No one would want him anymore except for Swenson's people.

And they would not stop looking for him. This much Cooper knew for certain. Something had been set in motion that could not be easily stopped. It was not even clear if killing the right person would make a positive difference. Perhaps he should kill Swenson. Most likely it would make things worse than they already were.

A part of him considered what it might be like to head across the Atlantic and set up somewhere like Spain. He had never been there but he was told that it was a country with many of the same attitudes as Mexico. There were no *maquiladoras* in Spain, no *colonias*. Cooper wondered if he could make a place for himself there. He spoke Spanish with a Mexican accent, knew Mexican customs and lived as a Mexican of means. How different would that make him?

Across the aisle from him, one of the passengers had fallen asleep. The man's head was rolled over sharply at an angle and he snored as if someone was strangling him. Cooper tried to ignore this.

For the first time he thought of Lorena.

She would be away from Ciudad Juárez now, that much he was certain of. She would be in Palmilla and she would be waiting for him. He wanted this to mean nothing to him but it did regardless. Before he killed Ruíz he might have been able to walk away from her, but they were bound up by what they had planned and what they had done.

They would not be watching her. Cooper comforted himself thinking of that. They were concerned with Bingham, not with other deliveries Cooper might have made. The only people who might have an eye on her were Barriga's people, but why would they? Of course they wanted to know who had killed Ruíz but she would not be a suspect. If they knew about what Ruíz had done to Lorena maybe things would be different but they didn't know.

Cooper understood with certainty that he would go to Lorena before this was done. Even if it were just to say good-bye, he would go. They would not have much time together; Swenson's people could never know of her. He wished there was some other way.

His mind was roving over Europe now, though he knew it was just a dream. Maybe he could take Lorena with him. She was not tied to her father anymore and a daughter couldn't stay with her mother forever. But it was just a dream. Some time ago he'd made a choice to make Central America his place. He could not lift himself out of that place and simply become someone new. He was embraced by Mexico, entrapped by Mexico. And they were chasing him home.

55.

The bus reached El Paso in the evening. The station here was like the stations of most cities, dumped into a dirty section of town that serviced trains and commercial business. Cooper used a public telephone to call for a taxi and when the driver arrived he paid the international fare to be taken across the Bridge of the Americas.

Though he didn't ask the driver to take him there, he was taken to the Avenida Juárez among the tourist businesses, bars and strip clubs. Cooper didn't object. He got off on a corner near a little restaurant serving "American food" and styled like a '50s diner. It was the middle of the week and the place was empty.

Only a few dedicated partiers walked the street. Cooper dodged talkers trying to drive business into their clubs and stopped at a *farmacia* serviced by an inter-city bus that shuttled senior citizens across the border from El Paso to Mexico, where the same drugs were available for far less.

Cooper bought a bottle of ibuprofen and took six of them with water from a drinking fountain in the back of the store. His shoulder was hurting and he'd begun to wonder if maybe he'd pulled a stitch fleeing the gunmen in San Antonio.

There were plenty of hotels catering to clients by the hour or the day. Cooper took a little of his remaining money and rented a room for the night. He hadn't allowed himself to sleep yet and when he lay down on the little twin bed he fell asleep almost immediately. He dreamed dark dreams that he couldn't remember when he stirred awake.

When his time ran out, Cooper paid for another day. He took a long shower in the dirty stall in the bathroom and afterward he checked his stitches by feel. They all seemed to be there, but the flesh was puffy and swollen and twinged when he touched it. All his prescriptions were lost with his bags, so he had no antibiotics anymore.

He spent the time mostly sleeping, venturing out once to get something to eat after the sun went down. Eventually he would have to move on to Monterrey but he was slow to leave this place because at least here he was anonymous.

Another taxi and another bus, this time headed for Monterrey. This bus was not as clean or spacious as the one he'd taken to El Paso, but like the one before it was a shield against the people looking for him. The bus was fuller than the El Paso bus, as well; Cooper had to share the seat next to him with another passenger, a woman. He let her have the seat by the window.

The bus made many stops along the way with passengers disembarking and more coming aboard. Every time they stopped Cooper thought of the Mercedes loaner he'd left behind in San Antonio and how it was a fingerprint that tied back to his entire life. He was angry with himself, but at the same time he knew he was being foolish; there were too many, and he was not a fighter.

His seat was hard and uncomfortable, but he didn't take the chance to get off the bus when it made long stops along the way. There was something about being under the open sun that he was not ready to take, so he remained aboard. Only when they stopped in the evening did he venture out to buy a snack from vendors at the bus station. At no time did he sleep.

They reached Monterrey at night. Cooper felt dirty and his clothes were terribly wrinkled. Somewhere along the line he'd picked up a big black smudge on the elbow of his jacket. Still, the cab driver did not look at him strangely when Cooper gave an address two blocks away from his apartment.

After the cab dropped him off, Cooper walked until he could approach his building from the rear. He was very aware of the gun in its waistband holster and how few rounds he had left for it. He did not want to have a shootout in the lobby or in his own apartment; he lacked the energy for it.

He lingered in the mouth of an alley for a long time watching the front of the place. Cooper wanted to walk to the door and head in, but he forced himself to be patient for over an hour, until finally he emerged from the shadow of a dumpster and did it.

The doorman greeted him as always. Cooper chose the stairs instead of the elevator and took eighteen flights of steps to his floor. He encountered no one on the way and was careful entering the hallway that led to his apartment. When he was sure no one was there, he went quickly to the door and let himself inside.

He stood in the darkness and held his breath. He heard nothing, saw no strange shadows where there should be none. Maybe they had been here and gone, or maybe he was still ahead of them. If it was the former then he was lucky, and if it was the latter he was luckier still.

When he finally turned the light on in the foyer he saw nothing disturbed. He took out his gun and moved from room to room turning on all the lights. He found everything as he had left it. This time he did not turn on the television, but left it dark.

Cooper did not want to relax too much. He could not sleep here, nor could he stay very long. Already he had taken a chance and to linger would be taking one chance too many. In the bedroom he changed out of his dirty clothes. Briefly he considered taking a shower, but even that would take too long.

There were extra magazines for his pistol in the gun safe. Though he would be leaving many weapons behind, he couldn't bring them all. Just the one would be difficult enough as he was planning to take a plane out of Monterrey as soon as he could secure a ticket. The pistol and the knife he could take with him.

He had another bag and this one he packed with essential items like clothes and cash. When he was safely away he would see about closing out his bank account and reopening one elsewhere, but for now his reserves would have to do.

Everything was packed.

For a moment or two he considered what he was about to do. He had lived in this apartment for years and been happy there. This had been his place to retreat when he needed time alone. Everything in its rooms he had chosen himself to furnish his life. All this would be gone, too.

Cooper wouldn't die for the paintings on his walls. He left them behind.

The doorman hailed a cab for him and then he was off to the airport. From time to time he watched through the rear window of the taxi but he saw only occasional headlights and none that looked familiar. The driver tried to engage him in conversation but quickly tired of one-word answers. The man put on the radio and they listened to jazz music.

Cooper would take a flight from Monterrey to Cabo San Lucas. That was his plan. He could rent a car from there and travel to Palmilla to find Lorena. Again he felt the urge to go to her and sweep her up and take her with him wherever he might go.

At the airport he paid the cab driver too much and waved off the change. He found a skycap to take his bags and told the man to take them to the AeroMéxico Connect counter. The airport was practically deserted at this hour. He found no one checking in.

There were no flights until the following morning. Cooper told the woman at the counter that this was not a problem and paid cash for the trip. His bags were checked. Now he was unarmed and perhaps they were watching.

Cooper went to the first-class passengers' lounge and had the bartender there fix him a drink. There were several overstuffed chairs with leather upholstery and he allowed himself to sink deeply into one while he sipped the whiskey. When he was finished he asked for another and then another after that. He wanted the soft edges of impending drunkenness and knew it would also help him doze here while he waited.

Eventually he did drift. He stirred briefly when a woman came to vacuum the carpets, but for the most part he was able to sleep the middling sleep that didn't bring dreams but let him rest. Hours later he woke to the smell of eggs and toast as the AeroMéxico workers set up a breakfast buffet. He ate the eggs with chorizo sausage and had toast smeared with butter. He drank coffee and orange juice and was fully awake again. When it was time for his flight he bid the attendant on duty farewell and went to the plane empty-handed.

56.

There was bright sun in Cabo San Lucas when the plane came in for a landing. It cut through the porthole windows of the plane and dazzled the eyes. When Cooper looked out he saw a line of beach against the bright blue of the Gulf of Cortez. And then they were bumping along a runway to a stop; the engines reverse thrusting and filling the cabin with an air-blasting roar.

Cooper did not like to fly. It wasn't that he was afraid of the flying itself, but rather the discomfort of it all. Even in first class the seats were not as comfortable as they could be and there was never enough legroom for him. Drinking at altitude or the smile of an attractive flight attendant sometimes distracted him, but for the most part he was unhappy and this time was no exception. After he flew to Costa Rica he would not fly again for a long time.

The airport at Cabo was not even an airport but an *aeródromo*. They didn't disembark through an extensible tube, but down movable steps on the tarmac itself. The heat blistered off the pavement underfoot and Cooper felt it through the soles of his shoes. The white of his jacket was brilliant under the sky.

He collected his bags and went from the little baggage carousel to the nearest restroom. He took a large stall and opened his suitcase. The liner was detachable and underneath were the pieces of his pistol. Cooper reassembled them while seated on the toilet and loaded the weapon when he was done.

The knife he'd simply put in an interior pocket. This went to its usual place. He felt better with it there.

Once he was done he closed the suitcase and went out to the rental-car desk. He would have to risk using his own card because taxis would not do for what he had in mind. He came away from the rental desk with the keys to a red Nissan. His bags went in the trunk.

Cooper sat behind the wheel for a time, his mind working. His plan was unformed and now he had reached the point where things had to take shape. He was feeling tired again and his shoulder had started to ache. Cooper ate ibuprofen and started the car.

He headed northeast along the coast. Another time he might have better appreciated the views he saw, but he was distracted by other thoughts. He saw few other cars on the road and he watched carefully in his rear-view mirror for anyone following too close. They could not be here. They wouldn't be here. This he kept telling himself.

When he had been to Cabo San Lucas in the past he stayed at a golf and beach resort between the city and San José del Cabo. It had been a few years, but he still remembered the way and drove there. The place was gated and he didn't have a reservation. He paid the guard at the gate 600 pesos and the man let him in.

The main structure of the hotel was distinctly Spanish in style and massive. There were little cabins dotted along the seaside and plenty of rooms in the building itself. Cooper remembered that many Americans stayed here and this was something he hoped was still true.

At the desk he paid another bribe to the man on duty to get an ocean-view room with a king-sized bed. He carried his bags to his room himself.

The room had a balcony and a broad set of sliding glass doors opening onto it. The air conditioner was on, but Cooper switched it off and opened the doors wide to let the breeze through. He had been on an airplane breathing recycled air and now he wanted something fresher.

He hadn't brought very much, but he unpacked his things into the closet and chest of drawers. The rest of the day stretched out before him, Palmilla was only a few miles away. Cooper thought of Lorena and for an instant he trembled.

Cooper lay on the bed and got real sleep to make up for the half-sleep he'd taken the night before. When he got up he helped himself to snacks and drinks from the minibar and went out on the balcony.

The water was beautiful. This he remembered from his last time. An archway of stone loomed over a nearby section of beach and Cooper saw people walking down there and others simply sunbathing. A few tanned bodies floated in the surf. He thought it would be good to swim here and smell the sea on his skin, but there was no time for that and he couldn't be sure his wounds wouldn't be affected. Besides, he didn't want to be away from Lorena anymore. There would be time enough for swimming when they were together.

He kept a few thousand pesos for his wallet and put the rest in the room safe. The door to the room had double locks and an electronic security system with a PIN he memorized. Cooper closed up the sliding glass doors reluctantly, set the alarm and left his room.

It had occurred to him that he didn't know where he was going. Palmilla was a small place, but it was dotted with resorts just like the one. He would have to ask questions, make himself known to the locals. He would have to spend money.

Cooper would do these things because he had to. Lorena was the last part of Mexico he would have and then he would be gone from here. And they would have to look long and hard to find him.

57.

Cooper was on the road in the red Nissan when his phone rang. Immediately his heart leaped a little thinking it was Lorena and he answered hoping it was she on the line. He answered.

"*Bueno.*"

"Cooper," Barriga said. He sounded far away, as if the connection was not good. There was a ringing sound behind his voice, like the echo of bathroom tile. "Cooper, can you hear me?"

"I hear you."

"Cooper, where are you?"

Cooper paused. "I think maybe it's better if I don't tell you," he said.

"Why is that?"

Of course Barriga had to know. He had to know that someone among Barriga's people gave up Cooper. They were the only ones who knew him, knew what he had done and where. They were not so close to Barriga that they knew Cooper's name, but they were close enough.

"I'd just prefer it that way," Cooper answered.

"You're going off the reservation, Cooper," Barriga said.

"Oh? I didn't realize I was on one."

"You know what I mean, Cooper. You're an asset to us. We've used you enough times. You're part of the organization now."

"I didn't ask to be."

"But that's the way things are. We're worried about you, Cooper."

"Why weren't you worried before you gave me Swenson's name? You said there wouldn't be any more favors. I believed you."

"Circumstances have changed."

"How so?"

Barriga sighed into the phone. "It would be better if we talked face to face."

"I'm not available."

An oncoming truck took up most of Cooper's lane. He slowed and pulled over onto the gravel shoulder until it passed. Barriga was quiet on the other end, but he was still there. Cooper felt the weight of him and when the man spoke again Cooper heard irritation. "What exactly do you want from my people, Cooper?"

"Nothing. I'm done asking for favors."

"We can work this out with Swenson's organization. There have been contacts since you met with them in San Antonio. That's why I'm calling now. The contacts have been quite fruitful."

"You're working with them now?"

"We've discovered that we have some interests in common, that's all. The point is you don't have to be out in the cold on this. We can bring you in, make things happen."

"I don't understand."

"I told you: we find you of value."

"Now."

"Always, Cooper."

"I'll have to think about it."

"Think about it, then. And consider this: if we didn't consider you an asset, we would be asking harder questions about Ruíz. That hasn't been forgotten."

"I didn't have anything to do with that."

"So you said. But it's an inconvenient piece of work, Cooper, and it feels very much like something you would have done. People have been asking questions. They're still asking them. I only have so many answers."

Cooper understood the threat implicit in Barriga's words. He glanced in the rear view mirror and saw the big truck vanishing on the horizon. Then he saw the flash of a car's windshield heading in Cooper's direction. Without thinking, he gave the Nissan more acceleration.

"Cooper, are you still there?"

"Yes. I don't know what to tell your people about Ruíz. I did what I was paid to do and when you said he wasn't getting a package I walked away from it. You know that's what I do."

"Not everyone knows you as well as I do. That's why you should come in. There are some people you should talk to. They'll understand once you've had a chance to explain it to them personally."

The car behind him was gaining. Cooper shifted in his seat so that his gun hip was slightly forward.

"Can I tell them you're going to speak with them?"

"Not yet."

"Then when?"

"As soon as I've managed to take care of things on my end. It could take a while, so tell your people not to wait up for me."

"I thought I explained to you that their patience isn't infinite."

"And I appreciate that, but I have to be careful."

"Cooper," Barriga said.

"Someone burned me on the Bingham job. I can't come in until that's resolved."

Barriga went quiet again. Cooper could hear nothing but the sound of his own engine. The car was even closer now, and the nose was beginning to take shape. He saw a woman's long hair streaming out of a convertible top.

"I'll tell my people," Barriga said at last.

"Okay."

"But there are going to be more questions, Cooper. Questions about your loyalty to our organization."

"I was never loyal to your organization," Cooper said. "I only wanted the money."

"That disappoints me to hear. We'll be in touch."

The line went dead. The car was almost on him. Cooper tossed the phone into the passenger seat and drew his gun. He touched the button to lower the window and kept the pistol against his leg

The car was a BMW convertible coupe and it roared into the other lane. The driver was laughing and the woman next to him flashed her breasts at Cooper. Then the BMW picked up speed and surged ahead. Cooper applied the brakes and let them go on.

His gun was still in his hand and his palm was sweating. He put it away and placed both hands on the wheel. Wind whipped at him through the open window.

He told himself again that they weren't here. He was far away from Juárez and Monterrey and no one knew to follow him. The only person who knew he would come was Lorena, because he hadn't yet broken his word to her. She believed in him and he would not betray that.

The BMW vanished ahead. Cooper drove on.

58.

There were many resorts and Cooper did not have enough cash to bribe them all. But he had learned a trick years ago that had served him well more than once: he bribed the workers.

He spent the day frequenting the working-class places in the tiny city of Palmilla. Like a coal town or a logging town, the industry here was tourism and almost everyone owed his or her livelihood to one resort or the other.

Cooper spread money around and asked questions. He bought beers. When it was dinnertime and the shifts changed he started over again until his wallet was empty and he'd talked with dozens. He drove back to his hotel in the dark.

When he reached his room he was careful. He let himself in slowly and looked through the hinges to the blind spot behind the door. The bathroom was clear and there was no one on the balcony. Looking through his things he found nothing disturbed. Later he refilled his wallet with cash. If he had to, he would go out and do the same thing all over again.

If he were anywhere else he would have been afraid to expose himself like this. He'd given his number out freely and though no one knew his name they would be able to identify him easily enough. He was the American with the money he wanted to give away.

He hadn't told them why he was looking for Lorena. That much they didn't need to know. He saw a look in some women's eyes that told him they were suspicious, like he was an ex-husband looking for someone he shouldn't. The men were more understanding.

Cooper took dinner in his room. He brought the food out on the balcony and watched the white surf curling in the dark. There were a handful of torches set up on the beach and a few people were having a meal served by the resort staff. Cooper watched them for a while.

After a time he went in and turned on the television. He had a choice of news channels and picked the one in English. For two hours he stared at the screen retaining nothing of what he saw until finally he was tired enough to turn off the lights and go to sleep.

In the morning he called room service for breakfast and had something light. He called the front desk asked if there was somewhere he could buy a bathing suit and he was told yes. Eventually he went down and selected a pair of trunks and went out to the beach while he waited for the phone to ring.

It was after four before he got the call. The man's name was Nacio and he had seen the woman Cooper was looking for. He asked if there was extra money for finding her and Cooper promised him there was. They would meet and Cooper would pay him 1,000 pesos for the tip so long as it was good. Nacio assured Cooper that it was good.

Cooper went back to his room, showered and dressed. He kept his gun with him. When he left the housekeeper was coming to tidy up. He left 60 pesos on the dresser for her.

The resort was not one of the new ones. It had been around since the 1950s and was built out to match. Like the one where Cooper stayed, it was zealously guarded, but money got him past the gates and fences and into the compound.

When he came to the front desk he asked for Lorena by name. A few hundred pesos passed across the counter were enough.

He found the little bungalow among a dozen others just like it scattered along the seaside. They were white, with tin roofs that reflected the sun, and their open doors and windows flowed with gossamer curtains caught in the offshore breeze. The Sea of Cortez was the color of lapis.

Cooper came down over a sand dune and approached Lorena's bungalow from the rear. He wondered what he would say to her when he saw her, and what she might say to him. He played a hundred scenarios through his mind in the time it took him cover two hundred yards. The soft sand gave way beneath his shoes.

Lorena had the shuttered doors at the front of the bungalow wide open. As Cooper approached the breeze reversed itself and the curtains there came billowing out like ghosts.

He thought to knock, but didn't. The curtains were sheer and he could see the shapes of furniture within. "Lorena?" he said. "Lorena?"

She materialized out of the interior of the bungalow in a while sundress. Her hair was up off her neck and she didn't wear any makeup. Cooper saw the girl in her then, but it didn't stop him from coming through the curtains to her.

They kissed and then their hands were all over each other. Lorena helped Cooper take off his jacket. His gun hit the floor when his pants dropped and he kicked out of his shoes. The dress lifted over Lorena's head. She was naked underneath. Cooper put his mouth on her nipples.

There was a short couch and Cooper pushed Lorena back onto it. She spread her legs. He put his head between her thighs and kissed her there. His mouth was full of the taste of her. He licked and sucked and pushed his fingers into her until he felt her whole body shiver. Then he lifted himself onto her.

Cooper wanted to be demanding with her, but he was gentle. He pushed slowly and let her put her feet in the small of his back. They took their time together and when he came he came strongly inside of her.

"I love you," Cooper said in her ear. "I love you."

59.

They stayed together in the bungalow for three days, long enough for Cooper to almost forget he had been anywhere else. They made love in the morning, afternoon and evening and spent hours together on the beach. Food was brought to them and they ate and made love again. It was exactly right.

When he tried to talk to her, she would cover his mouth with kisses. After a while Cooper stopped trying and they enjoyed each other without words. They slept naked under the slowly turning blades of a ceiling fan with the sound of crashing waves outside.

On the fourth day they spent the morning walking in the surf. Cooper wanted to hold her hand but she walked a little distance away from him, just watching the water. He found he had to speak. "I can't stay," he said and cleared his throat. "I said I can't stay."

Lorena didn't react to him, but she walked a little closer then.

Cooper stopped and Lorena stopped with him. He looked for her eyes and captured them. For a moment he was lost and the words were lost, but then he found them again. "I have people looking for me. I can't go back to Juárez."

"Why would you want to go back to Juárez?" Lorena asked.

"For you."

She came close and kissed him once and took both of his hands. "You have me now," she said. Lorena led him back to the bungalow and for a time there was nothing that needed to be said.

Cooper rested and even slept. When he awoke Lorena was moving around the bedroom. She was naked and her body was slim and sinuous. Lorena had a long waist and small breasts that stood high on her chest. She had unwaxed hair below.

He watched her for a while. She wandered from one thing to the next, only touching down for a few moments before moving to the next thing. Lorena reminded Cooper of a butterfly skipping over flowers and just as delicate. He could have kept on watching her, but she noticed him and came back to the bed.

When they were done again Cooper lay on his side, Lorena's back cradled against his. They were both perspiring, but the dry air wicked it away. The sheets smelled of sweat and sex.

"Some people are asking questions about your father," Cooper said into her ear.

"The same people who are looking for you?"

"No, not the same. Señor Barriga. His people. They want to know what happened to your father."

"He died."

"Not just that he died, but who pulled the trigger."

"They will never know it was you," Lorena said and she pulled his arm closer around her. His hand was on her breast. "That secret is ours. No one will ever know."

"That won't stop them from asking."

"Then let them ask."

"It's not that simple."

"Why not?"

"Because it's not. Some questions need answers no matter what."

"Then you will have to give them an answer they will believe."

"I wish it was that simple."

"I'm sure it can be. If you think."

"I guess I'll think about it."

They lay together for a long time. The sun crept across the room until its rays were almost horizontal across the room. The slatted windows raked shadows and light on the wall above them. Cooper wanted to get up, but he did not want to let go. He wasn't sure if Lorena was sleeping or not.

"Cooper?"

"Yes?"

"Did you mean what you told me?"

He did not have to ask what she meant and he shuddered a little. He hadn't said it again after that first time. He didn't regret saying it, but it was frightening because he had never said it before.

"Did you?"

"I did."

"How can it be true?"

Cooper frowned. "I don't know," he said. "I just know that I do. I can't explain myself. It doesn't make any sense to me."

"Do you understand if I tell you that I don't feel the same way?"

"I understand that."

"I could love you, but not yet."

"How long?" Cooper asked, and immediately felt foolish for asking.

"Not long."

"I see."

"My father told me he loved me. Every time he told me. It came to mean nothing to me because he said it so much. And there have been other men who've said it to me. I never believed them."

"I'm not your father."

Lorena raised his hand from her breast and kissed it. "I know."

"And I'm not other men."

"I know this, too. That is why we're together. I knew you loved me when you did for me what had to be done. And I knew then that I could also love you... just not now."

Cooper considered what she said. He hadn't thought of himself loving her when he killed her father, but looking back at it now he must have. The act made no sense otherwise. She had paid him, but he had already been paid not to harm the man. Some things should not be gone back on and he had known that then. Yet he had still done it.

"I want to be with you," Cooper said impulsively. "Not just here. I want to be with you. Not just now. I want you to come away with me. I have to go, but that doesn't mean we can't be together."

"Won't we be hunted?"

"I will, not you."

"Won't we be watched?"

Cooper fell silent. "Yes," he said finally. "Yes we would."

"This may be all we have. If that is so, then we ought to enjoy it. I don't like thinking about where we will go or won't go.

Do you understand what I'm saying, Cooper? I want to be here now."

"I understand."

"Good."

60.

He had to go back to his hotel for fresh clothes. On the drive there he thought only of her and how things would change when they could not be here anymore. Costa Rica was waiting for him, but he did not want to go.

At the front desk he extended his stay by another week and went to his room. Things were as he had left them, though the bed had not been slept in and the doors not opened to the sea. He gathered up what he would need and put them in a plastic bag for laundry. Then he left.

He found her out by the waves when he returned, standing in the surf and letting the beach sand engulf her feet little by little with each passing wave. Cooper went out to be with her and held her closely to him.

"Do you wish it could be like this forever?" Lorena asked him.

"You know I do."

"I feel the same sometimes."

They went back to the bungalow but this time they didn't make love. Instead they lay on the bed facing each other and held hands. Cooper memorized every part of her unlined face and imagined she was doing the same with him. Like the best of their times together, they were silent.

"If I tell you there may be a way to turn these people away — the ones who want to know how my father died — would you be happy?"

"Of course I would."

"Then there is a way."

"How?"

Lorena was quiet-faced for a moment and Cooper thought she might not speak again. He'd seen that expression before and usually she would close up and go away from him even when her body was still there. He felt like he knew her better than himself.

"You can tell me."

"There is a man. His name is Roldán Garcia."

"Yes?"

"When I told you there were other men who've told me that they loved me, I lied. There has been only one. Roldán Garcia is that man."

"Who is he?"

"He came to visit my father many times a year ago. When he was not in meetings with my father he spent time with me. My father encouraged this at first, but when things became too serious my father grew jealous. Before their business was finished they had a tremendous fight and he threw Roldán out of our house.

"Roldán, he told me that I could always come to him if my father would ever allow it. My mother, she thought Roldán was a fine man and she told my father so and that made him even more furious. The next time my father was with me... he hurt me."

Cooper had tried to put the image of Ruíz and Lorena together from his mind. It was easier to do when they were together, making love, and things were so different for them than it must have been between her and her father. Now he had the dark thoughts in his mind and they made him feel sick.

"If these men who did business with my father, if they could be convinced that someone else did what you did, would they leave us alone?"

"I don't know," Cooper said and it was the truth. "And there's still—"

"Only this problem, Cooper. The other men can wait."

"Okay. If it was possible to make Barriga's people believe that someone else was responsible for your father's death, I might be able to come to you, or you could come to me. It would take some time. It couldn't happen too fast. If they suspected anything...."

"They will believe me."

"What could you possibly tell them that would make them believe?"

"It's not just what I would tell them."

"I don't understand."

"I know my father was not just a landowner, Cooper. I know the people who came to visit him weren't looking for grazing rights. He was involved with crime, with drugs. My father was just a bigger fish than those that hack one other to pieces in the streets of Juárez."

"Who was Roldán to your father?"

"Roldán was a sweet man, but I knew he was involved with drugs, too. He came to my father for something to do with his business, just like you and Señor Barriga. When they fought, I overheard my father saying that Roldán was Sinaloan. Do you know what this means?"

"He's a member of the Sinaloa cartel."

"Yes."

Cooper considered. In Juárez there were two large drug cartels. The Sinaloenses came from the west, looking for a way to bring their drugs through *El Paso del Norte*, the North Pass into America. Hundreds of trucks passed over the bridges into the United States and scattered among those trucks were the drugs that fueled deals from border to border. The Juárez cartel guarded these routes and in guarding them from the Sinaloenses touched off a war that had killed thousands.

The year before there had been 5,000 killed. In the year thus far there had been 4,000. The cartels killed with knives and machetes and guns alike. Mutilated bodies and heads without corpses were scattered across the city. This was the violence Cooper wondered about when he thought of the United States and how its people would react. They had never known carnage like this.

It would make sense that Ruíz was a member of the Juárez cartel, but there was no way to know. If he made deals across the lines it was little wonder that Barriga and his people might have him killed. Things were taking shape now that had just been vague ideas before because Cooper hadn't asked questions. They paid him not to know, only to do.

"You're saying blame the murder on drugs."

"I'm saying we should blame a man who wanted me. My father refused him. That would be enough to make a man commit murder. Mexican men do not like to be denied. They will take what they want."

"I don't know."

"We can make Señor Barriga's people believe this. They'll stop looking at us."

"I don't know."

"It can be done!"

"How? All Roldán has to do is deny it."

"He can't deny it if he's dead."

61.

They slept. They ate. They made love. All but the last were satisfying. Cooper felt something between them and he could not name it. Whatever had begun with the talk of Roldán Garcia's death had not yet been undone.

Cooper was not afraid of killing someone. The fact that he did not know the man meant nothing to him. He had killed men before when he only knew their names and where to find them. It was the words from Lorena's lips that bothered him. This was not the same.

He had seen her father raping her. He had known the sickness and the impotent rage. Killing Ruíz was a release for him as for Lorena. Cooper did not want to admit it, but when he killed Ruíz it was the first time he felt he was killing for a reason.

There was money. She had paid him. But now she was here with him and her body was his. She wouldn't give him her heart, but he felt her wavering. When she loved him everything would be different again. When she loved him he would kill anyone for her. Or perhaps this was the thing he must do.

"Tell me more about him," Cooper asked one night.

They were on the beach and Cooper had gathered driftwood enough for a fire. The breeze off the water was cool, but the fire was warm. Lorena glowed bright yellow and orange. All this time in the sun had made her very dark. Cooper was the same.

"He was a gentleman at first," Lorena said. "But he became more insistent over time. I don't know why my father let it go on as long as he did. Even I was worried for myself. He was too... intense."

She described what Roldán looked like and Cooper tried to imagine him. He was a young man in his twenties, slender but strong, with longish black hair. He was clean-shaven and had light brown eyes. Cooper made an image that was probably all wrong. He saw that image with Lorena and it made him angry.

"The first time he told me he loved me, I didn't believe him. I was only fifteen. No boys had told me that. Roldán wanted to hold my hand all the time. He often tried to kiss me. I let him once. I think that was when my father knew."

"He saw you?"

"My mother saw us. I think she must have said something to him."

Cooper tried to remember Lorena's mother. He remembered that Barriga had been friendly with her in a way that made him think they had long been friends, but he wasn't sure what it was about them that made him think that. He remembered he had not seen much of either parent in Lorena.

"Why would your mother give you up like that?"

"I'm sure she didn't mean harm by it. How could she know?"

"Go on."

"The next time Roldán came to see my father they were arguing right away. My father called him *cabrón* and worse things. They fought all the way to my father's study and even then they were loud enough to be heard all through the house. I was afraid for him then, but my father let him leave without hurting him."

"He just hurt you."

"Yes."

Cooper's hands were in fists. He relaxed them.

"Roldán sent me letters after that. Several letters. He told me that my father was no good for me, but what could I do?"

"Did he know the secret?"

"No. Only you."

"Go on."

"In the last letter he said he wasn't going to write anymore because I hadn't written him. He told me that if I ever left my father that I could come to him and be safe. He sent me a key to his apartment in La Paz, and told me how to get there."

"He gave you a key to his apartment?"

"Yes."

"You don't have that key."

"I keep it with the rest. I have it here."

La Paz was not far away from Palmilla. He could make it there in a matter of hours. Already the wheels were turning though he had said nothing yet. He imagined the man, Roldán.

"Were you ever going to go to him?"

"No. He wasn't right for me."

"And you can decide that he should die just like that?"

"I'm not deciding just like that," Lorena said. "I know what this means. But you would do this for us."

"Tell me what you'd tell them."

"That I decided to go to Roldán and told my father. He shouted at me, he beat me and then sent men to beat Roldán. It was revenge for what was done to me, what was done to him.

Mexican men have killed other Mexican men for far less than that. And if he really is a Sinaloense, then he is familiar with death."

Cooper thought and then he said, "They won't believe you."

"Yes, they will."

"Why?"

"Because my father is dead. You said yourself they don't know why he was killed. This will give them the reason they're looking for."

"And how will you explain the two of us together?"

"That's a problem for another time."

"It's problem for *now*. I'm not killing someone just to kill them."

"You think they will never stop suspecting you."

Cooper sighed. "I know they won't. Not with us together."

"Then kill him to keep them from me."

She was watching him across the fire. Even without looking at her he could feel her gaze. He busied himself pushing the driftwood around by their unburnt ends. Something fell on his cheek. When he wiped at it, he felt a tear. "Goddamn it," he said.

"When they can't find a reason they will suspect my mother. They'll suspect me. The guards at my father's house will have their suspicions about my father and me. They'll talk. I'll be in danger."

"Shut up!" Cooper shouted. "I don't want to hear it."

"They'll come for me like they'll come for you, Cooper!"

"No! That's impossible. They have no reason to think you're involved."

"I *lived*, Cooper."

And there it was. Cooper did not have any words anymore. They would come for her because she was the only one who could know and when they were finished with her they would come for him. He could see it happen in his mind's eye, one step after the next. But if they thought Roldán Garcia had done it then it would explain her survival. It would explain everything.

Cooper got up from the fire and walked into the darkness. He splashed into the water up to his knees and stared out at the moon climbing into the sky. Again and again he thought it: *it would explain everything.*

He heard her coming up from behind and then she took his hand. "I'm sorry," she said.

"You don't have anything to be sorry for," Cooper replied. "It was just me, wanting things I can never have."

"They're things we both want."

"Is that true?"

"Yes."

Cooper turned toward her. The waxing moon reflected off the water lighted her. "Then tell me you love me."

"I love you."

He wrapped her up in his arms and held her as closely as he ever had, until he could feel her heartbeat against him and the heat of her body. "Tell me you love me," he said again.

"I love you, Cooper."

62.

He didn't have access to his tools. All he had was the pistol and his knife. It was enough for some of what had to be done, but not all of it.

They left the resort for the first time and went to Palmilla to see what little was there. Lorena wore her white sundress, the same one she'd worn when he came to her, and he let her convince him to buy a funny straw hat with a ragged brim.

There were vendors set up for the few tourists who made it away from their hotels and into the little town. Once politicians and movie stars had come to Palmilla for its sun and water. Something told Cooper that it wasn't quite the same anymore. Even in the height of summer they saw few people on their stretch of beach.

The tourists were staying away because of the violence, here as everywhere in Mexico. But the cartels hadn't stretched out their hands to the tip of the peninsula as they had elsewhere. It was as safe in Palmilla as anywhere, and perhaps safer. The city of La Paz was the same way. Once Cooper had considered living there.

Cooper thought about Roldán. Killing the man was not enough. There was a bloody standard to cartel deaths and this one could not be found wanting. Thinking about it made Cooper feel ill in a way that murder did not.

"Buy me a coconut," Lorena said.

They came to a vendor with a chest filled with ice and a pile of coconuts. He used a short-bladed machete to hack through the hairy shell in three angled swipes and planted a straw in the chilled milk. Cooper paid the man and they moved on. Lorena drank.

"You're quiet," Lorena said at last.

"There isn't much to talk about," Cooper answered.

"All right, then we won't talk."

Palmilla bored Cooper. He would almost rather be on the beach with nothing to do except watch the waves come in. Tourist junk was the same here as it was everywhere. He steered them back toward the car.

"Is it something I've done?" Lorena asked.

"No, it's not that. I don't talk much before... before."

"Are you afraid?"

"No, I'm not afraid."

"Then is it something else?"

"I don't know how to explain it."

"You don't have to," she said and she squeezed his hand.

When they were back at the car, Cooper paused. He realized suddenly that he had walked out in the open for the first time in many days without once looking over his shoulder. He looked now, all around, and saw nothing, but his skin crawled.

"What is it?"

"Just get in the car."

He got them moving and looked in the mirrors. No one was following. A minivan came down the street opposite them and Cooper watched it in the rear-view mirror until it was completely gone from sight before he allowed himself to pay full attention to the road. His palms were damp.

"What's wrong?"

"I didn't... I just... it's nothing."

"Are we in danger?"

"No. Nothing like that. I just forgot something."

"Is it all right now?"

"Yes, it's all right now," Cooper said and he checked the mirrors again.

They returned to the resort. Cooper rushed into the bathroom and splashed water on his face. When he looked at himself in the mirror he could see that the color had gone out of his cheeks and his hands were trembling. He started a shower for himself and stayed in longer than he had to.

Lorena was on the bed when he emerged. He joined her there and she made him forget everything for a while. They made love until both of them were exhausted and the day was almost gone.

"You don't have to hide from me," Lorena said. "Not from me, my love."

"I won't hide from you," Cooper said.

63.

The coconut vendor's knife cost him five dollars American. It was a heavy-tipped blade turned black from almost constant use and its grip was worn smooth after years of handling. At first it did not seem sharp, but Cooper drew his thumb across it and the metal cut him.

La Paz was a drive of decent length and Cooper started early. He'd changed out of the light, cottony vacation clothes he'd worn with Lorena and back into a jacket and shirtsleeves. The gun was on his hip beneath the jacket, the spare magazine on the other side. The coconut vendor's knife lay across the passenger seat like a dark promise.

The city was a small one, located on a great inlet from the Sea of Cortez. People had been living there for 10,000 years and left rock paintings to prove it. La Paz was beautiful and clean.

Cooper went to a restaurant called Las Tres Virgenes for the *comida corrida*. He ate huge helpings of beans and rice and spicy chicken tacos. After he was done he left a big tip for the waitress and then headed for the seaside.

He found a park by the water lined with bricks and palm trees. There were vendors here selling snow cones and soft drinks and churros and spicy snacks. Cooper ignored all of them and sat on a bench to watch the water.

Before he left he had listened to Lorena on the telephone with Roldán Garcia. If he had not known what she really wanted he would have believed her, too; there was nothing false in her voice. Afterward she made a map from the directions Roldán gave her. She took the key from her chain and pressed it into Cooper's hand.

Now he would wait. He would do nothing until the sun went down.

It was easy for him to disconnect now. This had happened too many times before and he had nothing he would call nerves. Those had vanished long ago. In its place was a stillness that he could not explain to anyone, not even himself. He was blank inside.

He made love to Lorena once more before he left her. Despite himself he'd cried. She didn't judge him, but held him to her breast until it had passed. Cooper apologized to her afterward. She pretended there was nothing wrong.

Cooper cried because he knew the time was almost up. He could not delay any more and she could not stay in Palmilla forever. Everything he had dreamed about would end before it had a chance to begin. They could not be together in safety, but they could be apart and live. He was buying that for them now.

The sun moved and people came and went. Finally Cooper went and got a cherry snow cone. He bit into the minced ice and winced a little as the cold went to the roots of his teeth. As always the cherry flavor collected at the bottom of the paper cone where he drank it like syrup.

Once again he was struck with the wandering bug and he took off across the park to look in shop windows. He found a bookstore where he browsed without reading a single title. A playground was full of children climbing and shouting. He stopped for a while there.

It wasn't that he had never wanted children, but that the subject had never been in serious contention. The women he was with were temporary, passing through his life without meaning beyond what they did for him at the moment. He could not imagine a life with any of them, but he could imagine it with Lorena.

She was young, but she would make a good mother. This Cooper knew without having to think about it. She was not a girl.

The young mothers at the playground did not look that much older than Lorena. Some of them were just as slender. Cooper could imagine her there among them, watching out for their son, careful of him in a way her parents had not been careful with her. Only he understood the gentleness of her.

He could not watch forever. Eventually the mothers took notice of him and some of them began to frown and talk. Cooper walked away then to find something else to occupy his time.

Cooper walked around in aimless circles, wider and wider, until he happened across a convenience store. Inside he found a two-liter bottle of Jarritos and purchased it with cash. He already had a roll of packing tape in his jacket pocket.

Finally he came back to the Nissan and drove until he was within a block of Roldán Garcia's apartment. The streets were busy here, but the commotion of cars and pedestrians was like camouflage and no one noticed him lingering behind the wheel of the car. The sun was not low enough in the sky and seemed to be moving slower and slower as the day wore on. He could not move until dark.

He busied himself watching the people who went past. Most of them were young because La Paz was a young person's city. They were dressed as professionals, but not too formally. If it hadn't been for the uniformly Mexican population he could have been in any trendy neighborhood in an American city where expensive apartments mixed with high-tech firms and scrappy start-ups. The people here had the same look of determination on their faces, as if everything in the world depended on them, but it hadn't resolved into the world-weariness of age. Cooper looked at himself in the rear-view mirror and wondered if he'd changed in that way.

The sun started to glare in his eyes. He put down the visor. Foot traffic slowed down as the business day ended. On the streets the cars thinned out. Cooper started to perspire and he didn't know why.

People came by the car in twos and threes. Eventually it was only singles and then finally there was no one at all.

64.

Cooper opened the door of the car. It was only when he was exposed to the night air that he realized how warm and stuffy it had been inside. He unscrewed the cap of the Jarritos bottle and poured the contents into the street where it foamed up and streamed away.

He still had fifteen minutes to wait. He brought out his gun and laid it on his lap. He took the packing tape from his pocket and tore off a long strip. This he wound around the open top of the bottle. When he had made a thick band of tape there, then he put the mouth of the bottle against the muzzle of the pistol. He began winding tape in layers around the end of the gun and the bottle, binding them together. He used almost all of the tape and when he was finished the wrapping bulged like a child's fist.

His watch counted down the time. When it was eleven o'clock, he got out of the car.

Cooper took off his jacket and draped it over the bottle and pistol. He had the coconut vendor's short machete tucked into his belt.

On the walk to Roldán Garcia's building he saw no one. There were lights in the windows but no one looked out. No cars passed down the street. It was as quiet as a city could become, as if all of La Paz was holding its breath. The moon was out and full.

Roldán Garcia lived on the third floor of his building. Someone had blocked the lobby door open with a brick. Cooper came inside and moved the brick so the door could lock shut. He went to the mailboxes in the shadow of the stairs to be sure Roldán was where he was supposed to be. There was no elevator.

He mounted the steps one at a time. At each landing he heard the sounds of life coming from the apartments around him. In some there was the white noise of a television blaring and in others the mumble of upraised voices muffled by the walls. This told him the walls were thick, but not too thick, and that he should be careful when delivering the package. Every door had a peephole. Cooper hoped no one was looking out.

When he came to the door he stilled himself. His breathing was even, his hands dry. He put his jacket back on and held the pistol loosely. The key was in his pocket. He took it out and held it for a moment. It was warm against his skin.

He listened. No sounds came from the inside. A pinprick of light showed through the peephole, so Cooper knew no one was watching him. He put the key to the lock quietly and listened again when it was home. There was nothing.

Cooper turned the key softly, twisted it back, pulled it loose. He barely made a noise. With his hand on the doorknob he turned so gently that it took almost a minute for the latch to click.

The door eased open. Cooper saw reflected light on a close wall and then he pushed the door fully wide. The smell of candles reached his nose.

The apartment had a short hallway that served as a foyer. There was a small bench with shoes underneath. The floors were wood. A mirror in an ornate gilt frame stood over the bench, a last chance to check one's looks before heading out the door.

Beyond the hallway the space opened up into a large room. Cooper saw a couch and a chair, the couch decorated with a colorful blanket tossed over the back. One step into the apartment and he could see a coffee table where two white candles burned next to a far red one.

Cooper pushed the door to. He stood still and listened. From somewhere out of sight he heard the short footsteps of someone being busy. He lifted the pistol and came into the main room.

The room had a glass wall made up of little panes that looked out over the street and to the buildings beyond. The wall had shades rolled up to the top, exposing the whole room from the inside. Cooper saw an easel with a cloth thrown over it and a row of stretched canvases stood side by side edgewise so that he could not see how they were painted. There was a second couch, a door that opened onto a bathroom and another that likely led to a bedroom.

Cooper turned left. An open doorway revealed a small kitchen. A pot steamed on the stovetop. A man was bent to the refrigerator and came up with a bottle of wine in his hand.

Roldán Garcia did not look anything like Cooper had imagined. He fit Lorena's description but his features did not come together the way they had in Cooper's thoughts. He had imagined the blank look when the man saw him and also the reaction when Cooper pulled the trigger.

The bottle was not the same as a sound suppressor. It contained smoke and gasses and the bullet blasted out the plastic base. Cooper hit Roldán Garcia lower than he wanted — through the neck — and the man reeled. The wine bottle crashed to the floor. Roldán fell back against the wall. The clock there jumped off its nail and fell.

Roldán had his hand over the wound, but blood escaped in jets and spurts between his fingers. He was trying to speak, but only little sounds came out. He had blood on his lips. Cooper advanced with his finger on the trigger but he could not fire again; the bottle was ruined.

The man bled out slowly, more slowly than Cooper anticipated. Eventually his eyes clouded over and then he was dead.

Cooper went back to the couches and stripped off his jacket. He peeled the shattered bottle and tape from the end of his gun. Back in the kitchen he caught Roldán by the ankles and dragged his body out into the main room. The man reeked of white wine and his pants were soaked in it.

He went to the broad windows that formed one wall of the main room and looked out. He could see across the street into the windows of the apartments. There was someone watching television. There was a woman exercising with a Wii. There was a man bouncing a ball across his apartment floor so his dog could catch it. Other windows were dark.

It took a few moments to decipher how they worked, but the blinds unrolled finally and Cooper closed off the windows to the street. The room seemed to shrink, like another wall had been dropped in. Cooper considered turning the air conditioning down.

Cooper undressed the body starting with his shirt. The buttons popped off when he pulled them sharply and he stripped the man down to his undershirt. He took off Roldán Garcia's shoes and socks, undid his belt and yanked on the wet pants until they came down. He left Roldán's underwear on.

He drew the coconut vendor's long knife and began to cut.

First he hacked through the muscle and bone at the shoulder joint of the man's left arm. It took more doing than Cooper expected and he was splattered with blood from the work. Finally the arm came loose and he tossed it across the floor to where a table set for two was waiting.

The second arm was easier. The flesh was still warm to the touch, but it was cooling fast. Cooper imagined Roldán Garcia's hand suddenly twitching and grasping, but his fingers were loose.

For the legs he started with the knees because they would be easier than the hips to displace with the blade and he was right. The black blade of the short machete carved through the ligaments and the lower leg came away. He repeated the feat on the other side. There was a pile of body parts gathering under the light of the dining nook.

At last he took Roldán's head by the hair. The wound in his neck was jagged and ugly and still leaked. Cooper cut torn flesh until he reached bone and then it was just a matter of hewing through the spine.

He took the head to the dining room table. He swept the dishes off onto the floor and planted Roldán Garcia's severed head in the center of the table facing the door. Roldán's eyes were rolled up under the lids so that his eyeballs appeared milk-white.

Cooper was bloody like a butcher at work. His shirt was thick with stains and his hands were soaked. The blade of the coconut vendor's knife dripped. Cooper drove it point-first into the table and it stuck there.

He went into the bathroom and left a smear on the light switch when he flipped it on. His fingerprints were everywhere but it didn't matter because soon he would be out of Mexico. They could search all they wanted but they would never find him.

Cooper caught sight of himself in the mirror. He had blood flecks on his face.

There was soap and much hot water and Cooper scrubbed his hands until they were clean even under the nails. He washed his face thoroughly and when he looked at himself again he did not look so pale and drawn. There was nothing he could do about his shirt; it was ruined. His pants were likewise spattered.

They would think the cartels had done it. They would see the broken pieces of Roldán Garcia's body and they would learn of his connections and they would put his name down in a file along with the countless thousands dying along the border. The cartels' reach extended to La Paz. Roldán Garcia was just another one dead.

Cooper came out into the big room again. His shirt was damp. His eyes fell on the canvases standing like a row of soldiers by the blind-covered windows. He went to them and looked at the first one and then the next.

Roldán Garcia was an oil painter. There were two paintings of flowers and another of fruit. Then he came to the life studies, women and men, and a nude. Something buzzed at the back of Cooper's mind and he swatted it away.

He took the cover from the easel. He felt sick.

Lorena sat beneath a live oak tree Cooper recognized. Take away the chair that held her and replace it with a table and it could have been him in the picture, enjoying a large breakfast. Roldán hadn't bothered to paint the camera on its tall, black pole, or maybe it hadn't been there when the picture was painted.

Cooper took the painting from the easel and checked the back of it for a date. There was none. The only thing was Roldán's name in a flourish at the lower right of the canvas. Cooper knew the dress Lorena was wearing; she'd worn it the first time they met.

He ignored the pieces of bodies and the headless torso and began to prowl the room, looking inside baskets and a few little jars on the mantel of a small fireplace. In the kitchen he turned out drawers and shoved around flatware looking for anything that might be hidden. He went through all the cabinets.

In the bedroom he checked under the bed and between the mattress and box springs. There were drawers in the nightstands and he looked in there. He found condoms, some change and a pair of keys on a ring. One matched up to the apartment key Lorena had given him. He did not know what the other one might be.

The bedroom had a walk-in closet. Roldán had good taste in clothes, but he owned no suits. Cooper rifled through the hanging clothing and then searched the few boxes the man had stored there. He found a pair of fancy shoes, a watch and some jewelry.

Roldán Garcia owned no gun. He had a baseball bat by the bedroom door, but that was the only weapon in the apartment. Cooper went back out to the main room. The air didn't smell of candles anymore, but of blood and butchered meat.

He could not be here anymore. He pulled on his jacket. The feeling chased him out of the door and down the stairs to the street. He found himself hurrying along the way to the car rather than walking calmly away from the scene. Behind the wheel of the Nissan he was hyperventilating and he saw colors in his vision. The engine didn't catch at first. Cooper cursed at it and slammed his hand on the steering wheel.

Back on the streets Cooper had to force himself to drive slowly. His ankle was shaky when he pressed on the accelerator. When he saw a police car he flinched, but they did not light him up. He wanted to be out of the city now, on the road back to Palmilla and with Lorena again. Questions pressed on him, but he didn't want to know their answers. He had to stop because he was hyperventilating again and didn't want to pass out behind the wheel.

When he could travel again he went calmly and the miles peeled away before him.

65.

The bungalow was empty.

Though it was early in the morning and the sun wasn't quite up, he knew the stillness there was not the still of sleep. Lorena hadn't closed the shutters for the night and the curtains bellied in the pre-dawn shadows. She was gone.

The bed was empty and looked as though it hadn't been slept in. Cooper went from room to room hoping he would find her but knowing he would not. When the sun came up he looked out to the beach, thinking she might have fallen asleep on the sand. She was not there.

Cooper stripped out of his bloody clothes and stuffed them into a plastic bag. He would take it with him and toss it out somewhere out of the way. He had blood on his skin where it had soaked through the material of his shirt. In the shower he lathered himself three times and though the stains were gone he did not feel clean.

He dried off with a big white towel and spread another on the bed before lying down. The night weighed heavily on his eyelids and despite himself he fell asleep for a long time. When he woke nothing had changed. The wind still carried through the open-sided bungalow and Lorena was still not there.

He entertained the idea that she had just gone away for a little while, that she would be back when her business was done.

Cooper knew this wasn't true, but the idea persisted another hour before he could maintain the energy for it no longer.

She had left nothing of herself behind. Even the sheets did not smell of her because they had been changed. It occurred to Cooper that he had not seen anything personal in the bungalow even when they had been together. She brought no mementoes of home, nothing that was hers except the clothes she wore. Cooper had more things that were his.

Room service came when he called and didn't remark on Lorena's absence. Cooper picked at his meal and then forced himself to eat heartily. He had no other way to pass the time, because maybe she might come back.

Cooper thought that something might have happened to her and that made his stomach twist up. She might have gone out and been struck by a car or had some other accident. Perhaps she was in a hospital. But the hotel would have told him something. She was just gone.

After a time he blamed Roldán Garcia for what had happened. The plan to kill him had been a shaky one, Cooper should have known that, but it was only now that he could see. Lorena had gotten frightened, maybe Cooper took too long to return from La Paz, and she fled back to Ciudad Juárez. Maybe this was so. He had no way to know for certain.

He still had his phone and she had the number. She might call him and tell him she was all right so long as he didn't leave the phone for a minute. He checked his voice mail just in case and scrolled through old text messages but there was nothing from her.

Cooper felt her absence keenly. As the day passed he developed a headache that forced him off the beach and out of the sun and into the shade of the bungalow. He slept again and when he woke up it was nearly dark. She was still gone.

Saying good-bye to her was important. When he left for Costa Rica that would be the end for them unless she came to him. He dreamed about that and of another beach farther south where exotic birds played in the foliage off the sand. They would make more love and she would get pregnant and have their son. They would be happy together and safe and no one would ever come looking for them because they would be smart, too.

It made him angry that he had never gotten a way to call her. He would call her now and she would tell him everything was all right. She wasn't gone for good, but just for a little while. If he lasted the night he could be with her one last time. That was the only thing he really wanted. It wasn't too much to ask.

But she was gone and she did not come back in the night and she did not call. Cooper waited until the moon passed and the sun came up again and he was still alone.

66.

He drove slowly back to the resort where he had his room. The car could go faster, but he was in no hurry to get anywhere.

The plan unfolded in his head: he would check out and head back to the aeródromo in Cabo San Lucas. From there he would take a flight to San José. He knew people in San José and he would be able to bring his resources together to buy another name. By the end of the month he would be someone else, someone the people from Texas wouldn't look for. Through his contacts he would find work and he would start all over again.

His phone vibrated in his jacket pocket and then it started to ring. Cooper nearly dropped it before he could get it open. His heart pounded. "Lorena?" he said.

"What?" said Barriga.

"Nothing. I thought you were someone else." Cooper felt himself deflate and the car went even slower. He could not summon the energy to press the pedal more firmly. "What do you want?"

"We've been waiting on you, Cooper. When were you planning to get back in touch with us?"

"I hadn't thought about it," Cooper said and it was true. The past few days had been about Lorena and nothing else. Until he went to La Paz the whole world could have fallen away and he would not have noticed. He did not need the whole anymore, he realized; he needed only her.

"We need a decision."

"I can't give you one."

"Why not?" Barriga said sharply. "Cooper—"

"I'm going away," Cooper said. "I'm shutting down."

"That's not necessary."

"Yes, it is. The Texas situation is... difficult to handle."

"I told you we could take care of that. There's no reason to do anything rash. My people are very interested in you, Cooper. They know you didn't mean what you said and they're leaning on me, Cooper, they're *leaning* on me."

"I don't have a choice."

"I don't, either. I'm making this call because I must."

"Don't do me any favors."

"You don't understand. I work for an organization. The organization makes demands on me the same as they do on you. We're only as free as we're allowed to be, Cooper, and you've been allowed a great deal of freedom."

"You have no idea."

"You need to come in, Cooper. You *must* come in. I'm not asking you anymore."

"I don't think you're in a position to make demands of me," Cooper replied. "You don't know where I am. You don't know what I'm doing. You want freedom? I'm free of all of it. You can tell your people to shove it up their asses."

Cooper cut off the line and tossed the phone into the passenger seat. It rang again but he didn't answer and when it rang for a second time he switched it off. He felt a pang when he thought of Lorena, but he would turn it on again at the hotel. She would call him. He was sure of it.

At the hotel he showed his guest pass to the guard at the gate and had the valet park the Nissan. He went to the front desk to check for messages, but there were none. She would call him.

He let himself into his room and before he had gone two steps he felt the man hiding behind the door.

Cooper froze. He heard himself breathing and beyond that, the gentle sounds of the man tucked into the blind spot by the door. "Turn around," the man said.

The man was Mexican, slight and short, with a thin mustache. His white linen suit was rumpled, as if he had not taken great care with it, and he wore a tie. The pistol in his hand had a suppressor screwed the barrel. He had flat eyes.

"You found me," Cooper said.

"It was not difficult," the man replied.

"Who are you from?"

"I come from Juárez. We've seen each other before."

Cooper searched his memory until an image of the man rose to his recollection. He saw the man in Ruíz's house, one of several men that passed anonymously during those long days of waiting. Cooper did not know whether to be relieved or angry, and instead he felt resigned as a man outplayed.

"What now?" Cooper asked.

"You get on your knees."

"I'd rather stand."

"It doesn't matter to me. *La Señora*, she only cares that it's done."

The pieces fit together easily. Ruíz was gone, but his family remained. Señora Ruíz was a *matrona*, a wife who ran her home as assuredly as any man. With Ruíz eliminated, only she could step up to take his place, and she would not tolerate a daughter who fled home to be with a man like Cooper. He should have known this, expected this, but he had been blind.

"How did she know it was me?" Cooper asked.

"I don't know. I was told only to look for a man. You are the one."

Cooper thought of Roldán Garcia, who died for nothing, but he did not feel guilt. He could not afford such a feeling. Not now, and perhaps not ever. "Let's get it done, then," Cooper said.

He waited until the moment he saw the man's finger tighten on the trigger before he moved. There was not much space between them, less than Cooper would have allowed, and when the gun went off the bullet passed close enough for him to feel it going by. The television exploded.

The man snatched his hand back, but Cooper had a hold on his wrist now and he turned into the man's body, twisting the gun across to point harmlessly at the bed. Another slug penetrated the mattress. Cooper jabbed his elbow back hard, twice, and then slammed the side of the man's gun hand against the wall.

The pistol fell and they were locked together. Cooper felt fresh pain in his shoulder where the stitches were stressed to the tearing point. They huddled face-to-face, forearms locked. Cooper brought his knee up into the man's crotch, and then kicked out hard. The man crashed backward against the wall, the breath rushing out of his lungs.

Cooper was on him before the man could move. He punched him in the throat, grabbed him by the side of the neck and whirled him around so that he tumbled across the floor into the scattered field of glass slivers that fell from the television. Cooper kicked the man hard in the side, then a second time when he tried to cover up. A finger-bone snapped where the man tried to block the blow away.

The man rolled over and scrambled for the fallen gun. Cooper fell on his back, his knees pressing the man to the floor. He landed a solid strike to the back of the man's skull and bounced his face off the carpet, then reached for the gun himself. It was beyond the man's grasp by inches. Cooper snagged it with his fingertips.

Two shots to the head ended it. The entry wounds were neatly punched holes, but the man bled from the eyes, nose and mouth as if the space behind his face had exploded beneath the skin. Cooper was panting, his shoulder on fire. He fell back against the bed.

It took minutes for his heartbeat to steady and his face was damp with sweat. The cut on his face stung beneath the bandage. He breathed heavily until his lungs no longer felt afire.

He gathered his things, those few that he had brought with him. The pistol he kept, though he packed it away. The room had not been anything but a place to him and he had not allowed himself to take up residence. When he was ready to leave, the only signs that he had been there were the broken television, the black circle on the mattress and the body. There was nothing he could do about any of them.

At the lobby he got his car from the valet and he drove away without speeding. His plan had not changed, but now he knew that Lorena was lost to him completely. It was not enough that the men from Texas were looking, not enough that now Barriga's people would want him, but when Señora Ruíz discovered what had happened in that hotel room, she would send another and another until this American, this unperson, was gone from her daughter's life. It could not be any other way.

He thought of Lorena all the way to the *aeródrome*, every mile and every minute that passed. He tried to reclaim the feeling of when they were together and there were no demands, no expectations. Before Roldán Garcia.

By the time he reached the plane he had almost managed to put Lorena in her place in his memory box where she could not be touched, where she could be taken out and admired for what she was. Just once he allowed himself to dream about a time when she would be free of her mother and they could meet again, but only once before he quashed the wish completely.

It would be a long time before he came to Mexico again.

67.

She had an evening flight from Cabo San Lucas to Ciudad Juárez. There was a car waiting to pick her up at the airport and ferry her back home. She wore dark glasses because she had been crying and she did not want her puffy eyes to show.

The flight had been long and she was tired, but she knew her mother wouldn't let her sleep when she got to the house. There would be questions and all of them would have to be answered before there could be rest.

It was eleven o'clock and right now Cooper would be in Roldán's apartment. Roldán would be waiting for her with flowers and maybe the stupid painting he'd done of her and he would expect her to make love to him right away. That was the way he'd been with her, always demanding, and then tears when he explained he could not help himself when it came to her.

Lorena wondered what it would be like when he died. Cooper was strong and he wouldn't flinch from it, just like he hadn't flinched when it came time to kill her father. He was like Roldán in some ways, but not in this. Roldán only wished he could be the man that Cooper was without trying.

She hoped Cooper would die quickly.

The car wound through the night and finally up the stretch of road to the house. All the lights were on in welcome and Rudolfo's replacement, Claudio, waited at the front door for her.

He held her door and told the driver to bring her bags inside. "Señora is waiting," he said to Lorena.

"I know," she replied.

The house smelled clean, as if all the windows and doors and had been thrown open and a breeze had blown through on a clear day. In the study there was still the lingering odor of her father's cigars, but there was nothing else that remained of him. If she closed her eyes, Lorena could remember the scent of his body, but she did not do this.

Her mother waited in the leather chair behind Father's desk. She had a book that she put aside. When she rose she put her arms out for Lorena and Lorena obeyed by coming to her for an embrace. "My baby," Mother said.

"Yes, Mother," Lorena said.

"Do you want something to eat? Something to drink? Let me get some *limonada* for us. Claudio, see that we get some."

"*Sí, Señora.*"

"Sit down," Mother said, and they retired to two great chairs that huddled near a cast-iron fireplace. "And take off those glasses, it's night."

Lorena took off the glasses and looked down at her hands. She could feel her mother watching her closely and she heard the cluck of Mother's tongue when she saw everything.

"You've been crying."

"Yes, Mother."

"You've been crying over that man? Cooper?"

There was no sense in lying. "Yes, Mother. It's nothing."

"No, it's not nothing. You are too good for a man like that. Too good for that Roldán Garcia, as well. You're lucky to be rid of both of them. An artist and a hired gun. They're trash. You were meant for better than they."

She did not agree, but it would do no good to argue, just as it had made no sense to stop the men who came to bring her from Palmilla back to Juárez. It would happen. The decision was made. Her task was to accept it. There was no room for dreams. "I won't cry anymore," she said.

"It makes me sick to think of their hands all over my daughter. You're a good girl, Lorena. Have I told you that? Even after all you have done, you are still my child. I cannot stay angry with you."

"Yes, mother."

"Ah, and here's the *limonada*."

Claudio brought the platter himself with a pitcher of light yellow limeade and two glasses. He poured for them. Mother watched Lorena until she picked up her glass and then smiled.

"Drink up. It will be good for your nerves."

Lorena obeyed. The *limonada* was heavy with gin and made her face wrinkle, but she swallowed and saw her mother smile. She forced down two more sips and then held the glass between her hands as it sweated.

"You're too dark. You spend too much time in the sun."

"I'm sorry."

"Do you want to wrinkle? You have to take care of your skin."

"I said I'm sorry, Mother."

"All right. It's done. The ugliness is passed."

Lorena had no answer for that. She looked down at her *limonada*, watched the ice slowly melt and shift. It was a long time before her mother spoke again.

"I understand it's been difficult for you. Everything that has happened. With this Cooper, with Roldán, with... your father."

Lorena did not want to speak of her father. She did not want to speak of any of them. Hearing Cooper's name made her feel pain she did know she could feel. He was dead now. They would never go to Costa Rica. They would never share a bed together.

"It's dealt with now," Mother continued. "All your problems are resolved. I will see to everything."

"I'm tired now, Mother. I'd like to sleep."

Mother reached over and patted Lorena on the arm. "Of course, *mija*. You go to sleep and tomorrow you will feel better about everything. Now drink your *limonada*."

Lorena did as she was told.

68.

The next day Lorena woke late and the sun was already shining brightly through her bedroom windows. She showered and put on a bathing suit and went down to the pool. She saw no one.

She swam laps until her arms were tired and she just floated. Out of the corner of her eye she saw her mother come out of the house and cross the lawn to reach her. She stood at the edge of the pool.

"You slept in this morning," Mother said.

"I was tired."

"And now you're swimming without breakfast. And it's almost time for lunch!"

"I'll eat something, Mother, I promise."

"See that you do. I'm going out to have lunch with someone and I won't be here to watch you. And I won't forget that you promised."

"You never forget anything, Mother."

"No, I don't," Mother said and her face creased into a frown. She lingered a moment, just watching Lorena.

"What is it, Mother?" Lorena asked.

"Nothing. It's just that... I do love you, *mija*."

"I know you do."

"Good-bye, Lorena."

"Good-bye, Mother."

Her mother vanished into the house. After a long time Lorena knew she had to be gone, in a car headed for the city to eat in some restaurant where the food was overpriced and company boring. Lorena would rather stay where she was right now and eat alone than be subjected to that.

She swam.

There was movement by the house and she saw Claudio emerge. He was with two of the regular men whose names Lorena did not know. They came heavy-footed, as if they had bad news to share. A part of her hoped it was a terrible crash and that Mother was dead.

She didn't hate her mother the way she'd hated her father. What Mother did to Cooper was because of her love for her, not out of malice or lust or any of the terrible things that drove Papá. But Mother didn't care, either. To her, a man like Cooper was to be dismissed forever to some purgatory where men who sinned were sent. Roldán could be exiled, but Cooper... he must die.

Lorena no longer felt close to Mother, though Mother still loved her dearly.

Claudio came close to the pool. All three men wore sunglasses to hide their eyes.

"May I help you?" Lorena asked.

He plunged into the shallow end of the pool feet-first and kicked up a wave that rocked Lorena. When he stood up he was only half-submerged and he sloshed across to her with the same flat expression he wore before.

"What are you doing? Don't you think you need a bathing suit?" Lorena asked and she laughed though it wasn't funny.

Claudio caught her by the arm and Lorena screamed. She could not pull away from him and when he got hold of the back of her neck she could not move, either. He forced her into the water. Her arms were free and she thrashed. She caught hold of his belt and pulled against it, but he could not be moved.

Lorena wished she hadn't screamed, wished she saved some extra breath. Bubbles sprayed into her eyes and then those were gone. Her lungs convulsed and she was breathing water. Her eyes were burning. She saw black dots. Claudio's hand was an iron bar on her neck.

And then she was gone.

69.

Señora Ruíz arrived at the restaurant Misión Guadalupe five minutes after his reservation time. The maître d' thought nothing of it and showed her to her table. Barriga was already there.

He rose from his seat and kissed her hand. "Narcisa," he said.

"Joaquín."

They sat down together and Narcisa Ruíz ordered a gin and tonic. Barriga already had a drink. For a while they simply sat and watched each other. Barriga's expression was unreadable.

Barriga broke the silence. "I'm sorry for your loss."

"It is done," Narcisa said.

"Was it quick?"

"They'll call it an accident."

"A wife who's lost her husband. A mother who's lost her daughter. It's the kind of thing tragedies are made of," Barriga said.

"I will go on."

"My people wish to know if you will see to your husband's interests."

"Of course. They are all I have now."

"That is good. And Cooper, is he also dealt with?"

Narcisa's face darkened. "He left my man dead. He is gone."

Barriga reached across the table and touched Narcisa's hand. "He won't come for you."

"How can you be sure?"

"Cooper is a man who needs no one."

"He wanted my daughter."

"No matter. One day he'll want someone else."

"I should send someone to find him."

"You never will. He will not be so sloppy again."

Narcisa considered. She sipped her drink. "Are you sorry you had to lose your man?"

"It was inevitable," Barriga said. "Besides, there is always another Cooper."

Printed in Great Britain
by Amazon.co.uk, Ltd.,
Marston Gate.